INSATIABLE

Book 1

AMETHYST WINTERS

Deviant Ink Publishing

ISBN: 979-8-218-51184-5 (Paperback)

Library of Congress Control Number: 2024919521

Any references to historical events, real people, or places are fictitious. Names, characters, and places are products of the author's imagination.

Front cover image by Yaşar Vurdem
Book design by GetCovers

Printed in the United States of America.

First printing edition 2024.

Deviant Ink Publishing
80 Seven Hills BLVD Suite 101
Dallas, GA 30132-0575

www.AmethystWintersRomance.com

To your battery-operated toys. May they rest in peace.

Caution & Trigger Warnings:

Panties may become slippery when wet. Proceed with caution.

If you need another warning, here it is:

Your pastor, priest, rabbi, and anyone you answer to will not like you reading this book. This is not for everyone. It contains very graphic depictions of things you may want to hide from people who are too afraid to explore their darker side. You've been warned.

As for you, you bad girl. This book is for you. Now spread my pages wide and come inside.

This is your last chance to turn around. Don't say you weren't warned.

- Toxic relationships
- Mentions of cheating
- Graphic violence/graphic Murder
- Choking kink
- Rough sex
- Self-harm
- Possessiveness
- Blood play
- Blood kink
- Impact play
- Mentions of rape, although not depicted in graphic detail
- Sadomasochism
- Inappropriate use of a knife
- Psychological abuse
- Violence
- Torture
- Voyeurism
- Mental illness
- Revenge
- Bondage
- Child abandonment
- Child abuse
- Exhibitionism
- Grief and loss
- Anal play
- Genital mutilation
- Voyeurism
- Degradation

- Dirty talk
- Stalking
- Spanking
- Unprotected Sex
- Cutting

- Death
- Foul language

"Don't you know I'll tear the world apart for you, little fox?"

TABLE OF CONTENTS

PROLOGUE

eing murdered by the love of my life was—how would you say—unexpected. That is until I found myself stuffed in a small box underground in the Georgia humidity. We had a heated love story. Some might call it a bit unhinged, but would I call it deadly? Absolutely not! So, imagine my surprise when the love of my life attempted to choke me to death while his cock was buried deep inside me.

I run my now calloused fingers along the splintered box, the four walls cutting my supply of oxygen. Darkness engulfs me. I close my eyes to drown it out and fight the tears that threaten to fall. What had I done? Was this a test? Had he gone mad? He had to have gone mad. But why? Was it the death of his mother? I mean, she had it coming. How dare she try to tell him to abandon our relationship and go back home to take care of her. Did she think I'd sit idly by and let her take him away? Could his grief have driven him to act so aggressively towards me? No, that couldn't be it. He loves me. He would never hurt me. I hoped he would never hurt me.

CHAPTER ONE
AYEMELINE

The local coffee shop, Out of the Brew, is the place for college kids to grab a tall, half-calf, non-fat, triple shot, soy, no foam, goat milk, sugar-free, extra shot macchiato each morning. I've never been into all that allure, however. I want my coffee to be strong and black. I need it today. I'd stayed up all night with Micah—the nerdy guy I had invited to my room last night. I was supposed to be studying for my English final. But halfway through my study session, I stepped out to get a slice of pizza, and I ended up with him inside me instead. I don't even know why it happened. He was there, and I was horny. This is why my study session took all night and not a few hours as initially intended. And it's why I am now at this coffee shop surrounded by these pretentious college kids, trying to get something that would keep me awake during my English final.

I'm used to being in a constant state of fatigue. My days were spent working at Loads of Laughter Daycare, and my nights studying and fucking, in no particular order. For this reason, my coffee is like a mother to me. Unlike my mother, it brings me comfort. And I have to have it if I intend to pass this final. After all, I have something to prove to my parents, who have labeled me the greatest regret of their lives. I have this burning desire to show them I could accomplish anything without their support; hence why I was at this ridiculous university with all these pretentious assholes. I do not want to be here. But what choice did I have?

I stand awkwardly behind two girls as they scroll mindlessly through their phones, neither one paying attention to the other, although it is obvious that they came in together. I shift from foot to foot, trying to find a comfortable position, my hands dangling by my side like they didn't want to be there. I fold my arms and drop them to my side again, trying to find comfort in a crowd of strangers. A girl I recognize from my sociology class bumps into my shoulder as she makes her way to the counter, never glancing back to see who she bumped into. The echoing sound of chatter fills the air as people converse with one another, hugging friends they haven't seen in the last ten minutes. The air feels heavy as sweat forms on top of my lip. I wipe it away, being careful not to draw attention to myself.

"What can I getcha?" The guy behind the counter stares at me.

I take a small step forward. "Um…coffee?"

He stares at me incredulously. "You want to be more specific, sweetheart?"

I hate being called "sweetheart" by strangers.

"Just coffee…black…with um…sugar."

"Juiced?"

"Huh?"

"Do. You. Want. Your. Coffee. Decaf or caffeinated?" He speaks to me like I'm stupid.

"Um…caffeinated."

He walks away to prepare my order, and I forcibly step back as a blond girl hurriedly steps forward to place her order as if I'm not there. Looking around, I recognize many of these faces from my classes. I'm pretty good at remembering faces; one never knows when that skill will be handy.

The constant *ding* of the bell that hangs above the coffee shop door forces me to shift my attention to the entrance. There walks in the most beautiful, tall, thick-bodied god—Ariel Yearwood—*my* Ariel Yearwood. My eyes water at the sight of him. This man is breathtaking. He is unfathomably delectable. I gaze upon the Herculean creature with sepia reddish-brown skin—its rich, warm tone contrasted exceptionally with his warm blonde curls. A dazzling smile reveals a slight dimple on one cheek. My eyes draw to his generous, pillow-like lips. I yearn to touch my finger to those lips. And his beard—oh gosh, that beard!

He walks up to the counter, places his order, and then plops down on a stool two tables from where I stand. In his hand is a music case, which he sits on the ground by his feet. He chats mindlessly with the friend he walked in with. They stand eye-to-eye. Both are over six feet tall, but Ariel is a lot broader than he is. His eyes wander around the room. They land on mine. We lock eyes, and suddenly, I can't move; I stop breathing. I cannot look away. There is something eerily calm about him. My stomach feels hot. My heart sprints and excitement weakens my knees. I've found him—my soulmate.

"Ari," the sudden howl of the guy behind the counter jerks me out of my stupor. *Ari. Ari.* I say his name over in my mind, as if the mere mention of his name will engrave him in my heart. He pushes himself off the stool and brushes past me. His comforting aroma of air-dried sheets coats my throat. Even after he walks out of the coffee shop, drink in hand, his clean, crisp aroma lingers. It is the scent of new beginnings.

CHAPTER TWO
ARIEL

She keeps gawking at me, wide-eyed, like a baby owl. Her light hair sits on a messy, stringy heap on top of her head. She looks like she is wearing the clothes she slept in—baggy gray sweatpants, flip-flops, an oversized T-shirt that reads "Love Never Fails" across the front in a retro 80's font. Even from where I stand, I can see her eyes appear pitch black. She's pretty. That is if I was into the unhinged, messy with a touch of homelessness look. But, oh my God, why is she staring at me so much? Does she know me from somewhere? My muscles tense. Something about her makes me feel uneasy yet familiar. It's in her eyes. They are her most powerful weapons, intense and penetrating. I want to look away, but I can't. My brain is telling me to look away—to run. But my curiosity is getting the best of me.

In the background, I hear a name being called repeatedly. Eagar to end this very discommodious interaction, I force my gaze over to the boy behind the counter. He looks to be a freshman—short, blond hair and excitement from his newfound freedom in college—something I never got to experience. The boy looks at her as he calls a name I'm sure he's pronouncing incorrectly. Her name? She does not budge.

A few moments later, a punch comes hard and fast to my side. "That's you, man," Remy says as he nods toward the boy. The counter boy holds up my drink. I get up from the stool, and my legs instantly become weak. How long were we staring at each other? I walk up to the counter, grab my drink, and bolt out of that coffee shop as quickly as possible. I need to get some air. Suddenly, it's hard to breathe.

"Dude, what was that?" Remy finally catches up to me after I bolted out of the coffee shop.

"What was what?" I say, feigning ignorance.

"You and that girl at the coffee shop. You know her?"

"I don't know what you're talking about, man. I'm just trying to get to class on time."

"Seriously? You were in a trance. Was it love at first sight or some shit?"

"Fuck you, man. I don't know that girl."

"Whoa! Don't come for me!" Remy holds his hands up in mock surrender. "I'm just saying it was weird. And the way you ran out of there..."

"Okay. Drop it, Remy," I say bluntly.

"All right. Don't tell me."

He walks beside me in silence. I feel bad about the way I reacted toward Remy. He and I have been friends since seventh grade. He lived next door, and although he went to a fancy private school and I went to the local public school, we became good friends. He was an even better friend after my parents divorced and my mom was given sole custody of my brother and me.

After my dad left, my mother became bitter and blamed my dad for everything that went wrong in her life. Pretty soon, she started resenting us. When my father stopped coming to see us, she no longer had someone to hurl insults at. So, my brother and I became her target practice. Hassan is four years older than I am. The year he turned eighteen, he left home, leaving me to take all the blows my mother threw alone. Remy has been the one constant in my life who I can always count on.

Remy's house was nothing like mine. He's always been the pampered only child of a loving, two-parent home. Even in the eighth grade, his mom baked cookies and read him bedtime stories. Remy knew my situation at home. He'd invite me over any chance he got so that I could escape. He is a good friend.

I know he cares about me. He's always the first to realize when something is wrong. "Honestly," I say, "I don't know who she was. I've never seen her before. It's just…" I pause, trying to find the right words. "It's just the way she looked at me freaked me out. I had to get out of there."

"I get it," Remy says, patting me on the shoulder. "I think you did the right thing. You don't want to get involved with these crazy girls around here. I think if you see her again, you should run the other way."

"Wow! It's not that serious, man."

"Trust me, Ari. You need to focus on you. She's obviously attracted to you, and you don't need that."

"I've never heard you speak so strongly against anyone before."

"She seems…weird. It's just a vibe I'm getting."

I remain silent. Maybe Remy is right. She was beautiful, though. Even in her unkempt state, I could see her beauty. But I know that's not what I need. Right now, my focus should only be on my healing journey, not some girl.

CHAPTER THREE
AYEMELINE

I can't focus on my English final. My mind is on my handsome god from the coffee shop, Ari. I keep repeating his name over and over in my head. I need to meet him officially, touch him, and hear him say my name.

"Time's up. Pencils down." I'm relieved to hear Professor Matthews end the class. My test paper remains blank, but I don't care. There are more important things I need to do. Like find my soulmate.

I grab my bag, fling it over my shoulder, and bolt out of the auditorium-style classroom. I don't even bother handing in my test.

"What's the rush, beautiful?" Micah stands directly in front of me, blocking my way.

"What do you want?" I ask with an exasperated breath.

"You," he answers dubiously. His lips curl upward in a half-smile intended to be sexy but one that comes off as sad.

"How original." I sideswipe him and walk off as quickly as I can.

"Hold up, Ayemeline." He sprints behind me. "What do you think about finishing what we started last night?"

"I thought we did finish."

"No, girl. I've got so much more to show you. I can eat that pussy like a grapefruit." He uses two fingers to push his glasses higher up his nose.

I halt and stare up at him. His hair clings to the sweat on his forehead. He repeatedly blinks as he waits for my response.

He is handsome with a smooth, sandy complexion. His hair is cut into a shadow faded cut while short, wispy, black ringlets sit on his head. He's tall with lean muscles that you would never guess were there until he removes his shirt. At six feet seven, I can see what a girl would see in him, even with the whole nerdy vibe he's got going on. What the heck?! My pussy could use a little attention. Judging by last night, he had the tongue of a hungry snake. After all, it's almost impossible to satiate my carnal desires.

***

Half an hour later, Micah and I are in my apartment, naked, with Micah's head between my thighs. As his tongue darts in and out of my pussy, I imagine it's Ari between my legs. I gaze down, surprised to find I no longer see black ringlets. In their place are warm blond curls. My arousal tangles with the need to touch him, to taste him. My soulmate pops my clit into his mouth and sucks. I'm not prepared for such intensity. "More," I moan, my breath coming out raspy. Obeying my orders, he inserts two fingers into my pussy as he continues to suck on my clit. He moans, and I feel the vibrations of his body on mine. My soulmate is here. He knows how much I need him and he has come for me. I place my hand on his head and push his tongue deeper into me. I need more. I feel my wetness leak out of me. The smell of arousal permeates the air.

Suddenly, his mouth and fingers are gone and are replaced with his long, thick shaft. He slowly eases himself into me. His thrusts are deep and fast. My breasts bounce with each thrust. He groans, and his warm, thick breath coats my skin.

"I want your cum in my mouth," I breathe. I want to taste him. Without missing a beat, he eases out of my pussy. I slowly lower myself to the ground in front of him. I grip the base of his dick and ease the tip into my mouth. I meticulously swirl my tongue around his head. He starts to shake. *Yes, baby. Feed me.* He grabs a fistful of my hair and vigorously pumps his dick into my mouth. He fucks my mouth like a possessed man. Pushing in one last time, he lets out a loud moan. "Oh, fuck," he whispers with a slight grunt as he lets his cum flood my mouth.

I swirl the warm, salty liquid with my tongue before swallowing. Some of his warm cum leaks down the side of my mouth onto my bare breast. "Damn, that was good," he drawls. Why did Ari's voice sound like…what the fuck? Before me is not my Herculean god. It's Micah standing there, dick out, still wet with my drool and his cum. He stares down at me with a look of satisfaction on his face. I instantly feel a pang of disappointment.

***

The stench of dirty diapers and germs permeates the air. I come to work feeling defeated. It has been three weeks since I saw Ari at the coffee shop. Three weeks of searching social media and the school website and even going to the coffee shop multiple times a day, hoping to run into him again. Being around a bunch of three-year-olds is not where I want to be. I want to be in his arms, touching his skin and taking in his scent.

"Ms. Cross," Suzette, the neediest child I have in my classroom, whines. "I can't do it." She is attempting to force a puzzle piece into a slot where it doesn't belong.

"How about we try another piece?" I kneel beside the little girl and offer her another puzzle piece.

She takes the piece from my hand and places it in the spot where she was trying to place the other piece. "I did it!" She shouts with a look of pure excitement on her face.

Kids are lucky to live in a world where putting a puzzle piece together gives them so much joy and excitement simply because someone told them this was an accomplishment they should feel proud of. Then they get older and realize that what you accomplish doesn't matter; no one will ever be proud of you. Because, to the world, you can always do more, no matter what you do. They'll soon realize that, but I'm okay with letting them believe their little accomplishments mean something.

"Oh my God, Suzette! You worked really hard on that. I'm so proud of you."

The little girl beams from ear to ear, her giddy excitement almost contagious. I know better, however. I will never fall into the trap of thinking that achievements matter.

My phone vibrates in my back pocket. I reached for it and read the message:

Dragon Slayer: We need to have a conversation.

I roll my eyes and put the phone back in my pocket. I have enough on my mind; I do not need added negativity. For the rest of the day, I ignore every text message, phone call, and attempt to contact me.

***

After my shift, I climb into my car and turn my phone on. It immediately starts to ping with incoming missed calls and text messages. Seven new text messages and fourteen missed calls.

Dragon Slayer: Did you get my message?

Dragon Slayer: Answer me, Ayemeline.

Dragon Slayer: We're worried. Where are you?

Dragon Slayer: At least respond and let us know you're okay.

Dragon Slayer: *angry face emoji*

Dragon Slayer: Why are you always so difficult? You're being ridiculous. Call me.

Dragon Slayer: I'm not doing this with you, Ayemeline. If you choose to ignore me, I will show up at your apartment and we can talk then. I'm not going to take any more of your disrespect. After all we've done for you, you continue to act ungrateful. Get off your high horse and call me immediately! This is not a game! *Angry face emoji*

I fling my phone onto the back seat. No way was I calling or responding. Did he think he could threaten me into calling him? The nerve!

I pull into my designated parking spot in front of my apartment. I rent an apartment a couple of blocks from campus. I much prefer living alone. And this is perfect. This is why I work at Loads of Laughter—to maintain a sense of independence—independence from my parents and peers. As I made my way towards my apartment, I see the tall, elderly man standing in front of my door. His pale white skin and ginger hair, similar to mine, make him easy to spot. Immediately, I want to bolt. *Was he seriously standing there waiting for me?*

"So you are alive and yet you decided to ignore me all day," he states brusquely.

"Hello, Father. It's so nice to see you." I give him a smug smile.

"Cut the bullshit, Ayemeline! I told you I'd be here if you didn't respond to my messages."

"Huh? What messages, FATHER?"

He rubs his brows together. "We need to discuss last weekend. Your mother is very disappointed in you. She wanted me to wait until I calmed down to speak to you. I wanted to wait to see if you would come to your senses and apologize to your mother. But, of course, that isn't something you're capable of doing."

"What," I fling my hand to my chest in feigned indignation. "Mother is disappointed in me? I've never experienced her disappointment before."

My father presses his lips together and crosses his arms. "Open the door so we can discuss this inside. Your neighbors don't need to know all our family business."

I hate for him to tell me what to do. But I also agree. My nosy neighbors do not need to be in my business. I enjoy my private, secluded life. The last thing I want is for anyone to think they know me. Reluctantly, I use my key to open my door. I hold the door open for him to enter. "After you, FATHER," I say, holding my hand out and bowing. I'd see red flames coming from his ears if we were in a cartoon. Or maybe he'd be surrounded by it. *Burn in hell, Daddy Dearest.*

He walks into my apartment, and I follow him, closing the door behind me.

"What the hell makes you think it's okay to embarrass your mom like that by not showing up to celebrate her birthday? Do you know how many friends from church were there asking where you were? What kind of daughter would simply not show up for her own mother?" His voice gets louder and louder with each phrase he speaks.

"How can I embarrass her if I wasn't even there, Father?" I keep my voice sweet and calm. I know my father hates it when I don't match his energy.

"You think this a joke?"

"No, sir," I mock, saluting him. "I would n..." A harsh slap cuts my words short. My cheeks sting from the impact. I'd like to say the assault stunned me but it didn't. I saw it coming the moment I noticed my dear father standing in front of my apartment door. I invited it.

Receiving that slap from my father restores my equilibrium. It makes me aware of my existence and assures me that he is aware of mine as well. I look him straight in the eye and give him a bright smile. A feeling of warmth spreads throughout my body. "Tell me how pathetic and worthless I am, Father."

His eyes widen as the realization sets in. "You are sick. You don't deserve anything we've done for you. After everything we've given you and sacrificed for you, your payment to us is to disappoint your mother and me. You never fail in that!"

"Are you saying I've succeeded at something, Father?"

My father glares daggers at me, his mouth curled up in disgust. Suddenly, he turns around and leaves, slamming my door behind him.

***

The angry orange ball in the sky sinks toward the horizon. Towering thunderclouds loom overhead as I walk to the Mexican restaurant. I need some tacos. I also need to release the fire that burns inside me. How dare he leave so abruptly? He didn't even have the decency to fight it out. Fighting with my parents makes me feel like I am visible.

I reach the restaurant and go inside as small droplets of rain begin to fall. The enthusiastic greeter greets me, and I want to slap the ridiculously wide smile off her face.

"I want to place a to-go order," I state monotonously.

She guides me to the bar, her ponytail swaying and bouncing with each step. *Maybe I should chop it off.*

The interior of the restaurant is homely. Art is displayed on the walls, and the smell of baked cheese invades my nostrils. A loud crowd takes over the whole left side of the restaurant. To my right is a table with four. Electric waves shoot down my arms when I realize who is at that table. My soulmate. He's sitting there with four other people. The person who catches my eye is the girl sitting beside him, giving him a flirtatious look. I look away quickly. I am furious. Who the fuck does she think she is? What is he doing with her? It looks like a double date. Is he fucking her?

When the bartender comes, I order three hard-shell carne asada tacos. I'm even more furious than I was when I came in. My mind is now consumed with how I will kill that little man-stealing bitch. But first, I must make sure he knows exactly who I am. When I walk out of the restaurant and notice him follow me, I smile. This is going to be easier than I'd planned.

CHAPTER FOUR
ARIEL

I notice her the second she walks into Zapatas Grill. She looks much more put together than during our first Out of the Brew encounter. Curly copper ginger hair is pulled back into a neat ponytail. Her medium tawny skin glows under the fluorescent lights of the restaurant. Light brown freckles faintly dot her nose and ascend just above her eyes. I study every feature of her face. Ever since I'd seen her, her face has taken over my dreams. I'm caught in her whirlwind and don't know how to get myself out. She doesn't notice me, however. She seems to be consumed in her world. She walks up to the bar counter and speaks quietly to the bartender. Her expression is empty. She looks straight ahead, past the bartender even as she places her order.

"Are you in?" I look over at Remy. His girlfriend, Brea, sits with her arms entwined with Remy's and her head propped on his shoulder. They both stare at me, waiting for a response. I look over at Brea's friend, who sits beside me, for clues about what they are discussing. *What was her name again?*

"What?" I ask, a little embarrassed. Once again, I let this woman take over all my senses. I'm just glad she's behind Remy so he can't see her or I wouldn't hear the end of it. I don't want to have to explain myself to him. I don't even know what I would say. *You know that random girl I had a stare-down with at the coffee shop? Well, she's been obsessively on my mind, and I don't know why.* Yeah, that wouldn't work. He'd want to analyze why I was drawn to her. He'd question me about my every move.

"We're going to grab some drinks at Timbers. You want to come?" What's-Her-Name volunteers.

"Seriously, dude?" Remy looks at me with squinted eyes as if saying, *Get it together, man.*

I look at What's-her-name because it is easier to address her than Remy. "I'm sorry. I'm tired, and I really need to get up early for class."

Remy glowers at me. Brea's been trying to set me up with her friend for a while and has been asking Remy to do the introductions. And at first, I was into it. But at this moment, I simply can't focus on her.

Over Remy's head, I can see her pick up her food and make her way to the door. I really shouldn't. I really, really shouldn't. But today, my feet and my brain choose not to work together. Before I know it, I'm excusing myself from the table and walking toward the door after her. I'm not trying to pursue her. I just need...something. I don't know what I need. I simply want to know who she is, to understand why she seems to draw me to her.

***

The rain is steady and warm as it hits the damp pavement. Her hair, which was in a perfect ponytail, is now slick and damp. It only takes me three large leaps to reach her, my long legs carrying me further than her short legs can. I wish I had brought my umbrella. Then I'd have an excuse to approach her.

We reach the crosswalk. I now stand side-by-side with her. Standing this close, I notice how small she is. Her five-foot frame looks so vulnerable in the rain. Suddenly, as if she were summoned, this tiny figure of a woman snaps her head toward me. I stare into her black eyes, trying to force words out.

She speaks first. "Were you following me?"

My laugh is uncomfortable. "Why would I do that?"

"I don't know. Why would you?" She cocks her eyebrow at me.

"I wasn't following you," I lie.

"We're just going in the same direction."

"I guess we are."

At the pedestrian walk signal, we both cross the street simultaneously.

"What's your name?" I ask abruptly after walking side-by-side in silence for the past thirty seconds.

She pauses. Turning her body around to face me, she stares right into my eyes with her cold, dark eyes. "Ayemeline." Her voice is mellifluous when she says her name, quite different from her suspicious tone when she first addressed me.

"Em-lean," I enunciate each syllable slowly. It tastes like honey on my tongue. The jagged, raised scar on her neck tells me she has a story to tell, that she fought something and won. It runs from her ear, down her neck, and disappears beneath her purple polo top. I have the sudden urge to reach out and touch it. Suddenly, I am. I don't know when I did it. "I...I...I'm...uh...I'm sorry," I stutter.

"What's your name?" She's calm. It's as if she didn't even notice I touched her.

"Ari. Ariel. But, um, everyone just calls me Ari." My speech is slow. Why can't I breathe? What is happening to me? She, however, seems oblivious to the turmoil going on inside me at that very moment.

She gives me a polite smile, and her eyes roam my body. "Okay, Ari. Do you want my number now?"

My eyes widen. I freeze in disbelief. Is she offering me her number? No, that's not what I am here for. I didn't follow her to start a relationship. I followed her to get closure—so she would stop haunting my dreams. I don't need her number. I am going to walk away from her and end whatever this is. "Yeah." My voice comes out breathier than I expected. I almost don't recognize myself.

Without warning, Ayemeline reaches into my jeans pocket and snatches my phone. She casually hands it to me. I use my thumbprint to unlock it. I watch as she taps out her number and presses the call button. She places the phone back in my pocket and walks away. And just like that, I relieve my lungs of the building pressure.

***

I'm soaked by the time I reach my dorm. I quickly get out of my clothes and put on dry boxers. I towel-dry my hair and body. After Ayemeline gave me her number and walked away, I decided not to return to the restaurant. I sent Remy a quick text letting him know I had an emergency and had to leave. He's called me five times since then, and I've ignored call. I don't want to have to explain myself. I wouldn't even know what to say. I reach for my phone and find his contact.

Me: Sorry, man. I'll call you tomorrow.

His response comes quickly:

Remy: What the hell, man?

Remy: What was the emergency?

Remy: Is it your mom?

I hold the phone in my hand, contemplating if I should use my mom as an excuse.

Me: Talk tomorrow.

Remy: sure

I scroll through my contacts, searching for Ayemeline's name. I can't find any contact named Ayemeline. Did she not save her number on my phone? That was strange. I check the recent calls list. The first contact name on the list is Remy, with one missed call. Below Remy was one outgoing call. *True Love*. Beside the name is a heart emoji. My cheeks warm as I stare at the contact name. She is a bold one. I select the name and click on messages.

Me: True love?

I press "send" and stare nervously at my phone. Why am *I* nervous? She's the one who had the balls to save herself as 'True Love' on *my* phone. I could call her crazy, degrade her, or delete her number.

The text startles me from my thoughts. I read the text message:

True Love: Is there a problem?

She is truly bold.

Me: I just think it's brave of you to save your name like that on a guy's phone you just met.

True Love: I know what I want.

Me: Interesting

True Love: Do you like wasting time? Or are you the type of guy who goes after what he wants?

I'm not expecting the conversation to go like this. Then again, I don't know what I'm expecting from this woman. With her, it's like my body isn't my own. It's as if I'm a different person watching myself do things that I have no control over.

My hands fly over the keys.

Me: If I want something, I get it. No wasting time here.

True Love: That's good to know.

True Love: Am I one of those things you want?

True Love: Because you're what I want. ijs

I've never met a girl this assertive and straightforward. The girls I've dated were more on the reserved side. They liked to pretend they were good girls. And most of them were, at least for me. Yes, they gave up the goods easily enough despite pretending they didn't do that kind of thing. But they were still good girls. Ayemeline is different, however. She reminds me of a bad girl—a *really* bad girl. I need to know how bad.

Me: We'd have to see. I'd need to get to know you first.

True Love: What part of me do you want to get to know first?

I chuckle.

Me: What part are you offering?

Who am I right now? I was taught to respect women—not treat them like objects, to be gentle with them, to wine and dine them, to protect them. But something tells me this girl doesn't need to be treated gently.

True Love: Take your pick 😉

Me: How about I take you out tomorrow night? Then we could decide.

True Love: Most definitely.

We plan to meet at a bar twenty minutes away from campus. I can't risk Remy running into us. I don't know why I felt the need to hide her from him. I'm not doing anything wrong, but some part of me knows my best friend won't approve of Ayemeline.

***

The next day is spent going to my classes. I try hard to avoid Remy. I even skip my comp class because I know there's a possibility I'll run into him. I'm anxious about my date with Ayemeline, the woman who calls herself "True Love" on my phone. Although every fiber of my being tells me to stay away, I'm magnetically pulled toward her. I have a desire to get to know this girl called Ayemeline. She's already proven herself to be different. Different doesn't have to be a bad thing. It might be just what I need.

****

After my last class, I return to my dorm to shower and prepare for the night. My plans halt when I reach my door. Remy leans against the wall, his hands in his pocket, and he looks less than happy.

"Hey," I greet him sheepishly as I open the door to my dorm. My roommate, Danny, isn't here, thank God. I don't need him overhearing Remy giving me the third degree.

"Are you fucking kidding me?" Remy barks. "My girl hooks you up with her best friend, and you bail on her and us. What the fuck?"

"I'm sorry, man. I had an emer…"

"Yeah, you had an emergency. What exactly was this emergency?"

I pause, not knowing what to say but not wanting to lie.

"What was the emergency, Ari?" he pushes.

"Look, I had to take care of some things. Tell…" I pause because I really can't remember the girl's name.

Remy looks at me quizzically.

"Tell…her…I said I'm sorry."

"Tell her? You don't remember her name, do you?"

I give him an apologetic look.

"I don't care if you're not into her. But you know Brea is pissed. Now she's on my ass because you're *my* friend. You embarrassed her."

"I can talk to Brea," I say apologetically.

"Please don't. Nothing good has ever come from you talking to anyone." Remy sits on my bed. "I just want to make sure you're okay. You've been…" He pauses. "Weird lately. Your mind is obviously elsewhere. You seem lost."

"I'm good."

"So why weren't you in your comp class?"

"I was hoping to avoid a lecture from you," I say honestly.

"Asshole," Remy teases. "I gotta go. Brea is waiting for me to bring her food. She's mad at me but not mad enough not to ask me to bring her food. What are you doing tonight?"

"I'm just gonna stay in and study."

Remy looks at me as if he is analyzing my answer. "Okay," he finally says. "I'll talk to you later."

"Later, bro."

Remy leaves, and I disrobe and jump in the shower. After my shower, I throw on a pair of slim-fit jeans, a gray T-shirt, and my gray and black colorblock hightops. We plan to meet at 7:00, and I want to get there early to watch her walk in.

***

I stand outside the restaurant, waiting for her. My hands tremble in my pocket. I don't know what to expect from this date. Will she be the shy girl from the coffee shop? Or will she be the daring girl from our text exchange?

There are plenty of passers-by to distract me while I wait. People walk eagerly to their destinations, sweat gluing their clothes to their skin. Even with a breeze, the air remains thick and humid. A haze floats over the crowd like smoke. Out of the fog, Ayemeline appears like an apparition. I watch as the girl who won't leave my thoughts crosses the street and walks toward me. The other pedestrians around her tower over her five-foot frame. She can't be any more than 120 pounds. Her curves are in all the right places. She wears a solid black pleated denim skirt with a big buckle around the waist, a white sleeveless top that shows a hint of a belly button, and a pair of black high-heeled platform boots. The laces on her boots connect to a buckle and what looks like doilies. Or is it lace? Whatever it was, she looks sexy. Her curly hair rests on her shoulders. She has it parted down the middle, with each side resting behind her ear.

When she sees me, she smiles. I smirk, remembering our conversation from the previous night.

"You look…" I can't find the words.

She gives me a concerned look, then raises one eyebrow.

"You look…good," I finish.

She smiles a genuine smile. "Thanks. So do you."

She is so tiny; I could hold her in the palm of my hand. I tower over her by at least a foot. I could pick her up and just sit her on my…*FOCUS, ARI*! How did my mind get there?

"ID, please," the big man at the door asks. I reach into my pocket for my wallet and hand him my ID. He hands it back and looks at Ayemeline. She looks at me curiously. I stare at her, wondering why she isn't handing the man her ID.

"I...I left my wallet at hooome." She drags out the last word and says it with a slight inflection as if she were asking rather than telling. Her voice is sweet and innocent—nothing like the aggressive lioness I've known for the last 24 hours.

"No ID, no entry. Please step aside." The man beckons the people behind us to step forward. I grab Ayemeline's hand and step out of line.

"Why wouldn't you bring an ID when you knew we were going to a bar?" I ask her, confused.

"They wouldn't let me in, anyway," she retorts.

"How old are you?"

"Twenty."

"Twenty? So why did you agree to meet at a bar?"

"I thought you had connections to get me in." She smiles flirtatiously, exposing the slightest space between her two front teeth. She is adorable.

I can't help but smile. Her disarming smile, her skin freckled beautifully against the oranges and yellows of the sky, and her eyes all make me lose my mind. I find sanctuary in those coal-colored eyes. The light reflects in them and makes tiny, white stars. Suddenly, I want to kiss her.

"Do you want to get something to eat?" She rests her hand on my chest as she speaks. She is so close. A tingling sensation runs down my legs.

"Sure," I answer. "We can walk to Java's."

CHAPTER FIVE
AYEMELINE

He is huge. Walking beside Ari, I take in this hulk of a man. He has to be over six feet tall and bulky. His chest swells beneath his gray T-shirt. When we walk inside the restaurant, his shadow nearly fills the room. All eyes turn to us, to him. His tattooed hand swallows mine as he leads us to the counter to order our food. His touch feels warm and electric. It's unexpected, but I welcome it anyway.

Java's is a small restaurant located three blocks from the bar. It's famous for its crispy lemon pepper wings and curly fries, which is the only reason I come here. We place our order at the counter, and Ari lets go of my hand to pull out my chair. I miss his touch the second he takes it away.

We sit perpendicular to each other. He looks at me with a smoldering smile.

"So, you're a freshman?" He says it like more of a statement than a question.

"Yes. And you are…?" My eyes land on his biceps, desperate to touch it.

"I'm in my last year. I graduate in the fall, but might stay to complete my Masters in music therapy."

I nod. "Why'd you choose that path?"

"I love music. I want to use it to help people."

"That's very altruistic of you."

"How about you? What's your major?"

"I don't have one."

"What are you leaning toward?"

Our order arrives, interrupting our conversation and I reached over and grab a fry from his plate.

"Don't you have your own?" He teases, popping a fry into his mouth.

I watch the outline of his jaw move with each bite, his thin, perfectly trimmed beard tracing his jawline. I reach over and touch it with the tip of my index finger. He turns toward me, and my finger is suddenly on his gorgeous, thick lips. His tongue sticks out slightly, and he kisses the tip of my finger with it. He doesn't say anything, but his tongue traces the tip of my finger.

It's a silent confession. Neither one of us needs to say a word. I can see the fire in his eyes. The restaurant is filled with patrons, but all I can see is him.

He pulls his tongue back into his mouth, and I feel a sudden chill in its place. Even without his touch, a jolt of heat zaps between us. I know he feels it, too.

He looks away suddenly as if he's just realized what he had done. But it's too late. I already see the flicker of longing. The true echo of his feelings rings in those bright, hazel eyes.

"So…what do you do for fun?" He stares at me, waiting for a response.

What do I do for fun? I mull over the question. I honestly don't know. What do I consider fun? Is there anything I truly enjoy doing?

I settle on the only answer that makes sense. "Sex," I say, giving him a seductive grin.

He cocks an eyebrow. "Really? Wow! Was not expecting that answer."

"Do you have a problem with my answer?" I ask.

"Not at all. I think many people would agree with you. They're just too afraid to admit it.

"What about you?"

He leans back in his chair. "For me, football and music."

"Nice. You play an instrument?" I ask, surprised.

"Yes. Violin."

Now it's my turn to cock an eyebrow. "I would never guess you were a violinist."

"Yup. Been playing for thirteen years."

"That's interesting. You'll have to play something for me one day."

"I'd be happy to."

I take a sip of my drink.

"What made you start playing?"

He gives a soft laugh. "It's a funny story, actually. I started playing because I had a crush on this girl who played violin. So I begged my parents for lessons to impress her or something. I ended up liking it. I joined my school's orchestra in sixth grade and all the way through high school."

"So you played football, and you were in the orchestra?"

He nods.

"Were you the biggest kid in the orchestra?"

He laughs. "Actually, I was."

The waitress comes by and refills our drinks.

"Thank you," he says to her as she walks away.

"So did you get the girl?" I try not to ask, but curiosity is eating away at me.

"No," he admits. "She never noticed me."

Good.

Like a train colliding into a building filled with people, a group of guys are suddenly at our table. They are dressed like frat boys fresh from a round of golf.

"Yo, Ari!" one of the boys bellows. He's short and stocky with greasy tendrils.

Ari looks shocked as he is suddenly pulled into reality. The guys study me. There are four of them, but their presence feels like twenty.

"Sup, guys!" Ari greets them with no enthusiasm in his voice.

One of the boys grabs a chair from the neighboring table and pops his ugly ass on it. My eyes narrow at the boy, but he doesn't notice. I anchor my attention on the other boys. They look at me as if I am a meal for them to devour. The tallest of the bunch, but nowhere near Ari's height, licks his lips. I flay him with a look that says— 'I will stab you in the heart and eat it from the tip of my knife.' His look does not falter. Instead, he grabs another chair and pulls it next to his friend.

"What's going on? Why are you here?" Ari asks with a bit of hostility in his voice.

"We came to get some wings," the first boy who invited himself to our table responds innocently.

"I mean," Ari starts, his voice growing impatient, "why the fuck are you here—at our table—uninvited?"

"I didn't know you had a girl, Ari," the Lip Licker says, ignoring Ari's question. "You holding out on us, man?"

"He's tryna keep all the bitches to himself." This comes from a guy who stands behind Lip Licker. He wears a red polo shirt and khaki shorts that reach mid-thigh.

"Fuck you!" Ari exclaims. His jaw ticks, and I see he's trying to hold on to all his self-control to not physically make them leave.

Right at that moment, two girls walk up to our table. "Who we fucking?" one of the girls asks. I recognize her. She is in my English lit class. She often sits right beside me, although we have never spoken a word to each other.

"Ari is being a prick because we wanted to meet his girl," Lip Licker advises condescendingly.

The girls' eyes focus entirely on Ari, and my presence is excluded. Their gaze lingers on his muscled tattooed arms. *Just try it, bitch. I'll chop your nipples off and feed them to your mother.*

Red Polo starts talking to the other girl. Some conversation about a party last night, yada, yada, yada. But English lit, she keeps trying to engage my man in conversation like I'm not there. I'm no longer listening to the conversation at the table because I'm fuming now. *How dare…*

My thoughts are cut off when I feel Ari's warm hand on my skin. He uses the tip of his finger and gently rubs back and forth on the inside of my thigh. My breath hitches, and instantly, I no longer care about the people at our table or the conversations. All I can focus on is his touch. I feel comforted and aroused all at once. His touch is like a heated blanket on my skin. I want to do very bad things to this man.

A surge of electricity shoots through my pussy as his fingers creep higher to just below the hem of my skirt. He traces light circles on my inner thigh as he gets closer to invading the space between my folds. I part my legs slightly to give him easier access. *Fuck! This is intense!* His nails dig into my skin, and I almost cry out in ecstasy. If he keeps this up, I'm going to have an orgasm right there in the restaurant in front of all his friends, in front of English lit bitch. I welcome the release. I need it.

His fingers climb higher and higher until he touches the seam of my cotton panties. I hold his wrist tightly. I need to hold on to something. He uses his knuckles to make small strokes along the lining, right where my clit is pushed against the restraints of my underwear. My breath quickens. I look over at Ari, and I see his chest's rapid rise and fall. He looks straight ahead. He looks toward his friends, but he doesn't see them.

He pushes his finger against my clit. It pulses under his touch. And then it is gone. I watch him pick up a fry with the same hand that kissed my most intimate area and place it on his tongue. My pussy pools as I watch his long, thick tongue lap at the French fry. His other hand covers the crotch of his pants. I stare at that spot, longing to replace his hand with mine.

"So, Reyna wanted to know if you were single." I level a glowing look at the girl, directing her question to Ari. She smiles at him flirtatiously. *Great! More people I need to slice up and bury.*

"No!" Ari furrows his brow and folds his arms.

"I'm just asking. No need for the attack, Ari."

I don't like the way my man's name rolls off that bitch's tongue. Why are they still there? As if reading my thoughts, Ari gets up from the table.

"Since you guys won't leave, we will." He takes my hand and leads me out of the restaurant.

We walk two blocks in silence until we reach a deserted alleyway. With one quick movement, he pulls me and stands before me with my back against the wall. He stares at me for the longest time, his body overpowering mine. "I'm so sorry."

"Don't be," I whisper into his chest. Our heated bodies press against one another. I feel the thud of his heartbeat against mine. His fresh, linen scent leaves me feeling unsteady. His luminescent eyes peer into the window of my soul. They caress every part of me. They not only see who I am on the surface, but they see the part of me that needs to be loved by him.

"Somebody may see us." His warm breath kisses my lips as he speaks, and I want to swallow it. I want to keep his breath inside me.

My lips quiver, opening to speak, but no words emerge. My heart gallops in my chest as he gently places one finger on my chin and strokes it back and forth. My mind becomes a cauldron of ideas of what I will do with this man. My body tingles, and I feel a jolt of intense electricity in my pussy. I jerk slightly as the electricity makes its way to my head. Ari's eyes drift downward; his probing visual caresses cause my nipples to push against the soft fabric of my top.

His forefinger dips lower until it hovers over my nipple. "I want you," he says, his voice sounding raspy. He is so close, so close I can breathe him in. Ari drags his eyes to my lips.

"Kiss me," I finally manage to breathe. He lowers his eyes and closes them. My hand reaches up to touch his cheek. Suddenly, as if he's broken free from a trance, he firmly grabs my hand.

"I need to get you home."

"What?" I mutter, still delirious from his proximity.

"We can't do this. I need to get you home."

One second, we are so close to sharing a passionate kiss, and the next second, Ari pulls away from me, refusing to even look at me. I don't understand what happened, but something shifted in him.

The night wasn't supposed to end like this. I should've had Ari between my legs now, but instead, I am left with just my Satisfier. Although it does the job, I still feel robbed of the experience the night had promised.

I know he'd felt the same things I'd felt at that moment. So why hadn't he taken what I knew he wanted to take from me? Did he think I didn't want him? This is fucking insane. I have to make it clear to him that I want him just as much as he's shown me he wants me.

CHAPTER SIX
ARIEL.

e walked in silence to Ayemeline's apartment. Her only acknowledgment of me was her hostile glare. With clenched jaws, she turned around and walked inside as soon as we made it to her door, leaving me there to think about how careless I had been.

Now I'm back in my dorm, wondering how the fuck did I let it get that far. I told myself I wouldn't get that close to another woman again—especially not this soon. I need to get to know her and understand her limits before I can ever be with her. Yet there I was on our first date, unable to resist her. In that alley, I was so close to taking everything she'd be willing to give me and even things she was unwilling to give. But I can't—not to her. Besides this isn't the plan. The plan isn't to fuck her. It isn't to become irrationally obsessed with a woman I barely knew. The plan is to get closure—whatever the fuck that means. As I sit here lying to myself, I realize I'm not even sure of my intentions when I first followed her out of that restaurant. I just knew I couldn't resist the chance to meet her.

Ayemeline consumes my thoughts entirely. I thought I could erase her from my mind if I got to know who she was. Stupid, I know. Now she has embedded herself in my mind and the deepest parts of my soul.

***

I strip out of my clothes, leaving only my red plaid boxers. I love the freedom of being alone in my dorm. My roommate hardly spends time here, preferring to crash at his girlfriend's apartment. I know nothing about her except that she's an older woman who graduated some years ago, but I'm grateful to her. At times like this, I appreciate not having to share my space with someone else.

I spend the rest of the night in bed, obsessing, as I have every night since the first time I saw her. Now, however, I have so much more to obsess over—her sweet, vanilla scent, the way her mouth curves up in one corner, and the way her midnight eyes twinkle in the moonlight. I obsess over her nose and smile at how they wrinkle slightly when she tries to think of what to say. I focus on the scattered freckles that decorate her unique features.

My hand reaches into my boxers. I circle the base of my cock with my hand and squeeze. I let out a loud groan at the sensation. I imagine Ayemeline's tight pussy clenched around my shaft. I stroke my dick up and down, and a warm bead of precum coats my fingers. I massage it along the length of myself and moan as my dick swells.

I think of those sweet rose-colored lips and the way they would feel wrapped around my dick. Then I imagine my hand wrapped around her pretty neck. I squeeze as I fuck her from behind. With each thrust, I squeeze harder, tighter. I no longer have control of my body as I continue to pound her pussy. Each time I pull out, I can see red coating my dick, and that makes me even harder. I increase my pace in and out of her pussy as I squeeze her neck. I need more. The harder I fuck her, the more I want. And I take more…and more…and more until her choked cries become silent, and all I can hear is our skin slapping together. More. Fuck! I need more. I take even more from her until I can feel it in my head and running down my spine. My body tenses as I explode deep inside her. I let out a beastly yell as my dick jerks and my whole body shakes. I let go of her neck, and she plops onto the bed—her eyes are open, but they see nothing. Her black hair encases her face. Black hair. Not red. Black. *Shit.*

I look down. My cum-soaked hand is still gripping my dick hard. Releasing my dick, I rush to the bathroom to clean up the evidence of my guilt as quickly as possible. *What the fuck is wrong with me?* I use a warm towel to clean myself. I try to be a good person. I really do. But it's like I'm constantly fighting myself for control. I need to get rid of my impure thoughts. Years of celibacy haven't helped eliminate these memories from my head. Until I could control these feelings, I could never be with anyone.

The vibration of my phone on the nightstand beside my bed interrupts my thoughts. I walk over and grab it. Sitting on the edge of my bed, I look at the screen:

True Love: So this is what we're doing now? Making my pussy wet then abandoning me to fuck myself?

My dick instantly hardens again. I picture her inserting those delicate fingers into her soaked pussy. Lying back on my pillow, I respond:

Ari: Really? Show me?

True Love: If you wanted to see, you should've come inside.

Ari: Give me another chance?? *sad face emoji*

True Love: Do you think you deserve one?

Ari: I don't.

Ari: But I hope you'll give me one anyway.

Silence. A minute goes by, and no response comes through. I continue staring at my phone willing it to ping again. Another minute goes by—then another—then another—then five. I hold the phone in one hand and grip the base of my cock with the other. I can't get the image of her fucking herself out of my head. My chest begins to feel restricted. Six minutes. *Did I fuck things up? She thinks you're an asshole, you dummy.* I squeeze my dick harder. *You fucking idiot.* But this is a good thing. I need to stay away from her. It's the best thing for both of us. It isn't worth the risk.

My phone rings. Looking down, I see **True Love** pop up on the screen. My heart leaps. I sit up hurriedly and select "accept" with trembling fingers, my dick still poking through my boxers. Her face lights up my phone screen. I smile when I see her, eyes glistening and the sweetest smile on her face.

"Tell me, do you think I'm too good for you, or you're too good for me?" She slightly raises one eyebrow in question.

"What?" The question catches me off guard.

"I'm trying to find a logical explanation for what happened tonight, and that's the only one I could come up with. So which one is it?" Her voice is soft yet demanding.

"Neither. It's just that…" I don't know what to say—how to explain why I had to get away from her as quickly as possible.

She stares at me, waiting for me to finish.

"We just met, and I thought we were moving too fast."

"Bullshit," she spits. Her smile drops.

"It's not…"

"Do you want me or not?"

"I do want you."

"So why are you such a fucking tease?"

I chuckle at that. "Maybe I want to make you angry. Let all that anger build up inside you so that when I fuck you, I can fuck you hard and long." *What the fuck am I saying?*

Her heated gaze lingers on me, and she smiles, which tells me she has many bad thoughts. "Prove it," she dares.

"I was stroking my dick thinking about you," I confess.

"Really? Are you stroking it now?" Her tone is now low and mischievous.

"Yes." My voice is barely a whisper.

"Mmmm," she moans, and I have the distinct impression she is touching herself.

My heart races as I watch her close her eyes and roll her head back. Her breath quickens. I stare, mesmerized at the sight before me.

"Are you touching yourself, you dirty girl?" A shiver runs down my spine as I spread pre-cum across my swollen head before dipping lower to caress my balls.

Her eyes lock onto mine. "You like it when I touch myself?"

"Yes." My voice is rough with lust.

"You did something bad today," she says in her silky voice, "you should be punished."

I groan and stroke faster. "What…" a short, jagged breath escapes my lips "kind of…punishment?"

"The kind that will have your cum drenching my pussy?" Her breath becomes uneven.

Our eyes stay locked on each other as we touch ourselves, our breaths growing rapidly. I stroke faster and harder. I need more. Although the camera stays on our faces, I can see her pussy in my mind, soaked with her juices, fingers deep inside down to the knuckles. My orgasm nears once again, the intensity increasing with each rough stroke.

"Are you gonna cum for me, baby?" Her voice is authoritative yet playful.

"Yes," I breathe out.

"What part of my body do you want to put your seed into?" Ayemeline's feathery voice gives me just the right harmonious melody to drive me over that ledge.

"On your pussy." A tingling sensation starts in my groin as a surge of energy rushes to my head. I squeeze my eyes shut as hot ribbons of fluid explode onto my hand and stomach. My legs go numb, and my head feels light. A second later, Aymeline emits a guttural moan as her shoulders convulse, then convulse a second time, then a third time. The last two convulsions become softer as she settles into a state of gratification. She inspects my face with hooded eyes. As my own wave of satisfaction hits me, I no longer care about anything else but her. I need her.

***

My phone vibrates against my wooden nightstand, making me jump out of a deep sleep. I'm agitated at the intrusion. My dream last night was filled with her—her eyes, her skin, her tight pussy wrapped around my…

"Yo, put that away and answer your damn phone!" Danny's voice leaves me feeling unsettled and agitated. How long had he been there? He feels like a voyeur now when my mind is filled with thoughts of fucking her. "Ari, snap the fuck out of it and put that shit away!"

I follow his eyes to my crotch, where my bulging erection is out on display. I frantically grab my blanket from my bed and cover it up.

"Why the hell were you naked?" Danny's tone sounds disgusted, but he wears a smirk that tells me he knows exactly why I'm naked.

"Why are you here?" I snarl. I give him that look that says he has no business being here even though it is his room, too. I wasn't expecting him. He's hardly ever in our room.

"This is my room," he answers obviously.

I glare at him, willing him to leave.

"Relax, man. I just came to grab a few things. I'm leaving."

I stare at him, waiting for him to leave so I can grab some pants.

"You gonna answer that or what?"

I glance at my phone, which continues to vibrate. Eagerly, I grab it, expecting to see True Love. I wrinkle my nose when I read who it is.

"Hey, Ma," I answer in a monotonous voice.

"Do you know how many times I had to call you before you picked up?" My mother's raspy voice comes through the speaker.

"I was asleep, Ma."

"Oh, I'm bothering you now?" My mother's snarl brings me back to my teenage years.

"No." I rub my neck and let out a loud, exasperated sigh.

I hear my mother's hacking cough through the speaker, wheezing between each one. I hold the phone a few inches from my ear.

"You don't even…*cough*…visit your mother. *Cough*. What if I die tomorrow? You'll never forgive yourself." She lets out a cough so loud it is as if her insides are expelling out of her.

"I have school." I fidget with the blanket that is covering my now extremely flaccid dick.

Through my peripheral vision, I see Danny waving frantically at me. I can't decipher what he's trying to tell me, so I just give him an exaggerated wave. He picks up his bag and leaves the dorm. I am glad to see him go. Having him watch me have an unwelcome conversation with my mother is almost worse than the exhibitionist show I unintentionally put on for him.

"I see you have your priorities aligned. Your brother abandoned me. Your father abandoned me, and now you're abandoning me. What did I do to deserve such harsh treatment in my life? I raised you. If you're in that little school of yours, it's because of me, you ungrateful son of a..."

"Did you need something?" I cut off her excessive droning.

"I don't need anything from you—not that you would care, anyway."

I rest my forehead on the palm of my hand and close my eyes.

"I can come by this weekend if you need me to."

"Don't do anything for me. I'll survive on my own. Maybe you'll come visit my grave when I'm dead."

"Ma, I have to get to class, but I'll see you this weekend."

"Of course you do."

"Okay, gotta go. Love you."

She let out a loud humph. With that, I quickly disconnect the call.

The call with my mom certainly put me in a different place from where I was the night before. I stare motionlessly straight ahead. The weekend is in two days, and I promised my mother I'd be there to help her with whatever she had called me for. It's often nothing but her desire for company, which isn't something I'm eager to give. My visits to my mother stem more from obligation and guilt and not from any desire to be around her.

***

The thunderous knock on my door shatters the quiet in the room. I stand, letting the blanket drop to the ground, and pull on a pair of boxers from my drawer. I have no idea where the boxers I had on last night are or even when I took them off.

"Yo, Ari. You in there?" Remy's voice comes through the door.

"Yeah, give me a second," I yell back as I pull on gray sweatpants and a white T-shirt. I fling my door open, and Remy walks inside.

"Bruh, your class starts in ten minutes."

"I'm aware."

"You just getting up?"

"My mom called."

Remy's nose crinkles at the announcement.

"Yup," I concur, "and it was a fun conversation, like always."

"Let me guess. She was calling to tell you how you're a bad son who doesn't ever visit."

"What else is there to call me about?"

"How can you abandon your sweet old mother like that?" Remy deadpans.

"I don't know. I guess I was just raised that way."

Remy laughs. "Good luck, man. You're gonna need it."

Once Remy leaves, I pick up my violin and play. It's been the one thing that has brought me some semblance of peace all these years. When I play, I am transported to another world where I'm happy.

Filling the space with music, I deliver a vibrato that grows harsh and brittle in its upper registers. The music is harsh and intense, but I don't care. I finish playing and set my instrument back in its case.

I'm scheduled to play tonight at the Brew, which features local performers once a week. I signed up for a featured spot three months ago and last week, they called me and offered me a slot.

I grab my phone and shoot Remy a text:

Me: You coming tonight?

Remy: I'll be there.

I contemplate inviting Ayemeline but I decide against it. Maybe I can give her a private show later. At least that's what I tell myself. But the real reason is that Remy will be there. And I feel that if she's there, I'd have to admit what I did to Brea's friend.

***

I usually look forward to the weekends. It is a time to get away from my classes and hang out with the guys. This weekend, however, is not one of those weekends. The fourteen-hour drive back home to

Iowa is something I try to avoid as much as possible. I know I will miss at least a few days of class, which is one of the reasons I try to avoid it. Not the main reason—but one of them nonetheless. I arrive at the home I grew up in, which never quite felt like a home, and I park at the curb. The lawn is covered in weeds and soda cans, the mailbox tilts at a sixty-degree angle, and my mom's car, which hasn't been driven in two years, sits in the driveway collecting rust.

I use my key to unlock the front door. Using force, I turn the key and push my shoulder against the door to open it. Walking into the living room, I realize this house will continue to feel worse each time I return home.

This house, which was once my mother's pride and joy, now looks like it should be featured in a hoarding documentary. Shelves line each wall, housing various books, figurines, trophies, and medals from the awards I'd won. I study my high school HOG award on the shelf, running my fingers over the gold lettering that spells out my name. I wipe away a thick layer of dust as I try to ignore the tightness in my chest. *Ghosts should stay in the past,* I tell myself. I jerk my head away from the trophy, focusing on my third and fourth-grade spelling bee ribbons. They are haphazardly taped to the wall above the fitted sheet-covered couch. I smile as I remember the look of pride on my father's face when I won those ribbons. He was so proud. On the other hand, my mother questioned why they were second-place ribbons and not first.

My brother, Hassan's, and my photos decorate the coffee table. My mother keeps his picture up, although as she proclaims, he is a good-for-nothing son. It is her way of fooling herself into thinking she cares about her sons more than she does. Keeping his picture up is part of her victim story. It shows that even though he doesn't care about her, she cares about him. That is a lie only she believes.

The kitchen, which is easily seen in our open-concept home, isn't any less overwhelming than the living room. Food is splattered all over the floor and table, a film of grease sits on the stove, and dirty dishes are strewn all over the kitchen counters and sink. I open the cabinet door under the sink and pull out a pair of yellow rubber gloves. As I slip them on, I can hear my mother's hacking cough coming from upstairs. Ignoring it, I grab a sponge, pour the little dishwashing soap left in the bottle, and wash the dishes.

After getting the kitchen to look more habitable, I climb the stairs to my mother's bedroom. The variegated orange carpet, which once was the lush rug my mother would forbid Hassan and me from walking on with shoes, now holds the stains of a life not worth living. I tried to get someone to come clean up while I was at school, but my mother always found a way to run them away. So I gave up, resorting to doing a quick clean-up whenever I came home.

"Ma," I call out as I approach the top of the stairs. The upstairs hallway is decorated with the same filthy carpet as the stairs. I get to the bedroom door and give it a gentle knock. No answer. I turn the doorknob and slowly open the door. My mother sits in bed with a book in her hand and stares at me with a "what the hell are you doing here" look on her face. "Hi, Ma," I greet, ignoring her expression.

"Why are you here?" She speaks brusquely.

"I told you I was coming."

She turns away from me and focuses her eyes on her book. "Go get me a glass of water," she demands without looking at me.

"Yes, ma'am." I walk downstairs and find a clean glass. I grab a water bottle from the fridge and pour it into the glass.

I hand her the glass back in her room, which she quickly takes from me. She takes two sips and places the glass on the nightstand beside her bed. I look at my mother. The woman who was once a dominating presence is now a withered shell of a person who can barely walk a block without stopping to catch her breath. Her body looks swollen, and her face is a lighter shade of pale than I remembered. At least she still has her mouth and that ferocious attitude. That is here to stay.

"Have you been taking your blood pressure medicine?"

My mother coughs into a tissue, and I can see the spots of blood that are left behind. "I have to take it with food."

"No, you don't, Ma. You don't need food to take your medication."

"Is that why you left me here to starve?" My mother sneers at me. I realize I walked right into her trap.

"What are you talking about? I have groceries delivered here every week."

My mother rolls her eyes and goes back to her book.

"Ma, you have to take your medication."

"What do you care? You want me to die anyway." I feel the pressure building in my head, as if I am wearing a hat that is two sizes too small. I walk over to my mother's dresser, where she keeps her medications, and inspect the prescription bottles. My mother should've been due for a refill in a few days, but her pill bottle is still full.

"You haven't been taking these."

She pretends to be completely engrossed in her book and ignores me. I open the bottle and pour a pill into my hand. I walk over to her and offer up my open palm. My mother's gaze lingers on her book. After a few seconds of ignoring me, I grab a napkin, place the pill on it, and place it on her nightstand. This is going to be a long weekend.

CHAPTER SEVEN
AYEMELINE

Six days. That's how long it's been since our date—since I've seen or heard from Ari. Six days of misery. Six days of isolation. Six days of frustration. I sent him a few messages, but he never responded. *Why is he ignoring me? Did I do something wrong?* Perhaps that whore he was with at the restaurant with distracted him.

My eyes land on Ari's best friend Remy, holding hands with the skinny pale girl. This is the same girl that was at the Mexican restaurant with Ari and the whore. They're engrossed in conversation as she uses her other hand to sip her paper coffee cup. Stopping beside a tree, he turns around to face her and lands a heated kiss on her lips. After what seems like an eternity, he pulls away and grips the edge of her T-shirt. The pale girl giggles as he nuzzles his face into her neck. *Get on with it. I don't have all day.* As if hearing my thoughts, they pull away from each other again and walk down the brick path toward the dorm. I follow a safe distance behind. If anyone knows where Ari is, it's his best friend. I'm careful not to be seen. I don't want Ari to think I am some type of psychopath who will stalk his friends.

They reach the girls' dorm and stop in front of it. They speak, but I am too far away to hear. Remy rubs her cheek with his knuckle. Then, he pulls away slightly, as if sensing impending danger. His brow furrows as he investigates his surroundings intently. The pale girl looks in the direction he is looking, a confused look on her face. She says something to him. He shakes his head, gives her a small kiss on the lips, and watches her as she walks into the dorms. Remy pulls out his phone and stands facing the dorms. He types out a message, holds it in his hand, and stares at it. *Are you texting Ari? Do you know where he is?*

Without warning, I'm pushed to the ground. A stabbing flash of pain emanates throughout my wrists and arms as it hits the ground first.

"You need to watch where you're going," the nasal voice says.

My nostrils flare as I glare up at the culprit. I recognize this girl as the whore from Ari's unfortunate double date. *Really, bitch?* She glares down at me and with a flick of her hair, she turns and walks away. There are students gathered on the lawn, all smirking and whispering to one another as they look in my direction. I get up and rub my hands together.

Looking around, Remy is nowhere to be seen. *Shit!* I've been playing nice for far too long. I tried to be good. Now she has just sealed her fate.

I'm in my apartment. "Bitch Better Have My Money" by Rihanna plays through the Bluetooth speakers. Red stains coat my phone screen. The energetic, crisp sound of the melody booms through my speakers. It's like a wave crashing on rocks. It pulsates throughout my body, and I move with the beat. It is thick and angry, flooding out from every part of the apartment at once. Red crimson inks my hands and clothes, symbolizing strength and vengeance. A drop of blood hit the cool, wooden tiles beneath me. I put one finger to my mouth and suck as I continue to dance. It is salty and slightly bitter, filling me with determination. I feel powerful in this moment.

Later that evening, I'm in his dorm watching him sleep. His chest rises and falls with each soft breath. With his mouth slightly parted, he lets out a sequence of soft baby whistles. A sense of peace overtakes his features. He hadn't noticed me when he came into his room that evening.

A duffel bag is flung in the corner of the room. He must've gone away. I slowly get up from the brown wooden chair in the corner of the room and tiptoe over to the bag. I unzip it and rummage through the oversized duffle. Clothes, toothbrush, a pair of shoes in a plastic bag, three pairs of socks, and a few pairs of underwear are all neatly folded and meticulously placed in the bag. I pick up the toothbrush, which is in a freezer bag. I open the bag and pull it out. I place it into my mouth and gently suck. "Mmhh," I moan quietly. Ari shifts in the bed, and I freeze. He stops moving, and I rest the toothbrush on the stack of folded T-shirts in the bag. I walk over to his hamper and pull out a pair of boxer briefs. I bring the underwear to my nose and take a slow, drawn-out breath. Linen and musk permeate my nostrils.

Unfastening the button of my jeans, I reach my hand into my damp panties—my pussy already moist from my arousal. I gently massage my throbbing clit as I hold the crotch of Ari's boxer briefs to my nose. He shifts again as I give a stifled moan of satisfaction.

I freeze as he stands. He takes a few steps toward the door, his back to me, and stops. He stands there for a few seconds. I hold my breath with one hand gripping his underwear tightly and the other down my pants. Suddenly, he opens the door to his dorm room and walks out, closing the door behind him.

CHAPTER EIGHT
ARIEL

I'd love to say the week spent with my mother flew by—that we connected as if no time had passed. But I'd be lying. That was the most grueling week of my life. It seems as my mother gets older, she becomes more unbearable. She's always demanded respect in a way that a mother should never require of young boys growing up. Now however, she is needy, demanding, and hostile. What I had initially intended to be a couple of days dragged on into a week. I spent that time cleaning, force-feeding her medication, drawing her baths, and cooking—all while my mother hurled insult after insult at me. To say I'm exhausted is an understatement. To top it off, the fourteen-hour drive back turned into a seventeen-hour nightmare due to all the traffic.

I open the door to my dorm, throw my duffle bag into a corner, and kick off my shoes. I drop myself onto the springy mattress. I'm just glad it's the weekend again. My eyes grow heavy, and my thoughts become more incoherent with each passing minute. My consciousness quickly ebbs away as I close my eyes and become dead to the world.

I don't know what day or time it is when I wake up again. The room is dark, with only the warm glow of the moon peering in through the window. I roll over on my back and feel the intense pressure in my groin. I get up to make my way to the bathroom. An eerie feeling overcomes me—like I'm being watched. I stand still and listen. Somewhere in the distance, a dog barks, and muffled music pulses through the walls. The lack of sleep over the last few days is making me paranoid. I open my dorm door and make my way to the hall bathroom.

***

When I wake up again, it is daylight. The sun warms my cheeks as it shines through the window. I pick up my phone to check the time. 3:12 p.m. *Had I really slept for almost twenty-four hours?* I also notice all the missed calls and text messages. When I was visiting my mother, I didn't have a minute to check my phone, and I was not in the right headspace to speak to anyone. I open my text thread and read the top two messages—Remy, two messages, and True Love, sixty-three new messages. *Sixty-three?* Shit! I keep fucking up with this girl. She is going to hate me. I open Remy's messages first since they are the quickest.

Remy: You still at mommy dearest?

Remy: Let me know when you get back.

Remy understands what it is like over there and doesn't demand anything more than I could give. Ayemeline, on the other hand, doesn't know what it was like. So, to her, my disappearing looks like an asshole move.

True Love: Hey

True Love: I had fun with you last night. Next time, we should try it in person.

My dick leaps at her words.

True Love: Are you doing it again?

True Love: Fucking me then ignoring me?

True Love: Are you going to respond?

True Love: You better be dead somewhere.

True Love: So I was thinking we could go out again. Maybe somewhere a little more private next time.

True Love: *winking face emoji

True Love: If you don't want to, just have the balls to tell me.

True Love: You better not be ghosting me.

True Love: *angry face emoji

True Love: I don't like being ignored, ARI!!!

True Love: Where are you?

True Love: Hey. Are you ready to talk now????

True Love: ??????

True Love: Did I do something wrong?

True Love: Is it me or is it someone else?

True Love: You're a fucking asshole. I hope you know that.

True Love: I DON'T ENJOY BEING FUCKED WITH, ARI!!!

True Love: Good morning, Ari. Call me when you're ready.

True Love: I'm going to bed. I'll be thinking about you.

True Love: I'm sorry for whatever I did. I can make it up to you.

Her messages continue this way for forty-two more messages. They are a mixture of anger, frustration, and sadness. A part of me feels bad for not responding to her. Another part tells me to run because what the fuck? What kind of person leaves sixty-three messages for someone after one date? My hand hovers over my phone screen, knowing I owe her an explanation. It isn't right to leave her with nothing.

Me: Hey. I'm sorry I haven't been able to get back to you. I've been out of town visiting my mom. Backspace. Backspace. Backspace. **My sick mom.** Send.

The response comes almost immediately:

True Love: No worries. I'm sorry to hear about your mom.

True Love: Is she okay?

Me: Not really, but it is what it is. How are you?

True Love: I'm better now. *smiling face emoji

Me: I didn't mean to ignore your messages. It's just complicated with my mom.

True Love: I forgive you.

True Love: But you know you have to make it up to me.

Me: I'll be happy to. *winking face emoji*

My phone buzzes with an incoming text message from Remy.

Me: I have to run, but maybe we could meet up later?

True Love: Definitely.

Me: Then we can talk about you calling me an asshole.

True Love: LOL. Let's pretend you didn't see that.

I smile and open up Remy's message:

Remy: Kyle said he saw you. You back?

Me: Hey. I passed out when I got back. What are ya'll up to?

Remy: A lot of shit went down. Come to the Brew.

Me: What kind of shit?

I put my phone down and grab a towel and some extra clothes. I need a shower—and some clean sheets. I make a mental note to change my sheets when I get back. After showering and dressing in a black Tee and a pair of black sweats, I grab my phone and head to the Brew. While walking to the coffee shop, I see a tree with flowers and teddy bears leaning against it. There is a picture of a girl beside the flowers. There is something vaguely familiar about the girl.

The campus is quieter than usual, and several students walk around with their heads downcast. Two girls hug while one cries on the other's shoulder. Shit must've really gone down while I was gone.

Out of the Brew's doorbell announces my arrival. Remy sits at a table toward the back with a red-faced Brea clinging to him. I make my way over to them. Remy looks up at me with raised eyebrows.

"You look like shit," he observes.

"Thanks." I pull out a chair and sit down. Brea's cheeks are soaked with tears. "What's going on?"

"Crystal's…dead," Brea says between tears and sniffles. She uses a tissue to wipe her nose.

My eyes narrow. "Who's Crystal?"

Brea gives me a death stare and sobs uncontrollably. She gets up and runs to the bathroom.

Remy looks at me with raised eyebrows.

"Was I supposed to know who Crystal was?" I ask, moving closer to Remy and leaning in.

"Dude. Sometimes I wonder about you."

"Seriously. Who was she?" I'm genuinely curious at this point. Apparently, this Crystal girl was someone I was supposed to know.

"Brea's best friend. The girl she set you up with. The one you ignored all night and left at the restaurant."

"Oh, *that* Crystal."

Remy looks at me and rolls his eyes. "You know Brea still hates you for that."

I smile as I remember the reason I ran out of that restaurant and everything that occurred because of that night.

"What the fuck are you smiling about?" Remy is staring at me.

I quickly wipe the smile off my face as best as I can.

"You make it really hard for me to vouch for you; you do know that?" Remy looks over toward the bathroom Brea has disappeared into. "I'm gonna go check on her."

"I'm gonna head out. This is a lot." After a week of pure hell, I need to be in a different state of mind and all this death and sadness isn't doing it for me. I need to see her.

***

Ayemeline and I agree to meet at her apartment fifteen minutes after I escaped the coffee shop. Her apartment complex is off-campus and within walking distance of various shops in the area. It is a cozy place with one oversized sectional that takes up almost the whole living room. Neon pink, green, and yellow pillows sit on a cream sofa. A purple fleece throw blanket is draped on the back of the sofa. The floor is covered with an oversized area rug with splashes of greens, yellows, pinks, and whites. I take a seat on her couch facing her pink sheer curtains. Plants and soft lighting surround me. The cozy yet colorful atmosphere of the apartment makes me feel instantly at peace.

"You brought your violin," she observes.

"Yeah," I say, smiling. "I figured I'd keep my promise of playing for you, you know, since you asked."

Her smile is loud and contagious. "I'm so excited. What are you going to play?"

"Oh, you want me to play now? Right out the gate. Okay. Sure. What would you like me to play?"

"I don't know. Anything."

I unzip my case, pull out my violin and bow. Ayemeline sits on her sofa, her eyes on me steady as glass.

I lift my violin to my shoulder and play a sonata. The music is romantic, passionate, and haunting. Her features are set in concentration as she watches my every movement. I take her on a journey of intense warmth and melancholy.

I close my eyes as I feel my heart slow. The smooth sound pours like water, hitting every corner of the apartment. I feel every note in my bones. As I finish playing, I watch her. She is tense with emotion.

I put my instrument down.

"That was…amazing." Her eyes sweep over me. "You are a whole package."

I feel the heat of her stare. "Thanks. I'm glad you like it."

"I loved it. I wonder what else you could do."

I smile at her flirtatious comment. "Nice place," I say, attempting to change this subject. My eyes explore my surroundings as I admire her apartment. The scent of vanilla fills the air. Her apartment smells like her. I have the uncontrollable urge to take a deep breath and suck it all inside my body.

"Thanks." She sits on the couch beside me, facing my direction. Her elbow is propped on the back of the couch, and her cheek rests on her hand. She looks at me and smiles. "I like you being here. You fit right in."

I give an uncomfortable chuckle. "Really?"

"Definitely." Her hand reaches out and tangles a string of my hair. I feel my cock make a small jump in my pants.

"I have a question for you," I say, eager to shift the erotic energy in the room. Shifting my body to face each other, I ask, "Why are you single?"

"Why are you?" she retorts.

"I asked you first."

She pauses, seeming to contemplate her answer. Then she reaches over and grabs the blanket to cover her lap. "I hadn't found you," she says.

I laugh. "That is a pretty cheesy pick-up line."

She watches me, unsmiling.

I straighten my features and try again. "You were waiting for me?"

"Yes." She furrows her brows above unblinking eyes. "I was waiting for you to find me."

I frown at her response.

"How about you?"

"Me? I don't know. Life. School. Family."

"I don't know what that means."

"It means I have a lot going on, so I never had time to really date."

"How about now?"

"Now? Now…I don't know. I think you just sort of…found me. I think…" *I'm obsessed with you. I need you. I want to melt inside you until we are one. I need to possess you.* "I like you."

She smiles the kind of smile that reaches her eyes and melts my soul. This girl, with her copper, ginger hair encircling her face and her eyes darkening when she looks at me, is undeniably breathtaking.

But something about those eyes—how she looks at me tells me she has already put her scent on me, marking me as hers. She seems to be a solitary creature—innocent and nonthreatening. As I stare into those coal-colored eyes, however, all I can see is black, and I know all that softness could easily turn to hostility if threatened, like a fox.

Her excessive text messages while I was with my mom tell me there is something about this girl that I should watch out for, something carnal and possessive. But right now, I can only stare into her eyes, bathe in her warm scent, and imagine what it would feel like to kiss her soft, rosy lips.

"You remind me of a fox," I muse.

"What?" She laughs.

"It's a good thing. You're cute. And foxes are my favorite animals."

"You have a favorite animal? Do you have a favorite color, too?" She teases me.

"Red," I respond frankly.

"Really?"

"Yup." I playfully tangle a piece of her ginger tendrils between my fingers.

She beams at me with undisguised lust. It takes everything I have to not give in to her gravitational pull. *Keep the conversation going. Keep yourself distracted.* "When was your last relationship?"

She looks at me and purses her lips, her smile dropping suddenly. Her face is like a child who has just discovered that Santa is not real.

"Bad question?"

"Very bad question," she mutters almost too quietly for me to hear.

"Why?" What is it about her past that she wants to keep hidden? I observe her closely. I want to know everything about her.

Her mouth opens to speak, then pauses to collect her thoughts before responding. "Because what happened in the past isn't important."

I narrow my eyes. "Don't you want to know about my past?" I question.

"Not really." I notice the slight shift in her body as she tries to angle herself away from me. She stares out the window, looking like she wants to jump out of it.

I raise an eyebrow at that. That's a new one. I've never had a girl not want to know about every detail of my past. "Okay..."

"Look." She looks at me. "I don't care about your past. All I care about is now."

"Is it because you don't want to share *your* past with me?"

She looks down at her hands and fidgets with her nails before leaping off the couch. "You want a drink?"

I grab her hand and pull her back down to me. I caress her chin and press my lips to hers. I smell her sweet vanilla scent. Then her tongue is in my mouth. I wasn't expecting that, but it is very much welcome, nonetheless. A surge of warmth fills me, and I'm left wanting more, needing more of her. In one quick movement, her hip straddles mine as she places her crotch directly on top of mine. *Shit. Stay in control.* My dick throbs and springs to attention under the warmth of her body. She pulls away and looks into my eyes, caressing my face. Slowly she leans forward, and our lips make contact once more. Her lips are silky and warm, like hot cocoa on Christmas morning. She parts them slightly, allowing me to slip my tongue inside this time. The intensity of the kiss is dizzying. Our breaths are heavy, and I feel the thumping of our heartbeats. My little fox's body quivers with need as she fumbles to unfasten the button on my jeans. I hold her hand and pull away from her kiss. She stares at me; her eyes are filled with questions.

"I'm sorry."

"If you don't stop fucking with me, you *will* be sorry, Ari!" Ayemeline's jaw clenches.

"I do want you. I just need us to take things slow…for now."

"Is it me?" Her lips are a quiver of emotion.

"Absolutely not. I've…um…I've…been…" I'm afraid of how she will respond. This girl has already proven to have a little fire inside her, and she isn't afraid to burn me with it.

Ayemeline looks into my eyes, our bodies still so close that I feel her stagnant breathing. "Please just say it," her voice is soft and shaky.

"I'm celibate," I blurt out, "for the past five years." I hold my breath.

"Wh…what? How? Why?" Her eyes grow impossibly wide.

"It's just a decision I made after high school. I…uh…needed to do this."

Ayemeline shifts off my lap and sits beside me. "Well, that's no fun," she mumbles under her breath. She rests her forehead on her hand and massages her temple. "I…don't really know what to say," she speaks slowly.

I'm quiet because I don't know what to say either.

"How long is this vow of celibacy going to last? I'm not trying to be insensitive or anything, but I need to fuck you. And I know you need to fuck me. So why are you torturing yourself?"

"I want to make sure my person is my person. I want to make sure whoever I choose to be with accepts me for everything I am. "

"I know that's not it," she says, staring pointedly down at my crotch.

"I don't have small dick insecurities." I feel the need to make that clear.

"I know. I can tell." Her eyes remain on my crotch where a bulge is reforming.

I lift her chin to force her to look at me. "Do you think you can handle me?" Her eyes glisten with her arousal.

She nods.

"Good. Then you'll have plenty of time to show me, little fox because I'm not going anywhere."

CHAPTER NINE
AYEMELINE

2 Days Prior

*M*uffled music pulsed from the lounge above us. The worn wooden stairs creaked as I made my way down them, alerting my guest of my arrival.

"Hello, friend," I said cheerfully as I skipped toward her. I popped my red blow pop into my mouth and gave it a deep suck. "Did you miss me?" A smile lit up my face.

She bit out a curse and tried to free herself from her restraints. A thick rope tethered her hands and feet to two polls, immobilizing her. Her body was splayed out on the thin mattress that lay on the basement floor—her arms secured above her head and feet tied to a bench that was bolted to the ground; I stood back and admired my work as I continued to suck on the candy.

I was so lucky to have found this place situated below a sorority house. When I initially stumbled upon it, I thought I'd use it as a safe space to escape the annoying drone of college kids' chatter. A few weeks after I arrived at school, a group of girls invited me to a party at the sorority house. Unbeknownst to me, it was part of their sorority initiation to haze a freshman. As soon as I found out what was happening, I left or tried to. I got lost in the house, trying to find my way out.

That's how I found this gem in the basement down a long corridor. The door was locked but the lock was easy enough to pick. Most girls didn't have the balls to venture to this part of the house. But I was never like most girls. Whenever I had a break between classes, I used this place to recharge my battery without any of the girls ever seeing me coming in or going out. And now, it was a place where I could distribute punishment to bad girls and boys.

The room was dim and smelled of decay. It was full of cobwebs and random nails jutted from the walls. The basement groaned, its wooden beams too worn and exhausted. The beams were filled with small cracks. Pipes ran across the open ceiling. Old partly torn boxes sat in one corner of the basement, and a laundry sink sat opposite them. A spider crawled out of the shadowy corner behind the boxes, and I grinned to myself. "We have another guest," I told her, her face emitting confusion.

The violent hum of the electricity streaked through the air, causing the lights to flicker. I looked down at my guest, tears staining her cheeks, and gently stroked her hair. "How are you feeling?"

"Please. Just let me go," she pleaded. "I…I'm sorry. I didn't mean to bump into you."

"Sweetie," I giggled, "this has nothing to do with you bumping into me. Do you really think I'd have you here for a simple fall? I'm not crazy."

"Why are you doing this then?" Her voice trembled.

I reached into my bra and pulled out a pink pocket knife. Her eyes widened, then darted around manically. She thrashed around again. She started to scream. I watched as the rope dug into her flesh. Climbing onto the mattress, I straddled her body. Pressing the edge of the blade to her neck, I leaned in close, my mouth barely touching her ear. "Shhhh. You can't make all that noise, little birdy. It's going to make me stabby."

The muscles in her jaw tensed, and her skin became chalk white.

"Good girl," I praised. I gripped the knife's handle with my fist and, with that same hand, softly touched the back of my hand to her cheek.

More tears streamed down her face. I smiled as I saw the desperation in her eyes, the desire to live. A surge of electricity jolted throughout my body. I did this. I elicited such a strong reaction in another individual. My heart swelled with pride.

"Please…" Her voice came out breathy and pleading.

"Shhhh…don't cry, sweetie. Don't cry." I brushed her hair off her face.

"Why? Why?"

I cocked my head at her. "You really don't remember me?

"I…I don't know who you are. Just, please. Let. Me. Go."

"I can't let you go. You are the final piece of the puzzle."

"I don't know what you're talking about. I…I didn't do ANYTHING!"

I rested the tip of my knife on her cheek and drew the smallest drop of blood. She whimpered, and her body shook.

"You…" I sliced a line from the bottom of her eye to her chin, "tried to…" another slice, "take everything away from me." Slice. Three lines of blood trailed down her cheeks.

Her body lay rigid, too shocked to move. The only movement I could see was the rise and fall of her chest as her breaths became shallow. She peered at me wild-eyed, unable to blink. The tears became heavier as they pooled around her eyes.

"You helped them take from me. Now I'll take your life from you." I made another smooth line, this time trailing down until I reached her neck. "Then, you tried to take Ari. I'll protect those I love." I raised my knife to my lips and slowly licked the blood off the spine.

"You're fucking crazy." She spat in my face, her saliva landing on my cheek.

I wiped it away. "That wasn't nice. You are a bad girl, and bad girls must be punished." I pulled her ear and used my knife to cut a piece off the top. "Maybe I should get five guys to hold you down."

Her eyes widened even further as realization hit her.

"You remember me now? You remember all those things you watched them do to me? You remember laughing as they took and took from me?"

My guest's mouth contorted into a grotesque scream. I rested the blade on her lips. Her screams were cut off abruptly. "I told you to be quiet, sweetie. Do you want someone to hear you scream? Oh, you know what?" I giggled. "Actually, no one could hear you down here." I gave her a sinister smile. "Anyway, I don't like to dwell on the past. Let's discuss the present. Now. Why were you with Ari at that restaurant?"

Her mouth opened and closed, but no sound came out.

"Answer me when I talk to you." I slapped her coldly, causing her face to turn to the side.

"My…my friend," she sobbed.

"Your friend, what?"

"We went out as friends. I don't…you can have him."

"I can have him?" I snorted, flinging my blow pop to the ground. "Sweetie, he's already mine." A slice to the side of her neck caused her to scream in agony, her body shook uncontrollably beneath me. "Calm down. Shhhh. It's okay. When we're bad, we must be punished, and you were a bad girl," I said in a motherly tone. I climbed off, kneeled beside her, and used my knife to slice her top and bra, leaving her veined, perky breast exposed. There was a blue tinge to the skin. My knife slowly made a shallow cut from her breast to her belly button. I looked at her face covered in a mixture of blood, tears, and snot. "You aren't so pretty now, are you?"

"Please…stop…please," she pleaded.

I bent over, leaned close to her ear, and spoke in a gentle singsong. "Don't worry, sweetie. It'll all be over soon."

****

Ayemeline, Age 6: Home

"Eight. Nine. Ten. Ready or not, here I come!"

I giggled from my hiding spot beneath the sheets on the bed.

"Hmm…I wonder where she is. Emmy, where are you?"

I shook beneath the sheets, unable to suppress my giggles.

"I guess she's not here. I'll just take a nap on this lumpy bed." My mother lay on top of the big, hard lump on the bed, being careful not to put too much weight on me.

More giggles.

"This bed sure is giggly and lumpy. Let me see what's under here."

She pulled the blanket back, and I leaped up. "Ahhhh!"

"Oh, there's my Emmy. I thought I lost you." She swallowed me in her arms and gave me several wet kisses on my cheek. "Okay, girly. Time to brush your teeth before they all fall out." My mother carried me in her arms to the bathroom.

"Can we read five stories?"

"Five stories? I don't think we'll have time for five, Emmy sweetie. How about two?"

"Four," I bubbled.

"Three stories and two kisses," my mother grinned at me as I thought it over.

"Deal," I said excitedly.

"Great. Now let's brush those teeth so we can get to those stories." She patted my back and put me down.

"Okay, Mommy. You get to pick a book this time."

***

My head rests on Ari's chest as we lay on my oversized couch. This is the fifth day in a row where we lie like this on my sofa, our bodies touching while we watch television. Each day he comes over, we take turns picking something to watch, then snuggle back on the couch, trying our hardest to avoid sex. Well, he's trying his hardest. I'm not. I want his cock so bad. He's intoxicating, and I don't know how much longer I can take it.

His movie choices are always sci-fi thrillers involving some sort of time travel, while I choose murder documentaries.

I plant my face into his chest and sniff his white T-shirt.

"Did you just smell me?" He chuckles.

"Uh…yeah?" I titter. "You smell nice." His fresh linen scent gives me a cozy feeling and lets me know this is exactly where I belong. It is soft, powdery, and warm.

"So do you, little fox."

I smile at his nickname for me. He thinks I'm cute, and I like it. No one ever cared enough to give me a nickname, except my mom.

"Hey," Ari interrupts my thoughts.

"Hmm?"

"I want to know more about you. You're like a closed book sometimes."

"What do you want to know?"

"Okay. Do you have any siblings?"

"You mean do I have a sister?" I lift my head and glower at him.

He looks at me with confusion, then an awareness of what I'm implying. "No. I just want to know if you were the only child or if you grew up with siblings. I had one brother, Hassan," he placates.

I rest my head back down on his chest. I feel the fast thump of his heartbeat against my face. "I'm the only child," I state.

"That explains a lot."

I raise my head to look at him again. "What does *that* mean?"

"It means I understand you. You strike me as a possessive person. You don't like to share."

"You say it like it's a bad thing." My chin rests on his chest while I stare at him.

"It's not. I don't like to share either."

I give him a coy smile. "Are you done with your celibacy yet?"

Ari guffaws, his chest bouncing up and down beneath me.

"You laugh, but I've got you pinned underneath me. I can take what I want. I can do it," I assure him.

Ari looks at me and raises one eyebrow, his dimple prominent on his cheek. "Really?" His voice sounds daring.

"Really." I reach down and push my tiny hands into the waist of his jeans. Ari's muscles tense and relax. I grab the base of his cock and give it a firm yet gentle tug.

"You're playing with fire, little fox," Ari singsongs.

"Maybe I like it hot," I purr into his ear.

He stares at me with hooded eyes.

His dick is powdery and soft. I can feel a small, wet puddle form around his tip as I make circles around it with my index finger. His breath hitches and he tilts his head toward the ceiling. Suddenly, I slip my hand out of his pants, and he looks at me, confused.

"Too bad you're celibate. Or that could have gone a lot further," I tease him. I lift my body off him and stand.

With one swift movement, Ari grabs me and pins me to the sofa. I am in a kneeling position facing the back of the sofa. Ari crouches down and kneels behind me.

His lips brush my ear. "You like it hot, little fox? You're about to burn," he growls.

Adrenaline pumps through my body as a surge of electricity runs from my pussy to my legs. It is painful but feels so good at the same time. He strokes my butt, then grabs the elastic of my waistband and slides them down to my bent knees. He reaches under my shirt and unhooks my bra, sliding it off with my shirt. Kisses trail from my earlobe, down my neck, to my shoulders. Then he bites into my neck hard. I gasp from the sudden surge of pain and pleasure.

Ari pulls my nipples as he bites into my neck. His hand trails from my nipple to my belly button—then further down to the opening of my pussy. His fingers massage my two lips as I feel him shift behind me. The sound of his belt buckle and his pants sliding down his legs makes the moisture pool between my legs. I feel fingers spread my pussy lips apart and slide back and forth from my clit to the entrance of my pussy. His fingers push inside me, and I buck, instinctively pushing my body against his hand.

"Ari," I breathe, my breath hoarse. I can't breathe—can't think— as his fingers push in and out of my drenched hole. I can feel his erect dick bulldoze my ass as his strokes get deeper and quicker, my breathing getting heavy.

Ari moans in my ear. "You like being treated like a bad girl, don't you, little fox? You like to be punished."

I nod, unable to speak.

"I know how to punish bad girls like you."

"Please…punish me," I breathe.

Ari chuckles in my ear. His fingers leave my pussy, and his massively hard dick thrusts inside me. I let out a loud moan. His dick drives into me hard and fast. I'm so full. He's so much bigger than anyone I've had in the past. *Oh, shit!* I feel like I'm being split in two. When I reached into his pants earlier and gripped his dick, I imagined him to be on the girthier side. But this feeling of fullness is one I've never felt before. It is unexpected.

"Fuuuck," I yell out.

His breaths warm my neck as his thrusts become more aggressive—each one deeper, longer, and harder. My legs quiver as I feel the rush in my pussy. Ari's hand reaches my throat and I instinctively lean my head back into him. He squeezes just enough to make me lose my breath slightly.

"Are you ready to cum for me, little fox? Are you ready to cream all over my dick?"

I nod as the feeling in my pussy grows more intense. I grip the back of the couch tightly as his giant hands encircle my throat, cutting off my air supply and releasing it again. My entire body quivers, and my muscles tense as my climax explodes out of me. I cum hard, one orgasm hitting me after another. He follows right behind me, his cock pulsating inside me. He let out a loud, throaty moan as he releases himself into my pussy. His cock continues to twitch and jerk inside me.

He leans forward and growls into my neck. "That feel good, little fox?"

Too exhausted to speak, my body collapses against his. He flips me to my back, spreads my legs, and kneels between them. I move my knees up and spread my legs further apart for him.

"So beautiful." His voice is soft and velvety. I feel the warmth of his breath on my pussy. His fingers gently graze my labia.

He reaches over, grabs my phone from the arm of the chair, and hands it to me. A few seconds later, a request for a video call comes through. Ari's name is on the screen, so I swipe to accept. On my phone is a video of my gaping, moist pussy. I look down at him between my legs and see that he is holding his phone toward my pussy.

"I want you to see how beautiful you are."

I smile and lean back against the couch, my body still weak and exhausted from my release. I watch his thumb spread my labia, exposing my pussy hole and his creamy cum inside.

"Squeeze for me."

On instinct, I clench my pussy. I watch as a dollop of Ari's cum oozes out and trickles down my ass. He collects it with his fingers, massaging it onto my clit.

"You're mine now, little fox."

"Forever and always," I mutter, my mind drifting to a state of euphoria.

CHAPTER TEN
ARIEL

I trace my fingers along the freckles on her back—a feeling of pride to be the one to be here—to experience her like this, vulnerable…mine. She lay on the bed beside me, her back pointing toward the ceiling and arms propped under her head like a pillow. Her big midnight eyes gaze into mine, and I know this is where I am meant to be.

Ayemeline flips onto her back, exposing her breasts. The conical-shaped, puffy, auburn-colored nipples make me want to bite down hard on those puffy mounds.

The purple tattoo, which covers the back of one shoulder, snakes its way under her arm creating an interlocked pattern of flowers beneath her breast. Her skin is covered in purples and greens.

My fingers hover over her tattoo right beneath her breasts. "Tell me about your tattoo."

She breaks eye contact and she stares into the distance, her eyes not focusing on anything. Her lips tremble as she speaks. "They're foxgloves. They're for my mom."

I raise an eyebrow in curiosity but remain quiet.

"My mom…she had them in her garden. Their purple color was always so beautiful to me."

I stroke her skin, tracing the outline of her tattoo as she speaks.

"My mom used to say, 'You never really know someone until you get close enough. Then you might find out that they're just filled with poison'—like the foxglove," she adds. "Pretty to look at but deadly on the inside."

I quietly play with her tendrils of red curls.

"My mom had trust issues," she simpers.

"We all have a little trust issue," I say, smiling down at her. "You know, there's so much more to foxgloves. They're called foxgloves because, as far as folklore goes, foxes would wear the flowers on their paws as they snuck into the hen house without waking the chickens. But the cool thing about it is although it's poisonous, it can also be medicinal. It's the dosage that makes it poisonous. Given the right dose, it can actually heal."

Ayemeline stares into my eyes as I speak, admiration shining through them.

"Foxgloves are used as the basis for heart medicine." My fingers brush the side of her cheek. "In a broken heart, it can help heal. But in a normal heart, it can hurt."

"What about you? Is your heart broken? Or normal?"

My eyes stay glued to hers. "There's nothing normal about my heart, sweetheart. I think I might need you to heal me."

"I can't heal anyone if I'm broken."

"You're not broken."

I place my thumb on the jagged scar that runs from her ear to her neck. She pulls my hand back.

"Don't do that," she says, gripping my hand tightly.

"Don't do what?"

"You're not allowed to touch me there."

I chuckle. "Did you forget, little fox? You're mine now. That means I can do whatever I want with you…I can touch you wherever I want, and I can fuck you however I want."

"Is that so?" she hums.

"Yup. Anything I want." My teeth sink into her sweet, warm flesh right beside the scar and draw blood.

She gives a pleasurable whimper—letting her hand rest on my arm.

A sultry groan escapes my lips as the copper taste lands on my tongue. My blood rushes through my veins like a pack of scared zebras.

"Ari," she moans. She tries to push me away when my bites become too intense for her.

"You said you could handle me, little fox." I bite down again.

She lets out a breathy moan.

I reach down and insert a finger into her pussy—her arousal evident in the way her wetness has leaked onto her thighs. I feel like

I've been waiting my whole life for this moment—to find a girl like her. The scent of her arousal fills the tiny bedroom as my fingers pump in and out of her pussy. Her wet noises echo in my ear, causing my dick to harden.

My dick throbs against her thigh—my cum moistens her skin, causing it to glisten.

I insert two more fingers; her pussy caresses and sucks them further inside her.

Ayemeline gives an open-mouthed cry, each cry getting louder and louder. She wets her palm with her tongue and reaches for my rock-solid cock. She strokes it a few times before reaching further down and squeezing my sack. I completely lose control, listening to the symphony of her erotic cries. Feeling it rising, I let thick globs spray onto her legs and coat her hand.

Ayemeline thrusts her hips toward my finger as I continue to bite, lick, and suck on the wound I've created on her neck.

She cums almost violently, shuddering and convulsing against me. Juices flow out of her pussy, coating my fingers and knuckles. Feeling the way her pussy clenches around my fingers as she cums—seeing the way her eyes roll to the back of her head—causes me to release myself again, spurting another load all over her hand. I pull my fingers out of her pussy and suck them into my mouth, savoring her arousal.

We both lay there, exhausted and satisfied. I gently brush my thumb to her lips before landing light, feathery kisses on them. Her beauty blows me away. My gaze focuses on her, and my whole body tingles. The world seems so far away while I'm lying here with her. I feel my existence shift, and I embrace it.

Pressing my lips to her forehead, I give her a gentle kiss. She winces when my hand brushes her scar. I kiss it.

"Your scar isn't a sign of your weakness," I breathe. "It's a sign of your strength…that you went through something and survived. You wear the mark of the foxglove on your skin. It's a testimony to who you are. Plants can't run away when stress comes. They have no choice but to become stronger through adversaries. That's what makes you extraordinary. You are a badass, little fox. I can sense that in you. I sensed it since day one." I plant another soft kiss on her forehead. "And now you have two scars," I tease.

Ayemeline darts her eyes and bites her bottom lip. "Promise me you'll never leave me," she says quietly. "I'm addicted to you now, and I don't think I can ever let you go." She gives me a shy smile, but it doesn't reach her eyes.

I grab her chin and force her eyes to look at me. "You're mine, and I'm yours…forever and always, remember?"

This time, her smile does reach her eyes.

***

"Dude, where have you been?" Remy runs up behind me and slaps me on the shoulder.

"I've been here."

"No the fuck you have not. A bunch of us wanted to hit up that club on Elk. I tried texting you to come, but you never responded."

There's no way I was going to tell him that I've been with Ayemeline every day for the past five days. I'd spent all weekend at her apartment making her scream my name, then after class, I'd rush over there—my body unable to stay away.

"Why are you being so elusive?" Remy stares at me incredulously.

"I've just been busy." I try to evade his probing eyes.

"I know this isn't about a girl."

"It's not," I answer too quickly. He cocks his head. "How's Brea?" I ask, attempting to change the subject.

"Fucked up. That was crazy what happened to Crystal, man. I didn't see it, but I heard someone carved out intricate designs on her skin with a knife. Hence the reason for the curfew."

"If there's a curfew, how were you gonna hit up the club?"

"Rules are meant to be broken, man." Remy laughs. "But for real though, Brea is really torn up about it. She went home the day after it happened. She said she couldn't be on this campus right now."

"What about her classes?"

"She spoke to her professors, and they're giving her time to grieve. I'm thinking of going down to be with her next weekend."

"That's good," I say monotonously.

I'm not focused on Brea or her dead friend…murdered friend…her friend was murdered right here on campus. I know I should be more worried, but the only thing I can focus on now is getting back to Ayemeline's apartment.

"Well, you ditched her at the restaurant, so I guess you don't give a fuck."

"Sorry, man. I have a lot on my mind."

"I'm sure you do," Remy says under his breath. "I'm gonna grab a churro," he states as he passes the churro stand on campus.

I follow him and stand in line. In front of us stands a five-foot little fox with beautiful ginger ringlets. I stand so close that I can smell her vanilla fragrance. My dick hardens immediately, and I shift my books to cover my crotch.

Like she senses my presence, she turns and stares straight up at me, her midnight eyes burning a hole into my soul. We stand there for longer than we should have, simply staring at each other.

"Uhhh..." Remy's voice breaks our trance. He looks back and forth between us. "Ya'll good?"

Ayemeline looks over at Remy and gives him a smirk, then quickly drops it.

Remy glares at her and then looks over to me. "I'm not in the mood for churros," he says and turns.

I should introduce him to Ayemeline. I feel bad for keeping her a secret from him. I don't really know why. She's beautiful—not at all a girl to be ashamed of. But Remy could sometimes be judgmental. He was the one who suggested I go celibate after my last relationship ended. He said it would be better for me.

What would be the big deal if he knew I was dating Ayemeline? Well, he'd want to know how it started after the whole coffee shop incident. Then I'd have to explain that she was why I left the restaurant that night, and that would either lead to more lies or judgment, both of which I am trying to avoid.

"Hold up," I call to Remy.

"I'm good," he says, waving his hand in the air as he continues to walk away.

I stare after him, confused at his obvious frustration. Did he already know she was why I ignored all his text messages the past few days?

"Your friend's a jerk." I turn and face Ayemeline, who's now facing the direction in which Remy had disappeared.

I rub my forehead, a little confused about what just happened.

"He's not. His girlfriend's best friend just died and he's just…" I try to justify his behavior.

She rolls her eyes. "He's just a jerk?"

"He doesn't even know about you, so what's he got to be a jerk for?"

"Why haven't you told him about us? Are you ashamed of me?" Her forehead creases.

"No," I whisper with a forced smile, not wanting anyone in line to hear us. I pull her over to the side. "I'm not ashamed of you." I pause. "So, the night you gave me your number, I was actually on a double date." Her eyebrows lower and pull closer together. "I was set up. Remy's girlfriend set me up with her best friend. I ditched her at the restaurant that night. It was wrong, but I had to meet you." I watch as her face relaxes. "Remy and Brea weren't happy. But I never told them why I left…that I met you that night. And now the girl I ghosted is dead…murdered. So, I guess that's why I haven't said anything about us. I don't want him to ask questions. But trust me, little fox," I lift her chin so she can look up at me, "I will never be ashamed to call you mine."

***

I pound on Remy's door, rapping out the beat to "Jingle Bells" before opening it and letting myself in. Remy sits at a small desk, books spread open in front of him and on the floor beside him.

I place my bag and violin case on the floor and sit on his bed.

"Where's Johnson?" I ask, inquiring about his roommate.

"Don't know," he responds, never looking up from his books.

"What's going on with you?"

He spins his chair around and looks straight at me, his eyes narrowing. "What's going on with me? Seriously?"

I take a quick deep breath. "I'm seeing Ayemeline," I admit, "the girl from this afternoon—and the coffee shop." I look at him waiting for a reaction. I see nothing. Then he turns and returns to his books as if I'd said nothing. "She's why I ghosted Brea's friend that night," I continue, feeling the need to get it all out at once. "I've been with her the past few days." Silence. "In her apartment." More silence. "Fucking."

As expected, that last word makes Remy spin toward me again—his eyes widening.

"That look," I say, pointing to his face. "That look is exactly why I didn't want to tell you."

Remy exhaled slowly.

"It just happened." I pause. "I like her. She's not like…you know. She's…different." He continues to look at me with a disbelieving expression. "You're killing me. Say something."

Remy exhales again. "I think…" He stares off at nothing. "You need more time. You don't just get over someone you truly cared about."

"It's been five years," I rush out.

"And five years is enough for you?"

I shrug.

"When did you decide to do this?"

"It wasn't a decision I made. She just…happened."

"And she's good with everything? With you?"

"I think so."

"You think so?"

"I can control myself, Remy."

"Can you?"

I look at him, and my jaw clenches. "I've been doing this therapy shit for five years. I'd like to think it's helping."

"I'm sorry. I'm looking out for you."

"I can control myself," I bark.

His eyebrows draw together and the skin between them becomes wrinkled. "I just want to make sure you're good," his voice trembles.

My frustration quickly dissipates at the worried expression on his face.

"I promise you, I'm good."

We both sit there in silence. I understand Remy's concern, but he couldn't possibly understand how it feels to be near her…to be inside her. It's been five years since my last relationship, and that ended in the most unfortunate of ways. I vowed I wouldn't lose control of myself like that again. And I won't. Ayemeline is the last person I'd ever want to hurt. I will do anything to protect her.

CHAPTER ELEVEN
AYEMELINE

Ayemeline, Age 10: Abandonment

*M*y mom lay on the hospital bed, a yellowish tint to her once milky skin. Her head, which once held beautiful ginger curls, was now bare. Her favorite purple nightgown draped her bony figure. She gripped my hand in hers.

"Emmy, sweetie. I need to tell you something."

I looked at my mom, eyes welling with tears. I wiped them away. I wanted to be stronger than this for her. She needed to see me strong. Maybe that would help her get strong too.

"I called your father. You're going to live with him."

"My…father?" I'd never met my father. I didn't know his name or what he looked like. My mom always told me that he lived far away, that's why I had never met him. But as I got older, I started to think that wasn't the whole truth. "I want to stay with you."

"I know, baby. But…you can't stay with me. I don't…" My mother trailed off; a single tear ran down her cheek. "I love you. I will always love you. But right now, I can't give you what you need. You need someone to take care of you. Who's going to make your favorite mac and cheese?"

My throat tightened as more tears escaped. I didn't want to live with a father I never knew. I wanted my mom. I watched her come to the hospital every week "to get medicine". She promised me the medicine would help her get better. But it didn't. The medicine made her worse. And now she was telling me she couldn't take care of me anymore.

I could no longer control myself as my body convulsed with an onslaught of sobs and tears. "I don't want to," I pleaded through tears. "I don't want to go. I want to stay with you!"

"Emmy, baby..."

"NO! If you make me go, I'm not your daughter, and I'm not your baby." I struggled to breathe between my sobs. I felt numb—like nothing was real—like nothing mattered. My throat was sore. I looked straight at my mom through blurry vision. I wanted her to understand that I was serious. I was not going to let her do this to me. I needed her.

My mom's lips trembled, and her mouth turned downward. "I'm sorry," she said, her voice hoarse and cracking. "I'm so sorry."

***

"I'm sorry. I used up all your cheese." Ari stands in my kitchen stirring a pot of cheese sauce.

"As long as it tastes good, babe, use anything you'd like."

I watch him as he stands in my kitchen wearing nothing but a gray pair of boxer briefs, his broad back on full display. He told me he'd come over to make me his famous mac and cheese, and he's delivering. I squeeze my legs together and watch his back muscles flex as he stirs the cheese sauce.

He turns around to face me—a happy trail of hair runs down from his belly button to the distinct man bush peeking out from above his underwear. "You want to try some?" He holds a sauce-covered finger to my lips. I part my lips, and he inserts the tip of his finger into my mouth.

I moan in pleasure.

"You must be hungry." His smile tells me he has something else he plans on feeding me, and it's not the food.

"Definitely."

Everything about this man makes my pussy wet and my heart skip. His pure hazel eyes rake over my body. He grabs me and pulls me close.

"I could put something else in your mouth. But you might choke on it."

"I know how to swallow." My voice has a kittenish quality to it.

His muscular arms pull me closer to him. Lowering his head, he sucks on the sensitive skin below my ear. His teeth sink into my neck, and I let out an audible moan.

"You must be half vampire," I exhale.

"Maybe I am, since I love to suck you dry."

A soft, rhythmic moan escapes my lips as I feel his tongue flick my ear. His dick leaps against my stomach. I push him away gently. "Your sauce is going to burn."

"Don't worry about that now." He wraps his fingers in mine and looks into my eyes. We hold eye contact for what feels like an eternity. His face is so close to mine that I feel his warm breath on my skin and inhale his comforting scent.

He hesitates, his gaze moving to my lips before meeting my eyes again. With one hand still wrapped around mine, he uses his other hand to tilt my head up slightly. His lips caress mine. Gentle kisses, like a feather, brush against my lips. His lips are soft, contrasting with the stubble of his rough beard. The electricity crackles between us as we share this moment. The soothing sound of the rain beats against the windowpane, wrapping me in its melodious embrace. This is what comfort feels like—what home feels like.

We part, and a flurry of emotions race through me all at once—excitement, hope, sadness because the kiss had to end. I watch him as he backs away from me, our eyes still locked.

"Better get back to cooking," he says, his voice is filled with regret. He gives me a cool, dimpled smile. His arms flex as he lifts the pot of noodles and pours it in with the cheese sauce. His arm muscles flex as he stirs the noodles with the sauce.

He has a full-sleeved blackwork tattoo on both arms that connects to a lion tattoo on his chest. The overlapping images seem to create a magical story so intricate that it's hard to tell where one ends and the other begins. I stare at his tattoos, mesmerized by their beauty, by his beauty.

I watch Ari pour the mac and cheese into a porcelain baking dish and place it in the oven. The savory aroma of the baked mac and cheese wafts through the kitchen while it bakes, emitting a fragrance rich in crispy, golden-brown cheesiness. It is a comforting, familiar scent that promises a meal that is both filling and deeply satisfying.

We eat picnic-style in my living room. Ari feeds me spoonfuls of mac and cheese. Each bite is smooth, crusty, and rich in flavor.

"You should cook for me every day. It's been a while since I had anything this good," I compliment as I savor each bite he puts in my mouth.

"It tastes like your mama's mac and cheese," he jokes.

"No. I didn't get good food like this growing up." I lower my head and stare down at my nearly empty plate.

Ari lets out a hearty laugh. "Really? How did you eat?"

I lift my shoulder in a half-shrug.

He stops laughing and looks at me, noticing my shift in mood. He scoots his body closer to mine until our shoulders are touching. "You can talk to me, you know?"

I hesitate as I contemplate what to share. "My mom died when I was ten, so…" I finally admit. "She used to make amazing mac and cheese. It was my favorite. My stepmother…she's a horrible cook."

"I'm sorry." He rubs my shoulder.

I twirl my hair uncomfortably, not wanting to feel these feelings around him. "It's fine," I say, my voice cracking slightly.

He takes my hand into his. "How did she die?"

I feel a tight ball in my throat as I utter the words. "Cancer."

Ari tucks a lock of hair behind my ear.

"My father and his wife took me in after she died, and she became the only mom I've known since," I admit.

"How was she? Your dad's wife? Was she nice to you?"

I wipe away the tears that threaten to fall. "I…I don't want to talk about this anymore." It's too much. I worked hard to bury these feelings, promising myself I would never feel them again.

"We don't have to if you don't want to." He leans closer, and I rest my head on his shoulder. I feel safe being so close to him. Nothing bad will ever happen again when he is around. He is someone I want to hold on to forever.

CHAPTER TWELVE
ARIEL

We lay together in Ayemeline's bed, the sheets warm and crisp. Her head rests on my chest. Her hair is the perfect blend of chocolate and the sweet scent of vanilla. It is nearly impossible to resist. I close my eyes and take a whiff of her beautiful red curls. She is intoxicating—everything about her. I let out a sultry groan.

"Did you just sniff me and then get hard?"

I chuckle. "I guess I did."

"Hmm…interesting." Ayemeline slides her hand down my torso to the thick patch of hair on my groan. My dick hardens at her closeness.

"Don't start something you can't finish, little fox."

"Who said I can't finish it?"

My dick jerks.

Ayemeline lifts herself off me and slides down my body. With one quick movement, she takes my throbbing erection into her mouth, the suddenness of it catching me off guard. The rigid flesh pulsates as she wraps her tongue around the tip. I look down at her and catch her beautiful coal-colored eyes gazing into mine. They sparkle with need, and my body trembles.

Her tongue flicks across the tip of my dick. I continue to watch her as her warm lips swallow my dick. I bite my bottom lip as euphoria overtakes my whole body. My breathing is ragged as she licks and sucks my cock. She digs her nails into the flesh of my thigh, and I let out an erotic groan.

"Shhiiiiiiiiitttt," I exclaim, my eye never leaving hers.

She pumps my dick in and out of her mouth. Her right hand slips to my balls and squeezes them gently. One finger starts to massage my perineum as she sucks. My dick is completely inside her mouth.

She lets out a soft moan of pleasure and I feel the surge of my orgasm nearing. I need more.

I pull her up and force her on her hands and knees. I push her ass up so that it is raised slightly higher than her head. Kneeling behind her, I worship her plump ass. I stroke the powdery soft skin and kiss each cheek. Her salacious moans tell me she's enjoying the attention. She rests her head on her arms as I salivate at the sight before me.

It is a beautiful sight, her before me, ass in the air, ready to give herself over to me, to trust me. I hold each end of her rear in my palms and kiss the space between them. I feel her moisten on my lips. My fingertips stroke the opening of her pussy as my thick tongue runs over her forbidden hole. She squirms and shakes at the intrusion.

"Ari!" The harmonious purr of my name on her lips floods me with all kinds of emotions—pleasure…joy…adoration. Love?

I insert my finger into her warmth and her pussy squeezes around me. She wiggles as I stroke her ass with my tongue. I taste her arousal as I penetrate her ass with my tongue, pumping in and out vigorously.

I smack her ass and flip her onto her back. I spread her legs and admire her swollen pussy lips.

With labored breaths, she pleads, "Ari...please...fuck me." She pushes her center upward toward me.

"So impatient, little fox." I caress the thin landing strip of soft light-colored hair on her pussy and trail a finger down her slit. She lets out a hoarse moan.

"Ari." There's that sound again, the sound of my name on her sweet fucking lips.

I bend forward and kiss her lips, gently pushing my tongue into her mouth. As we kiss, I guide my swollen shaft into the entrance of her pussy and push in.

Ayemeline moans against my lips as I pump in and out of her, my dick growing with each stroke.

I grunt as her tight pussy squeezes my dick. *Fuck, it's so tight. I think I might die.*

"More," she pleads.

I chuckle. "You want more, little fox? You sure you can handle it?"

"Yes...please," she begs with a shaky breath.

I accept the invitation and thrust hard inside her, my scrotum slapping against her ass with each impact. Her moans get louder and louder until they are pleasurable, uncontrollable cries. I continue to pound her mercilessly as she grips my arm, digging her nails into my skin. Our skin pummels together, making squishy, slapping sounds with each intense thrust.

Her hips move erratically. I see blood on my arm where she is gripping, glistening red in the light streaming in from the open bedroom window. My hand goes to her throat and grips tightly, restricting blood flow. This is pure need. I need her—I need this.

I push deeper into her. The world becomes dark around me as I give her what she pleads for. All I can hear is the chorus of aggressive moans of pleasure.

"I like it when you scream," I say as I pump deeper… harder… faster.

"Oh my God," she chokes out.

"You're so wet, little fox. You make me so hard."

She grabs my wrist with her hand. Her eyes widen as I pump inside her, never slowing my pace.

"You're such a good girl." My dick swells even more as I look into her glistening eyes. At this moment, there is no world. It is just me and her. "Cum for me, little fox. Cum all over my cock."

On command, Ayemeline writhes and jerks beneath me, her pussy clenching my dick with each orgasm. Unable to hold back anymore, I unload into her pussy, loosening my grip on her neck. She reaches down and pulls my dick out of her. Getting up from the bed, she crawls over to me, grabs my dick, and slides it into her mouth. I stare down at her as she licks my cum and hers off my dick.

"Good girl," I moan as she licks her lips, a look of pure satisfaction in her eyes.

We collapse on the bed, both breathing hard and shaking as the wave of our climax subsides.

"Can you play for me?"

"You want me to play a song for you?"

"Yes."

"I don't have my violin."

She pouts.

"But I can go get it."

CHAPTER THIRTEEN
AYEMELINE

*H*oly shit! That was fucking intense. Ari transforms into a different person when he's inside me. Everything about him is different at that moment—the way he speaks to me, the way he touches me, and especially the way he pumps into me, and I love every second of it. He takes control of my body and gives me exactly what I want, what I deserve.

After we're done, he returns to his dorm and grabs his violin. He plays so beautifully. He's a complete anomaly. Here is the big all muscle guy, who appears to be rough. Yet, he plays the most beautiful, delicate music on his violin. Each time he plays, a bit of my soul melts into his.

I prop my head on my palm and watch as he sleeps, his eyes flickering, his mouth slightly parted, his breath soft. His thick, dark brows pinch together. I wonder what he dreams about. He looks to be in a deep sleep, but not a peaceful one. I caressed his thin, perfectly trimmed beard that traces his masculine jawline. "Don't worry, I'm here," I whisper to him.

I can't believe this man is finally mine. He is here, in my bed. I don't know what I did to get so lucky, but it must've been something so good. It's been so long, but everything leading up to this moment is worth it.

Ari shifts, and his eyes slowly open. I look down at him and smile.

"Good morning, my love," I croon.

He smiles that sweet smile, his dimple making an appearance.

"Were you drooling over me while I slept?" he teases, his deep, groggy voice making me shiver.

"I was not drooling over you, sir. I was simply admiring what's mine."

"Hmmm…" He pulls me into him and kisses my nose.

"You're so cute."

"I better be more than cute, based on the way you fucked me last night."

Ari titters. "Yeah. That was…are you good? Did I hurt you?"

I smile. "Oh, Ari. There's nothing you could do to me with that dick that I wouldn't love."

He chuckles. "That's good to know."

***

An hour later, after our intense make-out session in my bed, we finally make it out of my apartment and walk to our classes.

"Later, I can come over and cook you dinner again."

"I'd love that," I say with the biggest grin on my face. I am truly happy in this moment with him. "So, where'd you learn to cook like that?"

"My mom. She wanted to make sure my brother and I knew how to cook. She said she wasn't raising a man-child."

"She definitely raised a man." Eager to learn more about him, I ask, "Is your brother older or younger?" This is a part of him I don't know very much about.

"He's four years older than I am. He left home at eighteen and never came back. He's been living in California ever since."

"Do you see him often?" A helicopter blades the sky above us. Ari pauses to observe it.

"Yeah, I go see him occasionally," he says, his eyes still raised toward the sky. "And he always comes down for my birthdays."

"Are you guys close?"

"We are. We don't see each other often or even talk that much, but I think we're still close."

"You think?"

He looks at me. "He and I have different opinions on things. He doesn't really speak to our mom, and he doesn't understand why I do. But I'm the only person she has in her life right now. I can't just abandon her like he has. He doesn't get it."

I look at Ari as he speaks, his jaw ticking. "Are you doing it out of obligation or love?" I have to ask because something tells me it wasn't because he wanted to.

Ari sighs. "I'm doing it because it's the right thing to do. I do it because I'd want someone to do it for me."

I squeeze his hand. "I get it. You're a good person."

A group of girls walk towards us, snickering into their hands.

"Hey, Ari," they singsong as they pass.

Ari tilts his head back as a greeting. He looks over at me, noticing the look of anger on my face.

"Don't worry about them," he reassures.

"Did you fuck them?" I clip, my eyes piercing right through his.

"Really, Ayemeline!" My name sounds harsh on his lips. I'm getting used to hearing his pet name for me. I didn't like his use of my given name now.

I remain silent.

"You do remember I told you I was celibate before you?" His voice is softer now. "I didn't lie about that."

"I'm sorry."

He stops and faces me, cupping my face in his big hands. "I don't want you to ever feel like I'm not with you. It's me and you—fuck everyone else. I got a taste of you, and I'll never be satisfied with anyone else. You're mine and I'm yours, remember?"

I nod and he gives me a gentle kiss on the lips.

"Good," he says, his aggressive tone returning. "Now don't ever ask me shit like that again."

"Yes, sir," I say teasingly. But I know he means what he says.

***

I sit in class listening to Professor Matthews analyze *The Great Gatsby* through a theoretical framework or something like that and question why I'm even bothering with these classes. My sole purpose in being here is Ari.

"Your papers are due in one week," Professor Matthews drones on. "If you're choosing topic A, I need you to think about the depiction of Tom Buchanan as a representation of the American upper class. If you choose to go with topic B, the depiction of love and desire in *The Great Gatsby*, focus on love's vital role in the book. Dive into Gatsby's romantic attachment—Myrtle's relationship with Wilson—*really* get into it."

I let out a long, exasperated sigh.

"Which one are you doing?" Micah, who sits behind me, leans forward to speak to the back of my head.

"I don't know," I say, without turning around. I couldn't care less about this paper or this class. I just want to get back to my apartment and have Ari pound my pussy like it is our last day on earth.

Professor Matthews dismisses the class, and all the students noisily pack their things. Once the seat beside me is vacant, Micah slides into it.

"You've been avoiding me?" He looks at me, waiting for an answer.

"No, I haven't."

"You haven't responded to my texts. I missed you."

I look into his emerald green eyes; the same eyes that used to soak my panties now do nothing to excite me. "I have a boyfriend now. I don't think he'd want me responding to your texts."

A look of surprise registers on his face but is quickly replaced with a neutral expression. "Since when?" He tries to pretend it doesn't bother him, but I know it does.

"Few weeks."

He nods as if contemplating his next words. "I thought...I thought me and you were...you know...something." His eyebrows lower and pull closer together.

"Were we?" I look at him. During the time I've known him, we've been nothing more than fuck buddies. He'd never suggested anything more than that. We'd meet up at my place or his dorm, fuck, and go our separate ways. What he was insinuating to now was completely foreign to me.

He gives a pronounced sigh. "Maybe you had a different perception than I did."

"Were we exclusive, Micah?" I know the answer to that question. Neither one of us had ever discussed exclusivity.

Micah glances away from me and swallows hard. "No, I guess we weren't." With an enigmatic quirk on his lips, he says, "I'm happy for you." Then, he stands and walks out of the classroom.

***

Professor Matthews looks in my direction as I walk down the stairs toward the front of the auditorium-style classroom.

"Ms. Cross, may I have a minute of your time?"

I give an audible exhalation. "Sure."

I stand in front of his desk while he shuffles through some papers.

Still looking down at the mountain of papers, he addresses me. "You know your grades aren't so great in my class. You need to get an A on this paper to pass."

"You're wasting my time telling me something I already know," I respond incredulously.

He looks up at me then and gives me a coy smile. He moistens his lips with his tongue when his eyes meet mine. "It's my job, Ms. Cross, to keep my students on track."

"I got it," I say monotonously.

"I don't think you do. You need to start taking my class seriously." His eyes rake over my body.

"I'm not going to fuck you again," I respond bluntly.

His eyes widen as he looks toward the door, ensuring no one heard me.

"Are you serious?" he says in a loud whisper. "I'm not asking for...that. What happened was a mistake! It won't happen again."

"You mean if I got on my knees, pulled your dick out, and pushed it to the back of my throat until I gagged, you'd stop me?" My eyebrows pull together, and I pout my lips.

His eyes burn with desire as he bites his bottom lip. I almost see the blood rushing to his dick. "I'm married." He says it like he is trying to convince himself.

"Didn't stop you before."

Professor Matthews shifts from foot to foot. "I just need you to focus on your grades for this class without trying to fuck your way to an A." His tone is clipped.

"Be nice to me, Professor Matthew," I say, my tone soft, "I know your secrets."

His nostrils flare, and I see the veins pulsing in his neck. One side of my mouth rises as I meet his gaze. I press my palm to his cheek. "I'll see you later, love."

***

As soon as I leave class, I send a text to Ari:

Me: Hey, Babe. I'm out of class. I need you.

I stare at my phone screen as I wait for his response. After what seems like forever, Ari responds.

Ari: I'll call you later.

Me: Why?

Me: Where are you?

I stand there, waiting for his response. Nothing comes through. Tired of waiting, I press the call button. After two rings, I'm sent to voicemail. *Are you fucking serious?* I let out a long, frustrated sigh and tuck the phone into my back pocket. Then his text comes through:

Ari: It's loud. Can't hear you. I'll call you back once I get out of here.

My stomach growls, and I realize I haven't eaten yet. Ari and I were too preoccupied this morning to think about food.

Reaching the sub shop, I instantly regret my decision to come here. The place is packed with students. I prefer to go as far off campus as possible to avoid the crowd. Today, however, I don't have the energy to walk. My stomach needs food now. I walk into the sub shop and am instantly surrounded by conversations and braying laughter. Music blares from digital players and laptops. In one corner, a guy hacks out a noisy bronchial cough. I don't want to be here. I move to the counter and place my order with the girl who stands behind it and prays she's fast so I can get out of this place.

As I wait for my Cajun chicken sub with extra Jalapeños, I glance around, spotting Micah sitting at a table alone. He tilts his head back in greeting when he spots me. I give him a ghost of a smile and look away, focusing my attention on the other customers.

As I look around, I am not prepared for what I see. Pure utter shock overtakes me but is quickly replaced by blinding rage. I press my lips firmly together as I approach the table. There is Ari, sitting at a table with some girl. My whole body feels hot in that moment. All I can see is black.

***

Ayemeline, Age 12: Isolation

Black. Black. Black. All I could see was black. I was trapped in this closet for so long that I was beginning to think my stepmother had forgotten about me. She was angry because I refused to eat her food. I hated liver and onions, but she insisted on making it every other night. She told me I couldn't get up from the table until I finished it. When I refused, she shoved my face into my plate, dragged me by my hair, and threw me into the closet.

This was the punishment closet. She only used it when my father was out of town for work. When I tried to tell him about it, he lectured me about respecting my "mother." He didn't believe me. He never believed me because she acted like a loving mother when he was around. But I knew she hated me. She told me herself. She hated that I was a product of my father's infidelity. She hated that she couldn't have children of her own. But most of all, she hated that she was left to take care of me, a constant reminder that the man she loved once loved someone else.

A cold shiver weaved its way down my spine as I lay on the floor of the box-like room, knees pulled up to my chest. The familiar darkness engulfed my weak body. I watched as the light seethed its way into the closet through the cracks underneath the door. The door opened quickly, and a plate of hard taco shells was shoved inside before closing again.

"Mommy," I sobbed, a single tear escaping. "Please come back. Please…I need you."

I could hear my stepmother's voice in my head. "No one will ever want you. Everyone will always leave, just like your mother."

***

"ARE FUCKING KIDDING ME?"

Ari swings around suddenly, and his eyes meet mine. "What are you doing?" He grimaces at me.

"You ignored me because you were here with this bitch?" My voice is loud enough so that the customers around us hear. I don't usually react this way, but at this moment, I can't control myself. I sneer at the girl who sits beside him, occupying a high top.

"Excuse me," the girl sneers back at me as she rolls her eyes.

Ari holds his hand up to silence her.

"Ayemeline, you need to calm the fuck down," he says, tightening his grip on my arm.

"Don't tell me to calm down. You know what? Fuck you. You want to play? We can play!" With that, I violently pull my arm out of his grip and walk away.

As I make my way to the door of the restaurant, I make eye contact with Micah, knowing he will follow me out. That boy is a sucker for a girl in distress.

I reach the sidewalk when I hear Micah call my name.

"Yo, Ayemeline, hold up!"

I stop and turn around to face Micah.

"Are you okay?" His eyebrows raise as his eyes search mine.

"I'm fine," I lie.

"Look, if you need to talk, I'm here."

Over his shoulder, I see Ari walk out of the restaurant. Our eyes meet. It is at this moment that I lean in closer to Micah, grab the back of his neck, and kiss him—letting my tongue enter his mouth.

As his tongue wrestles with mine, a great force grips my arm tightly and pulls us apart.

"She's mine," Ari growls deeply toward Micah, his eyes full of venom.

CHAPTER FOURTEEN
ARIEL

She fucked up. She fucked up big. I feel the veins pulsing in my neck as I walk into her apartment, carrying the duffle bag I'd retrieved from the storage unit I kept. After that show she put on at the restaurant, I ordered Ayemeline to go home. Surprisingly, she obeyed. She opens the door and steps back, giving me space to walk in.

"You fucked up, Ayemeline." I bare my teeth at her.

"You had no right…"

"Did I give you permission to speak?" My voice booms throughout her apartment.

She is silent, pinching her lips together.

"You embarrassed me today. You made a fucking scene over nothing."

She doesn't speak. She stands there, staring into my eyes, hers getting darker.

"I told you never to question me again, but you didn't listen."

Her mouth opens and closes, but no sound comes out.

"You know what happens when you don't listen, little fox?"

Ayemeline bites her bottom lip.

"You get punished. You're going to understand that there are some things I won't tolerate. You will not accuse me of being unfaithful to you. You will not accuse me of having feelings for anyone else but you."

I walk toward her. She stands her ground, her eyes never leaving mine.

"So now I'll have to teach you a lesson you will never forget."

I reach out and grab her by the neck. She lets out a soft moan and I can see the need in her eyes.

"You like being controlled, don't you, little fox?"

I gaze into her coal-colored eyes, searching for a hint of fear. I see nothing. I grab her by the hair and force her body into position so that her back is leaning against my chest.

"These are the rules of your punishment. One, you will not cum without permission. Two, you will only respond to me with 'Yes, master.' And three—you'll enjoy every fucking minute of your punishment. Do you understand?" I yank her hair back toward me, forcing her eyes to look up at me.

"Yes..yes, master," her voice is breathy with need.

I lean down until my nose touches her neck. "I can smell you, little fox. Your pussy needs this."

She whimpers, "Please…master."

I smile, enjoying her arousal.

I let go of her hair and pick her up, carrying her to the bedroom. I set her down. "Strip," I demand.

Her eyes never leave mine. She slowly lifts her shirt over her head and tosses it to the floor. I watch as her perky tits bounce once free from her top. My dick throbs in my pants. She unbuckles her jeans and pushes them down her legs, exposing her pink pussy, the thin landing strip of soft red hair making me want to bury my face in it. Her mound is thick and plump, and I can see her clit protruding from between her two slits.

"Get on the bed," I demand when she is fully naked. "On your hands and knees, ass in the air."

She obeys like a good little fox, and the monster inside me roars to life.

I watch her asshole pucker up at me. *Shit! I need that ass.* Her pussy glistens with her wetness as it pulses.

Leaving her there, I return to the living room and grab the duffel bag. I walk back into the bedroom. Unzipping the bag, I pull out a wooden paddle. I walk toward her, paddle in hand.

"Beg me to spank you," I growl into her ear, using the paddle to stroke her dangling breast.

"Please…" she pleads. "Spank me…master." Her voice is a cross between a hoarse whisper and a sensual moan.

I feel a drop of pre-cum escape my tip. "Good girl," I growl into her ear.

I gently caress her ass with the wooden paddle, letting it stroke each cheek separately before allowing it to slide down to her pussy. Her juices collect on the paddle, leaving a wet spot.

A gasp escapes her lips as the paddle connects with her engorged clit.

"You like this, don't you, little fox?"

"Yes, master."

"You remember the rules?"

"Yes, master."

"Good girl." I stroke her hair and praise her for accepting her punishment.

I start lightly with the wooden paddle. I use more force with each strike until her moans become loud grunts. I watch her ass reddens, the skin reddens under my punishment. I feel the uncontrollable urge to bury my face in that ass.

"You weren't such a good girl earlier, were you?" *Strike*.

"No…master…I'm…sorry."

"And for that, you must be punished." *Strike*.

Ayemeline squirms under my strike.

"Don't you dare move!" *Strike*.

She is still, like the obedient little fox she is. Her welted skin is like a work of art.

A sinister smile reaches my lips. This is what my soul thirsts for: the pain. I've locked it away for so long, afraid to let it out. Now, with her, I feel free. It's liberating to know I've finally found my person who would accept me for me, all of me. Because of Ayemeline, my monster is free to roam.

"How does your ass feel, little fox?"

"It burns, master."

"Good."

I walk over to the duffle bag and grab the tiny, purple felt bag. I pull out the silver and pink butt plug. Walking back over to her, I gently insert the butt plug in her ass.

Ayemeline flinches and yelps at the unexpected intrusion but does not move from her position on the bed.

I admire the small pink heart decorating her asshole.

She moans in pleasure once it's fully in, finally getting comfortable with its placement. A drop of liquid leaks from her pussy. Before her cum can fall onto the bed, I put my hand out and catch it on the tip of my finger. Lifting my finger to my lips, I tastes her sweet arousal. My dick gets even harder in my pants.

"Get on your back," I demand, my voice gruff.

Ayemeline rolls over to her back and spreads her legs. Her pussy glistens more than I had ever seen a pussy glisten before.

"You're so wet for me, little fox."

"Yes, master." She speaks as if she was trying to catch her breath. I can sense her oncoming orgasm.

"Don't you dare cum without permission," I warn.

"Yes, master."

I use my middle finger to massage her pussy, stroking up and down along the slit. I lift my finger and watch her wetness connect to my finger and stretch.

Smack. I spank her pussy, causing her to yelp loudly. I repeat the action, watching her squirm under my control. Wet, slurpy sounds fill the small bedroom, and my dick pushes against the restraints of my jeans. I think it might burst.

A hard slap lands on her clit, causing her to scream.

"Please…I need to cum."

I lean in close to her ear and insert two fingers into her soaking wet pussy. I growl into her ear. "You cum without my permission, little fox, and you won't be able to sit for a week."

Ayemeline moans louder as I pump her pussy faster. Her pussy sucks my fingers deeper inside as she clenches her walls around me. I hook my fingers in her pussy.

"You want to cum for me, baby?" I purr into her ears.

"Yes…master…please."

I smile as I jam three fingers into her drenched hole. She moans as I twist my fingers around inside her. She squirms, obviously losing control.

"Do you think you deserve to cum?"

"I'm sorry…I…please…master. Let me…cum." Her breathing is heavy as she pants out the words.

Four fingers. I pump deeper and harder. My whole fist buries itself into her insanely tight hole. I sunk my teeth into the warm, sweaty flesh on her neck and suck.

"Yes, little fox," I croon. "Cum for me."

Finally, as if waiting for that release for a lifetime, I feel a gush of liquid coat my hand. I pull my fingers out and smack her clit as she squirts, spraying her hot fluid all over my hand and soaking the sheets beneath her.

"You're a squirter," I muse, delighted at that discovery.

She smiles at me, her eyes brimming with tears.

I hold her legs up, close my eyes, and lick up and down her slit.

"You taste so good," I say, returning to wipe her tears.

I kiss her gently on the lips, letting my tongue penetrate her mouth. She accepts my mouth, sucking on my tongue. I pull away and stare into her midnight eyes. The dim lighting from the moonlit room makes her eyes sparkle. A warm breeze passes over us through the open window. My gaze flicks to her lips before meeting her eyes again.

Ayemeline inhales deeply, molding her body against mine. The faint smell of vanilla and arousal fills the air. It is the perfect blend.

I hesitate. Drawing in a shaky breath, I tilt her head slightly. "I love you, little fox."

Her smile is like a thousand fireworks lighting up the night sky. "I love you, Ari," she whispers.

My lips gently meet hers again, and my tongue lazily explores her mouth. She moans against my lips as I stroke the back of her neck. This girl keeps me wanting more, needing more. I have an insatiable hunger for her. The more I have her, the more of her I need. She is my peace, my salvation. She quiets the voices in my head—the regret, the guilt. All of it is silent when I am with her.

"By the way," I say with my lips still close to hers. "That girl from the restaurant—she's my cousin."

CHAPTER FIFTEEN
AYEMELINE

I make my way up the stairs of the townhome I spent most of my childhood in—regretting every step. My father watches me make my slow ascent to the door.

"Are you going to continue dragging yourself up the stairs, or are you going to come inside?" He crosses his arms, clearly irritated at my lack of urgency. *Perfect. That's exactly what I want.*

I don't say a word. I simply look at him and smile while I continue my slow pace. I don't want to be here, and I want to make sure he knows that.

My dear old father practically threatened me to come home so I could apologize to my dear, sweet stepmother for missing her birthday. I agreed because I figured I needed to play nice, at least for a little bit, if I'm going to ask him to pay for my apartment.

I started working at the preschool to gain some independence from them, but my work was proving to be unsatisfying. Every day, I go to work pretending to be a jovial, energetic person. I hate pretending. It's so draining. And the more I do it, the more I feel the life draining out of me. I'm left with two choices—either suck it up and slowly die inside or ask for help. He owes me, anyway. I'm his daughter. He missed out on supporting me for the first ten years of my life. He has some catching up to do.

My stepmother sits on a dark leather recliner in the living room, sipping what I assume to be tea with a shot of tequila, her usual drink.

"Hello, Mother dear. You're looking younger by the minute." I grin broadly and perform a little curtsy in front of her.

She looks up at me, her eyes narrowing, and takes another sip of her alcohol-infused tea.

"Cut it out," my father barks from the entry of the living room.

"Ignore her, dear. She's trying to get under my skin."

"Me?" I gasp, bringing my hand up to my chest. "I would never."

My father's face tightens as he watches me furtively. He doesn't have to say it, but I know what that look means: *Get your shit together.*

I take a deep, slow breath and summon all the kiss-ass energy I can muster. "I apologize for missing your birthday. I was selfish, and you are the most beautiful queen in the universe." *Shit. I was so close.*

My stepmother turns her attention to my father, who is still standing at the entryway, looking annoyed. "Dear," she says, completely ignoring me. "Would you mind getting me another cup of tea?"

My father gives me another look that tells me to behave and makes his way to the kitchen.

"You know," my stepmother begins, "you think you're so cute with that disgusting attitude. But remember…No one likes a bitch." She gives me a sinister smile.

"You found people who like you," I deadpan.

Her smile drops immediately.

Before she can spew the words I know she is dying to throw at me, I walk out of the living room, leaving her alone to mutter profanities under her breath—something she would never do around my father.

How she'd managed to fool him into thinking she was a loving mother all those years is beyond me. Maybe he's just stupid. Or maybe he chooses not to see her for who she really is. Either way, I hate him for it almost as much as I hate her for all the years of torture I endured under her thumb.

After dinner, my father and I stand at the sink while he washes and I dry. My stepmother takes her usual seat in the recliner, sipping her tea and watching reality TV.

"You know," he begins, "your mother loves you. You're like a daughter to her. You know she couldn't have her own child, so she's taken you in and cared for you like you were her own. The least you could do is show her some respect."

I scoff at that. *Was he serious right now?*

"Don't do that. What other woman do you know would take you in under the circumstances?"

"You mean what other woman would allow the child of her husband's whore to live in her home?"

"Ayemeline," he seethes, his tone sharp like a knife.

"I'm sorry," I say quickly. I'm not doing a very good job at sucking up.

Rage flows through him like lava. I need to put out the fire.

"I know she's done a lot for me, and I'm grateful." I'm laying it on thick.

He looks me over, some of his rage subsiding. "I need you to try harder to show your appreciation. I want you two to have a good relationship. That's all I ever wanted."

I highly doubt that. "I know," I say, feigning remorse. "I'll be better. I promise."

This seems to appease him because he goes back to washing the dishes.

I just need to behave the rest of the night before I can ask him to take over my rent. I can do it. I hope I can.

❋❋❋

Ayemeline, Age 14: Humiliation

"Show me yours first and I'll show you mine."

I stood in the tiny utility closet, unsure of what to do. Karo stood before me, a huge grin on his face. He was the boy of my dreams. I never imagined a senior would ever be interested in me. All my life, I'd been an outcast. I never fit in with the popular kids and I never fit in with the not-so-popular kids. Everyone saw me as different—weird.

I was elated when Karo asked me to be his girlfriend in the cafeteria yesterday. And when he asked to spend time with me alone in the utility closet, I shook with excitement. He was the first boy who had ever expressed an interest in me.

"Are you scared?" Disappointment spread over his features.

"No, I'm not scared." I didn't want him to think I was some scared freshman. I slowly loosened the buckles on my denim overalls and let them drop to my waist.

A smile spread across his face.

"Now the shirt," he said, pointing to my white Disney princess T-shirt. I hated my clothes. It was one of many things I hated about myself. My stepmother said these were the clothes appropriate for young girls my age. No one my age dressed like this, though. It was like she tried to humiliate me—and it worked.

I tugged the T-shirt over my head, struggling as it got caught in my puffy pigtails. After getting it off, I reached back and unfastened my bra, letting my nub-like breasts free. A cold draft hit my bare skin and I shivered.

"You have tiny tits." Karo chuckled as he stared down at my A-cups.

I suddenly became self-conscious of my body. I wrapped my arm around myself to cover up my breasts.

"You can't hide them." He pulled my arms down away from my breast, exposing them once more.

"You said you'd show me yours." My voice shook as I shuffled from foot to foot.

"Fine. But you're going to have to play with it if I show you."

"Play with it?" My eyebrows drew together. I had no idea what he meant by "play with it."

"Don't worry. I'll show you." Karo unbuckled his pants and let them drop to his ankles. He quickly pulled his boxers down. His dick popped out like a bobblehead.

I gasped at the sight of it. It was thin, long, and surrounded by dark hairs. I had never seen a dick before. This was so different.

"Get on your knees," he demanded with a grin.

"Why?"

"I'll show you. Do you trust me?"

I nodded my head, unsure if I actually trusted him or not.

"So get on your knees."

I got on my knees in front of him, his dick a few inches from my face.

"Open your mouth."

I looked up at him, confusion written all over my face.

"Just do it." His voice was stern.

I wasn't willing to make him think I was some stupid freshman, so I did as I was told: I opened my mouth.

"Wider."

I opened wider. With one quick movement, he plunged his dick into my mouth. I gagged at the sudden intrusion but was eager to show him I was a woman who knew what the fuck was going on, even though I had no clue.

"Don't use your teeth," he barked as my teeth scraped his dick. "Just lick it. Like a lollipop."

I stuck my tongue out and licked the underside of his salty dick.

"That's good," he grunted. "Keep going. Put it in your mouth and suck it like a Tic Tac."

I clamped my mouth around his dick and sucked it into my mouth. Karo pumped in and out of my mouth—long, slow strokes in and out. I felt the moisture form between my legs as he moaned and caressed my head. I was making him feel good. I, a freshman, was making him, a senior, lose his mind from the pleasure I was providing.

I sucked harder while he pumped his dick deeper into my mouth. My drool leaked from my mouth onto my bare breasts.

"Oh, fuck." Karo let out a loud grunt and he released himself into my mouth. Warm, salty liquid sprayed into my mouth, and I quickly pulled away, coughing and gagging. What the fuck? The thick, white liquid dripped from my mouth to the floor as I continued to cough.

Suddenly, the utility closet door swung open, exposing us to a group of kids staring at us and laughing. I scrambled to grab my shirt but couldn't find it on the ground where I'd flung it. I looked over at Karo to find that his dick was tucked neatly back in his pants. He held up my T-shirt with a sinister smile on his face.

"Is this what you're looking for," he said, dangling my shirt above his head.

I got to my feet, covering my exposed breast with one hand and trying to snatch the shirt out of his hand with the other. He was too tall, and my efforts were in vain.

"What kind of dirty whore would let a guy come in her mouth?" one of the girls said from the other side of the door as she twirled her blonde hair through her long, manicured fingernails. A bellow of laughter filled the doorway as more kids came to see what all the commotion was about.

I searched Karo's eyes, hoping to see the same guy I came into the closet with earlier. I hoped to see some sort of remorse for what he had done. There was nothing there. There was only the look of victory as he tossed my shirt to his friends and walked out, leaving me there topless, covered in drool and cum.

CHAPTER SIXTEEN
ARIEL

The fresh morning air is refreshing. Ayemeline and I walk hand in hand, admiring the crystal-clear pond. The air still smells wet after the morning rain. The sun filters through the clouds, giving her skin a glittering glow.

It had been a couple of days since I last saw her, and God, did I miss my little fox. She told me she needed to spend the weekend with her parents to convince them to pay for her apartment.

"If you needed money, you could've come to me, you know."

"I could've?" Ayemeline looks at me like she doesn't believe me.

"Yeah. You can ask me for anything. Better than crawling back to your parents. I know you didn't really want to do that."

"It's fine. My dad agreed to help me with my rent. Now I can quit my job."

"And spend more time with me," I say, pulling her into an embrace.

"Oh my gosh, you two. Get a room."

The voice comes from behind me. I swing around ready to wreak havoc on whoever had the nerve to interrupt us. I smile when I see Brea dragging Remy towards us. Brea is a sweet girl. She definitely doesn't deserve my anger.

"Hey, guys," I say.

"Ari," Brea chastises. "You never told me you had a…uhhh…girlfriend?"

"She's not his girlfriend," Remy responds before I can say anything.

Ayemeline's eyebrows pull up slightly. Then, a smile curls her lips.

"Uh…okay." Remy's sudden outburst confuses me. I have a feeling he isn't a fan of Ayemeline, but I can't understand why.

I turn to Brea and say, "This is Ayemeline…my girlfriend."

I look over at Remy, waiting for his response. I haven't admitted that to him yet, so introducing Ayemeline as my girlfriend is strange.

Remy's jaw tenses, and he continues to glare at Ayemeline.

"It's so nice to meet you, Ayemeline," Brea says, oblivious to the tension between the three of us. "Oh my gosh, you guys are so cute. You should come to the fair with us."

"They're busy," Remy offers again.

I glare at him.

"We'd love to join you guys," Ayemeline says with a big grin plastered on her face. "We don't have anything else to do."

I thought I was going to spend the day fucking you in every hole. "Are you sure that's what you want to do?" I ask, trying to persuade her to change her mind.

"I'm sure," Ayemeline says gleefully. "I'd love to get to know your friends better, you know, since we've been spending so much time together."

She gives me a seductive smile, and it almost makes me want to fuck her right there in the park—it doesn't matter who's watching.

"Okay," I manage to say.

✱✱✱

The fair is a myriad of colors and lights. Rich scents of greasy fried foods hurdle through the air. The streets are alive. The resounding sound of carnival music, screams, and laughter is exhilarating.

Brea is well-versed in shades and palettes and spends most of her time talking to Ayemeline about the latest makeup trends. I can tell by the expression on her face that Ayemeline doesn't know half of what Brea is talking about, but she pretends to be interested anyway.

A woman walks past us, and the aroma of her funnel cake's deep-fried dough and sugar invades my nostrils. "I'm gonna get a funnel cake. You want one?" Remy gestures to the funnel cake stand.

"Nah, I'm good. Trying to stay away from sugar, babe," Brea responds.

"Right." Remy tightens his lips.

"I want a funnel cake," Ayemeline turns toward Remy.

"Have your boyfriend get you a funnel cake, sweetheart," Remy hisses.

Brea glares at Remy. "Really, babe? You don't have to be so rude."

Ignoring her, Remy turns on his heels and walks toward the funnel cake stand.

"I'll grab you one," I mouth apologetically.

I jog after Remy. The smell of hamburgers competes with the smell of hotdogs as we pass each food stand. I catch up to him just as he reaches the line and observe him before speaking. "What's going on with you? What's your issue with Ayemeline?"

Remy stays quiet for a minute, then mutters, "I don't have an issue with your *girlfriend*."

"Why'd you have to say it like that?"

"How did I say it?"

I watch him as he tries to avoid my eyes. "I'm trying to understand why you don't like her."

"I never said I didn't like her."

"You didn't have to. I'm so confused. Why..."

"I just don't think she's..." Remy gives a deep, slow exhale. "I don't think you're ready to be this deep in a relationship."

"It's been five years. Look, I know you're trying to look out for me, and I appreciate that. But I've got this. She's not like Julia. She's so…different."

"Did you tell her about Julia?" Remy looks at me with raised eyebrows.

"No," I admit.

"Why not?"

"How would that conversation even start?"

"You tell me. She's *your* girlfriend and all."

"Geez, Rem, cut it the fuck out."

Remy turns and faces forward, crossing his arms over his chest.

"Just give her a chance. You'll like her. I promise you will."

Remy scoffs. "I'm sure I will."

Remy and I have always been great friends. He's been there for me during the toughest parts of my life. Now, however, it seems as if our friendship is changing. I can't put my finger on it but ever since Ayemeline came into my life, I feel like I'm losing a little piece of our friendship, and that hurts.

We walk in silence back to the girls, each of us holding a plate of funnel cake.

I hand Ayemeline my plate and she takes it with enthusiasm.

"Thanks, babe." I watch as she places a piece of the sugary treat on her tongue, powdered sugar sticks to her lips. Without thinking about where we are or who is watching, I lean in and lick the sugar from the corner of her lips. Ayemeline moans against my mouth, parting her lips to invite me in.

"Oh my gosh, you two. Do you need some privacy?" Brea's voice interrupts us.

"Yes," I growl instinctively.

Ayemeline stares into my eyes, telling me exactly what she wants me to do to her without using words.

"Okay," Remy's irritated voice chimes in. "Maybe we should separate."

"No, I don't want to be separated. We came here together," Brea says in a nasally voice.

"Actually, we should go our own way," I say, my eyes never leaving Ayemeline's.

Ayemeline covers her mouth and giggles like a nervous schoolgirl.

"We'll meet up with you guys later," I say, grabbing Ayemeline's hand and pulling her toward a rollercoaster.

"We're getting on a ride?" Ayemeline's confused tone makes me smile. She has no idea what is in store for her.

"Yes."

"You got me all wet. The only thing I want to ride now is you."

"You are such a horny whore, aren't you, little fox?"

"Always for you."

We pass people waiting in line, ignoring the grunts and profanity thrown our way. My size often intimidates people, so I know we won't have any issues.

We show the man working the ride our unlimited ride bands and climb aboard, pulling the lap bar down and securing it into place.

"I've never gotten on a roller coaster before," Ayemeline confesses.

I look at her, confused. "Really?"

"Nope. It's always been the one thing that made me nervous the first and only time I'd ever visited an amusement park. I don't know. Maybe it's the loss of control."

"That's funny. Because when you're with me, you have no control." I give her a devilish grin.

"With you, it's fine. You can control my body all you want."

I can't resist. I kiss her then. It is a full-bodied, soul-sucking, take-all-of-me type of kiss. It is the type of kiss that makes it clear that she is a part of me, and I am a part of her, and I have no intention of ever letting her go.

The ride starts to move, regrettably forcing us apart.

"Oh my gosh! Oh my gosh! Oh my gosh!" She grips my arm tightly, burying her face in my shoulder.

"Don't worry. I've got you, love. I won't let anything happen to you. Not now. Not ever." I rest my hand high on her bare thigh, forcing the short skirt she wears to hike even further up. My fingers trail the inside of her thigh, and I push her legs apart.

"What are you doing?"

"Helping you to relax. Now just breathe."

The ride ascends a steep climb and gravity pushes my hand further up her thigh. My fingers brush the lining of her panties. Ayemeline's breath hitches.

"Ari," she breathes. Her hand grips my arm tighter as I push her panties aside and explore the inner and outer lips of her pussy with my fingers. I gently pull on one lip and then the other. "You're doing this now?" She whispers to me while she looks behind her, making sure no one can see what I am doing to her.

"What? You don't like an audience? You have such a fat, wet pussy. Let them watch you cum," I breathe into her ear.

Ayemeline gives what sounds like a moan-type scream as the ride starts to tip forward, ready to make its first drop.

Just as the ride starts to descend towards the ground, I insert two fingers into her pussy. It is so slippery and warm. I wriggle my hand further into her, enjoying the feel of her around me. It feels as if I am plummeting to my death as the wind whips all around us. It is exhilarating—everything about it—the thrill of the fall, the satisfying pain as Ayemeline's nail digs into my arm, the insatiable hunger I feel as her thirsty pussy clenches around my finger.

I pump my fingers faster as the ride twists and flips us upside down. With two fingers, I press firmly into her pussy—up, down, side-to-side. It is getting hard to distinguish between Ayemeline's moans and her screams. This is by far the best ride I've ever been on.

CHAPTER SEVENTEEN
AYEMELINE

Exhilarating. Thrilling. Terrifying. Those are the words that describe what it feels like to be on the rollercoaster with Ari while he fingers my pussy into oblivion.

The ride picks up speed and I feel his fingers plunge deeper. I don't know if he can get any deeper. My wetness leaks from my pussy to my thighs. The air flowing around me gives me chills and I grip him harder, trying to bury my screams into his arm. I tense as the ride makes another drop, and his finger hooks into my pussy. If he doesn't stop, we'll have to explain to the ride attendant that I didn't pee myself on this ride.

Shit, this man is going to be the death of me. I've never felt anything like this. Playing on the edge of fear was always something I'd enjoyed. But this is not simply playing on the edge. This is bathing in the middle of fear. The combination of the ride and his fingers give me the sense that I can fly. Our bodies pull from side to side, forward and backward. His fingers, however, are relentless, gliding in and out. Fear and pleasure envelop me as I near my climax.

"Cum for me," Ari whispers in my ear, causing a surge of energy to shoot through my pussy. His penetrating fingers become harder, deeper, and more vigorous as the ride drops us and loops us around. With each thrust in, his knuckles push against my clit.

We soar through the air, the speed of the ride causing me to fly off my seat slightly, making our whole bodies vibrate. And just like that, I cum. My whole body convulses, and my eyes roll back as I let out a scream that is part overwhelming pleasure and part harrowing fear.

The ride comes to a stop, and I look over at Ari. Still trying to catch my breath, I watch as he lifts his fingers to his mouth and sucks my arousal from them. Watching his eyes roll back while he tastes me on his fingers makes me squeeze my legs together to keep from soaking the seat again. God, I love this man.

***

We are in the car making the fourteen-hour drive to Ari's mother's house. It is as if no time has passed. Being with Ari feels safe. It doesn't matter what we are doing or where we are, his presence alone can calm all the demons in my head. It is moments like this that make me feel as if I don't have to fight for his love. He gives it freely.

His hand rests on my thigh as we drive. The plan was for us to spend the weekend together but after his mother's phone call, he insisted he drive up to see her. He told me he didn't want to leave me behind because even a couple of days of not seeing me was too much for him. I feel the same way. That's why I am happily making this trip with him. Besides, meeting his mother is kind of a big deal, right? I tangle my fingers in my hair with one hand as the other hand rests on Ari's hand on my lap.

"Nervous, little fox?"

"Ummm…a little," I confess shyly.

"Don't be. It's not that serious."

I stare into the side of his face, confused. *What does he mean it's not that serious? Is he not serious about me?*

"What I mean is," he starts, reading my thoughts, "is that my mother's opinion of you doesn't matter. She won't like you. She doesn't like anyone. But that's not going to change how I feel about you."

I sigh, relieved I don't have to win her over. "Well, that's good to know."

"My mother is a bit…" He pauses, trying to find the right word. "Difficult."

"Difficult?"

"She can be a bit needy and angry. She's sick. It's her heart. And that causes her to be a bitch."

I laugh like a braying donkey choking on water. I did not expect his word choice.

"Your laugh is super hot, little fox."

I smile at him, his sexy dimple giving him this innocent charm. I know he is far from innocent, though. "You're super hot." I reach over and squeeze his balls.

"Don't make me pull this car over."

"I won't stop you," I respond flirtatiously.

He is quiet for a while, squeezing my thigh every so often.

I roll down the window, letting the faint smell of pine waft into the car. Hundreds of brown, majestic trees pass us by, their branches stretching up to hug the blue sky. The undisturbed landscape gives me a sense of tranquility. This isn't my past or anything I have done. This is a fresh new beginning—a beginning with Ari. This is a life of pure serenity, a euphoric sense of freedom.

I lean my head back on the headrest and allow the cool breeze to fondle my skin. I close my eyes and listen to the wind rustling like a melodic harmony.

"I wanted to ask you something." The tender tone of his voice is warm and inviting, like the first day of spring.

"Hmm…?" I tilt my head towards him so I can look at the side of his face.

His voice tumbles out softly. "We didn't talk about this before. We probably should've." His fingers rub back and forth on my thigh.

I remain silent, giving him time to find his words. Whenever he is trying to think of the right words, he will pierce his lips together slightly, as if he is ensuring the words don't escape prematurely.

His eyes are steady on the road as he talks. "We haven't discussed birth control, and we haven't been using condoms."

"You don't want me to have your babies," I tease.

His lips bear a semblance of a smile, just enough to show me that he is enjoying the idea. "Definitely one day. But not now. I'm not ready to share you yet."

I inch my body slightly closer to him and rest my hand on his thigh. "It's fine. I have an IUD."

"You do?" He turns to face me.

"Yup."

"Since when?"

"It's been a while."

"What do you mean 'it's been a while'? How long is 'a while'?

"Four years," I say.

"Four years? You got it at sixteen? How? Why? I don't think I even want to know why."

The muscles in his jaw tick.

"My parents made me do it. They didn't…trust me."

"Ok. I've heard enough."

"Is my Pookie-boo getting jealous?" I know he's upset, but I can't help teasing him a little.

"NO! I'm getting pissed the fuck off. I don't ever want to hear about some other man touching you. Not now. Not ever." His body becomes rigid, and he grips the steering wheel so hard that his knuckles turn white.

"Noted," I say incredulously.

We ride in silence the rest of the ride to his childhood home. The peace I had previously felt has now vanished as memories of the past flood my brain. I want to tell Ari everything, but I'm afraid. Would he still love me if he knew everything about my past? Would he accept me?

Hands holding my arms tightly against the bed as they each take turns pushing their tiny pencil dicks into me invaded my thoughts. The cacophony of my screams as I beg them to stop, their laughter, their grunts as they push in and out of me—it is all so deafening. As hard as I try, I can't stop a single tear from falling. I don't want to be there in the past. I don't want to live through that again. I never want to remember. But here I am, thrown back into a past I'd tried so desperately to escape.

I don't know when he stops the car or when he pulls me in, but the next thing I know, I am in Ari's arms. My head rests on his shoulder as he gently massages the back of my neck. Rocking me back and forth, he whispers, "I love you."

A great tremor overtakes my body at the sound of those words and tears race down my cheeks. My body is wracked with an onslaught of sobs and tears, drenching his shirt. But this time, they're tears of relief, relief that he can still love me in this moment.

Those three simple words from his mouth pull me out of the darkest hole and put my pieces back together again. He is all that is natural and good. His love is my forte, that protective wall that surrounds me and makes me feel like no one and nothing can ever touch me again. I know, at that moment, I can be free with him.

Still trembling, I slowly pull away from him, letting my eyes rest on his lap. I can't look into his eyes when I share this part because a part of me still feels shame like I am damaged because of it.

"I...I was pregnant." My voice trembles as I speak.

Ari tilts my chin up and forces me to look up at him. "Look into my eyes when you speak. Please look into my eyes and know that nothing you ever say to me will change how I feel about you. Don't ever doubt that, little fox."

I reluctantly look up, the sun brightening his angelic hazel eyes.

"When I was sixteen," I speak slowly, "I got pregnant after a group of boys from school..." I pause, unable to find the right words.

Ari takes my hand and strokes the back of it with his thumb.

I sniffle and push back the tears that threaten to fall again. "They thought it would be funny to take turns...I didn't want to, but there were too many of them for me to fight off."

Ari squeezes my hand slightly. My head falls. It's so hard to look into his eyes. He uses his free hand and tilts my head back toward him. "Eyes on me."

His eyes are glassy as he stares into the darkest parts of my soul.

"I found out I was pregnant, and my dad forced me to have an abortion. That's why I got the IUD. He wanted to make sure it didn't happen again."

"What happened to the guys?" Ari queries, his voice is softer and quiet, almost like a whisper.

"At first, I didn't tell my dad the whole story of what happened. So, he thought it was consensual. I guess I was too scared to say it out loud. Or maybe part of me didn't think he'd believe me. But then it came out. Rumors spread around the school about what happened.

They bragged about how easy it was for them to do what they wanted to me. News spread and got back to my dad. He asked me about it. That's when I told him what actually happened." I take a deep breath, trying to muster up the courage to continue. "My dad reported it. But it didn't matter. They got some big-shot attorney to represent them, and they walked free. I don't even remember that lawyer's name, but I remember his face clearly. I remember the proud look on his face when he shook their hands."

Ari's mouth clenches and his jaw ticks.

"So, those motherfuckers got away with touching you!" His voice is now thick with anger.

"Not exactly." I'm reluctant to tell him what came next. "I…I took care of it."

His eyes implore me, trying to find the answer to the questions that lay just behind his eyes.

"They're dead," I choke out.

He blinks repeatedly, his eyes tracking from my eyes to my mouth and back up again.

"How? What do you mean they're dead?" Ari sputters, although a part of me knows he knows the answer to that question.

We sit quietly while he tries to make sense of what I'd just shared. It is the loudest silence as anxiety takes over my body. *Had I shared too much with him? Shit! Shit! Shit! Why did I say that? What the fuck is wrong with me?*

After the most excruciating silence, he says, "I'm glad you did it because I would've had to take care of them myself if you hadn't." He smiles, his dimple more prominent than ever. That sweet dimple captivates my soul.

I cock my head at him, amazed at his response.

His laser-like focus peers into my darkness. He leans in and gently brushes his lips to mine, letting me feel a hint of him. When he pulls away, his gaze consumes me, sending tantalizing prickles up my spine.

"I'll do anything to protect you, little fox," he says, brushing my lips with his thumb. "And don't you ever forget it."

I nod, believing his words wholeheartedly.

***

I must've fallen asleep because the next thing I know, Ari shakes me.

"We're here, little fox."

"I'm awake," I somnolently exclaim after letting out a huge yawn.

Ari walks to the passenger side and opens my door. He takes my hand and helps me get to my feet. My sluggish body weighs me down as I try to wake myself up to examine my surroundings.

"You better wake up. You'll need to be fully awake to deal with my mother."

"I can't wait," I deadpan.

Ari grabs my bag and his and leads us up the stairs. Walking into the house, I notice his childhood home is not what I imagined it would be. It is unkempt in the worst way. This home is like a hoarder's nightmare.

The shock must have registered on my face because Ari says, "Yeah, I know. It's a mess. I try to help whenever I come, but I can only do so much when I'm so far away."

"This house needs a whole cleaning crew," I blurt out, then cover my hand with my mouth. "I'm sorry," I mutter.

"It's fine. I know it's bad. I've hired several cleaning crews, but she always scares them away. I've given up at this point."

"Wow. Your mom must be a dream."

Ari smiles, but it doesn't quite reach his eyes. "I think you could handle her."

It's obvious he thinks I'm stronger than I feel.

I walk over to the shelves that house several trophies and ribbons. "You played football?"

"Yeah, in high school," Ari laments as he looks up and down the shelf.

"But you don't play now. After all these awards, shouldn't you be playing D1 or something?"

"Another time, little fox. Let's get these bags upstairs."

Ignoring him, I walk over to the photos on the wall. I notice a young Ari smiling with his hand around the neck of a much bigger kid, a much bigger version of himself.

"Is this your brother?"

"Yeah. That's Hassan."

"You look so much alike." I smile at the picture, trying to imagine who Ari was back then. My eyes skim over several other family photos, including one that includes who, judging by the uncanny resemblance, I presumed to be Ari's dad. Something is so familiar about that face. I feel like it's more than him looking like Ari. My stomach clenches although I'm not sure why. "Your mother seems to keep everything,"

"Yup."

I look at Ari, and his solemn expression suggests he prefers not to go down memory lane. I understand that all too well.

"We could bring the bags up now," I say, putting him out of his misery.

He immediately picks up our two duffel bags and approaches the dingy stairs. I don't want to stay in this house. But that isn't something I want to say to him. I understand he feels obligated to be there. And if he is here, this is where I need to be, no matter how much the place makes my skin crawl.

We make our way to a larger-than-expected bedroom. Unlike the rest of the house, this room is immaculate. The bed is perfectly made, with a black down blanket and two perfectly rectangular pillows. There is a dresser against the wall opposite the bed and a desk right below the only window in the room. Two grey nightstands sit on either side of the bed, each holding a simple lamp. This room is the opposite of the home, it is the perfect image of minimalism.

"Is this your room?"

"Yup."

"Wow. It's…clean," I marvel.

"It's the one place that's missing my mother's touch. It's how I'm able to stay here, having my little sanctuary in hell."

I'm relieved that his room doesn't resemble the rest of the house. It also feels like I'm getting a better sense of who Ari was, his life before me.

"I'm going to check on my mother. You want to meet her?" His voice is weary. I noticed that the second we walked into the home, it was as if some invisible pressure weighed him down.

"Sure," I agree reluctantly. Walking into the home makes me feel anxious about meeting the woman who can devote her life to living like this.

We walk down the hall to the bedroom at the far end of the hall. Ari cracks the door open slightly.

"Ma? You awake?"

A hoarse cough comes from the bedroom.

Ari pushes the door open more and walks in. I stand at the doorway, unsure of whether I should wait to be invited in or walk in like I own the place. I opt to stand there and wait.

"Who the hell is this?" Her voice is raspy and choked, like a woman who smokes ten packs of cigarettes a day and has bronchitis all at the same time.

"Ma, this is Ayemeline. She's…my girlfriend?" The heady smell of mothballs, peppermint, and eucalyptus with a side of staleness greets me at the door.

Slowly walking towards her, I extend my hand to shake hers. "Nice to meet you, Ms. Yearwood."

"I'm ain't no fucking Yearwood," she fumes.

"Yearwood is my father's name," Ari explains.

"I'm so sorry," I apologize.

"She didn't know, Ma. No need to be rude to our guest."

"She's not *my* guest."

"It doesn't matter. Just show her some respect. She came all this way to meet you."

"I didn't ask no one to come here."

I'm starting to understand what Ari tried to warn me about. This woman is relentless. She is the one who interrupted our weekend alone to have Ari drive fourteen hours because she claimed she needed him. Now she has the audacity to say she didn't ask anyone to come. *What a bitch!*

I stand there, unsure of what to say or do next. I shift from foot to foot, afraid to make eye contact with Ari's mother.

"Did you take your medication?" Ari walks over to the dresser, where a considerable amount of prescription medication lay. He picks up the bottles, one by one, and examines their contents.

"I'm not a fucking child, Ari. I know how to take care of myself," she scolds.

I see Ari's shoulders visibly slump.

"You act like a child. I mean, I know you're not, but sometimes you act like one," Ari vacillates.

Ignoring him, his mother looks at me up and down, her mouth pouting like she smells the stench of a rotting corpse. "Girlfriend, huh? I thought you weren't going to do the girlfriend thing ever since you killed Julia."

I cock my head and look over at Ari, who is suddenly frozen.

"You didn't tell her about Julia?" His mother coaxes; a huge grin plasters on her face.

Without turning around, Ari speaks through gritted teeth. "Ayemeline, go wait for me in my room. I'll be right there."

I pause, frozen for a few seconds, before I force my feet to move. *Who the fuck was Julia?*

CHAPTER EIGHTEEN
ARIEL

*I*t's becoming abundantly clear that my mother was put on this earth for one sole purpose: to make sure my life is utterly as miserable as hers. Rage flows through me like molten lava.

My mother sits up in bed grinning at me. "It's not good to keep secrets from your girlfriend, you know."

I can't speak. I'm immobilized by rage. All I can do is stare at her while my irritation crackles, a mounting vortex swirls inside me. I want to explode. I want to pick up the lamp beside her bed and hit her over the head with it. I want to keep hitting her until the blood explodes from her brain. I want to suffocate her with my fury. But I don't do any of that. I stand there, frozen to one spot.

"You're just like your father," she drones. "So weak."

"I'm not weak," I finally mutter. I turn to walk away, no longer being able to be in the same room as my mother. I need to breathe, to get away from her. *Why couldn't I be more like Hassan? He left and never looked back. Why couldn't I do that?*

"Because Hassan is a bad son," I hear my mother's voice say in my head.

I walk down the hall and stand behind my closed bedroom door, too afraid to open it—to see Ayemeline. *Why did I have to bring her here? Did I expect my mother to be happy for me that I'd finally found someone to be with? That I was finally free from the demons that had haunted me for the past five years?*

The bedroom door opens slowly as if she senses me on the other side. Her deep, dark eyes bore into mine. Ayemeline takes my hand and gently pulls me into the room. Once I am fully inside, she shuts the door, walks over to the bed, and sits, folding one leg under her.

"I told you my secrets. Now, you tell me yours." She speaks softly and gently.

I rub my head and close my eyes, unsure of what to say.

"Just talk to me, Ari."

I walk to the bed and sit down beside her. This is the moment where I need to cut myself open and lay bare for her to see who I truly am.

"When we'd just met, I told you that I was celibate."

Ayemeline nods, her eyes never leaving my face.

"In high school, I met this girl…Julia. We dated for a while, and things were great…sort of. I liked her and all, but…I always felt…like I needed more."

She looks at me as if she understands.

"I'd try to convince her to try different things with me," I continue. "In the bedroom. But she was never comfortable. We were just into different things. She never understood the satisfaction I got from inflicting and receiving pain through sex." I pause, giving her a minute to digest my words.

"It can be difficult for people to understand because it can seem scary," Ayemeline clarifies.

"Exactly," I affirm. "I tried introducing her to the lifestyle, and she called me disturbed. She wanted no part of it. But at the time, I thought I loved her, so I didn't want to give up on getting her to see the pleasure in it all. I was selfish, I know. I never really considered her needs."

"You were young. We're all a little selfish when we're young." Ayemeline rests her hand on mine.

"Yeah, well, I really fucked up with my selfishness. I finally convinced her to play. I used my popularity as a football player to get my way with her and other girls in school. So, eventually, it became easier to convince her to do things that I wanted to do. I've always been drawn to breath play. So, I decided to try it on her." I need to catch my breath but also get it all out before I chicken out. "I knew she had a heart condition, but being young and stupid, I didn't think it would affect our sex life. During one of our scenes, I just…blacked out. When I came to, I found her lifeless body beneath me. I had strangled her to death, and I couldn't even remember doing it. Turns out sometime during…you know…she went into cardiac arrest. It was…horrifying. That's why I was afraid to touch you after our first date. I was afraid of hurting you."

Ayemeline remains quiet for a while, staring at our two hands entwined. "You could've told me," she finally says.

"I didn't think you'd understand. And I didn't want to lose you."

"You wouldn't have lost me."

"I know that now." I squeeze her hand in mine.

"It was an accident. You didn't mean to hurt her."

"But it happened and that scared the shit out of me. Then I met you and I'm just…I'm obsessed with you. I think, what if the same thing happens to you? What if I hurt you?"

"I enjoy your pain, Ari. I enjoy being dominated by you. You could never hurt me."

I lift my head to look at my girl, the woman who unleashed the monster inside of me with no remorse. "You are amazing, you know that?" I lean over and place a light, feathery kiss on her lips. She kisses me back.

"So what happened after you found out she was dead," Ayemeline asks, pulling away from our kiss.

I exhale sharply, not wanting to relive the story but needing to get it out. "I called an ambulance. I hoped there was a chance she was not dead, just unconscious. Anyway, I ended up losing my scholarship. I was charged with involuntary manslaughter. My parents made sure she got the best criminal defense attorney to defend me. Thanks to my attorney, I was able to…" I pause my nattering. I want to tell her everything, to pour my soul into this woman. But I know I can't. "I was able to walk." I shudder, wondering if I shared too much. I hope she can't read me, or she'd know I'm keeping so much more from her.

"Hey," she says, touching my chin. "In the car, you told me you'd do anything to protect me, remember?"

I nod.

"Well, just like you've got my back, I've got yours. And just like you didn't judge me for my past, I won't judge you for yours. We're the same, you and me. We understand each other, even if no one else does."

I smile. That is so true. We fit together like a puzzle. All the paths I took in life, whether good or bad, have led me to her. All the suffering, the loss, the ghosts of my past—they are all worth it to be with her.

"Don't ever hold back from me, Ari. I can handle all of you."

Smiling, I take her hand, kissing her knuckles. "That's so good to know, little fox."

***

Two days with my mother are enough to make me want to jump off a cliff, but having Ayemeline with me made it a little more bearable.

I can tell Ayemeline doesn't care for my mother just as much as my mother doesn't care for Ayemeline. However, it seems Ayemeline's hatred far surpassed that of my mother's. Her eyes darkened with rage whenever she looked at my mother. I tried my best to keep them apart as much as possible.

I'm happy to finally be away from that place once again. As Ayemeline sleeps beside me on her bed, I keep replaying the conversations over the last couple of days. My heart weeps for my little fox and everything she's been through. At the same time, I've come to realize that this woman who lays beside me is so much stronger than she appears to be at first glance. She doesn't let things happen without consequence.

I never asked her for details regarding the incident with the boys. She said those boys were dead. She said she took care of it. But how? My mind goes back to Brea's friend, who I was on a double date the night I first spoke with Ayemeline, and how she was found dead. I look over at her sleeping form, lying there peacefully, this tiny ball of innocence. Who is this woman? And what the fuck am I doing here with her?

CHAPTER NINETEEN
AYEMELINE

Class is uneventful. As usual. Professor Matthews makes a point of repeatedly calling on me, just to piss me off, even though I'm pretty sure he knows I'm not paying attention. Micah, who had always taken the seat behind me, has relocated to the other side of the classroom. Whenever I look in that direction, I notice him looking over at me, always turning at the last minute so I wouldn't catch his stare.

He doesn't speak to me or address that jealous kiss we shared in front of the restaurant. Neither has he tried to text me. I'm pretty sure Ari scares him. Ari is significantly larger than Micah. Although Micah, at six foot seven, has a good five inches on Ari, Ari must have at least 100 pounds or more of pure muscle. Micah is what one would consider a lean-fit guy made for playing basketball, although he much prefers being at the computer screen or with his nose in a book. Meanwhile, Ari is nothing short of a beast in human form. Whatever the reason, I'm glad Micah has chosen not to pursue me as he had in the past. I like him and I don't want to see the hurt look in his eyes whenever I turn him down. He sometimes resembles a puppy who was chastised for relieving himself on the carpet.

"Micah and Ayemeline." Professor Matthews's voice snaps me awake, and I'm suddenly alert.

"What?" I mumble incoherently, trying to figure out what I missed.

"For the group project, you two will work together." Professor Matthews paces the front of the auditorium-style classroom as he speaks.

"What the…" *What project? Had I not been paying attention for that long that I had no idea what he was talking about?*

The girl beside me snickers, obviously amused by my confusion. I look over at her and glower, feeling the intense desire to chop her tits off and choke her with them.

"Class dismissed," Professor Matthews announces.

The students shuffle loudly as they pack up their belongings. I look over at Micah with eyebrows raised as if to ask, "What the fuck is going on?" His gaze gives away nothing.

I make my way to the other side of the classroom over to him.

"Do you know what we're supposed to be doing?" I ask, reaching him.

"We have to pick a project and work on it. Together."

"I gathered that much. What project?"

"On The Great Gatsby. We have to decide together." He doesn't look at me while he speaks. He continues to put his books in his bag.

"Seriously? Fuck. I don't want to do that."

"I know you don't," Micah says, his face free of all emotion.

"What are the options?"

Micah nods his head toward the projection screen in front of the classroom. On it, there are four topics to choose from: Topic A: The Geography of Desire, Topic B: Poetry Connections, Topic C: Eulogy for Gatsby, and Topic D: Modernism in Art and Literature.

I groan, dreading that I must be bothered with this.

Micah picks up his bag and starts to head out of the classroom without a glance in my direction. Following him out, I tug on his arm.

"Why are you being so cold?"

He swings around and finally looks at me. He says nothing. He looks at me, his eyes seeming to stare a thousand miles away.

"Micah?" I search his eyes. Nothing. Shaking him, I shout, "Micah! Is this about the kiss?"

Micah's eyes finally focus on mine. They appear to have a thin film of water on them.

"Are you…okay?" I'm beginning to worry about him. He is here but not here at the same time.

"I'm fine," he mutters, his voice barely audible. "We can decide later. I have to go." And with that, he turns and walks away, leaving me utterly confused.

The way he is acting doesn't seem to be about fearing Ari. He seems to be in pain. That wasn't the first time we kissed. Heck, we've done so much more than kiss. I've also rejected him before. That isn't new, either. So why is he acting like I killed his dog?

***

By the next class, I decide that I need to speak with Professor Matthews about this group project. I haven't spoken to Micah since that day in class when it was assigned to us and I feel it isn't a good idea to work with him, considering our history and the way he's acting toward me.

I walk into his office, ready to plead my case. And if that doesn't work, well, that's where the art of manipulation and blackmail would come into play.

"Ms. Cross," he greets, a devilish grin decorating his face.

"I need to speak to you about the group project," I say, getting right to the point.

"What about it?"

"I don't want to do it. And I can't work with Micah."

"Because you're fucking him?" His tone is serious, and the grin is now gone. It is replaced with a scowl.

"What? That's none of your fucking business, Troy." I spit out his name.

Professor Matthews walks around the desk toward me.

"You see, you're wrong, Ms. Cross. It is my business." His fingers grabs the hem of my shirt, pulling me into him.

"Don't fucking touch me." I smack his hand away.

The devilish grin returns. "So now I can't touch you. I guess you don't need anything from me, then, huh?"

"Are you trying to blackmail me?" I hiss, lifting my chin to meet his gaze.

"Why would I do that? This is merely an exchange of services."

"You fucking pig. I'm not going to fuck you. That was a mistake. I promise you it will not happen again."

"That's a shame, Ms. Cross. You had so much potential. I hate to see you give up on it."

"You're disgusting. Maybe your wife needs to find out about your extracurricular activities."

Professor Matthews laughs. He just stands there and laughs. It sounds like what it would sound like if lions could laugh, his protruding belly bouncing up and down.

"Ms. Cross. Sweetheart." He rubs my cheek with his knuckle.

I smack his hand away, enraged at his reaction to my threat. "Don't. Touch. Me."

Professor Matthews stares at me, amusement in his eyes. "If you tell my secret, I'll have to tell yours. And you don't want me to tell yours, Ms. Cross. You see, if you tell my secret, my wife will leave me. But I can always get her back. However, if I tell your secret…" His hand reaches up to cup my chin, "your life is over."

My eyes focus on him, trying to figure out what he knows. *Is he bluffing?*

"You're so quiet all of a sudden, sweetheart. What happened to that disgusting tongue of yours?"

"I...I don't have any secrets. I don't know what you're talking about," I say, injecting steel in my voice.

"Of course you do. I'm pretty sure you know exactly what I'm talking about."

I stare, unable to form a logical thought pattern. This conversation has taken a turn in a direction I wasn't expecting.

"I've been watching you very closely, Ms. Cross. You aren't as innocent as you pretend to be. I'm pretty sure Crystal would agree."

At the mention of her name, my eyes widen. *What the fuck? Does he know what I did to her?*

"Ah...now you're getting it. So you see, Ms. Cross. We both have our little secrets. But unfortunately for you, one of us holds more power here. And it's *NOT* you."

I stare in disbelief. My brain won't allow my mouth to speak the words I want to say, to deny his accusations.

"Don't worry. Your secret is safe with me. That is as long as you play nice."

Professor Matthews walks around his desk and jots something on a piece of paper. Folding it up, he hands it to me.

"You're free to go," he says with a wave of his hand.

I hold the paper and leave his office, my legs feeling like they could give way and collapse under me. After I turn the corner away from his office, I unfold the paper and read the words he scribbled on it. *Queens Inn. Room 220. 10 p.m.*

CHAPTER TWENTY
ARIEL

I know something is wrong the minute I see her. Her eyebrows are pulled up and together, and she has not spoken much since I arrived at her apartment. She sits on the couch, staring into a book, never turning the pages. I sit beside her, pulling her feet into my lap. I work each foot one by one, stroking and manipulating the muscles of her feet with my fingers.

Ayemeline looks up at me, the worried look I saw in her eyes earlier even more prominent.

"Thank you," she mumbles.

"Anytime, little fox." I try not to probe, allowing her to process her feelings. I want her to come to me when she is ready. But I hate seeing my little fox so distraught. I want to fix it for her. It doesn't matter what it is.

"I need to take care of something," Ayemeline says, suddenly pulling her feet from me and standing. She puts on her shoes.

"Wait. Where are you going?"

She looks at me apologetically. "I…I need to take care of something. Something important."

"I can go with you."

"You can't."

"Why not?"

Ayemeline hesitates, her eyes searching for any excuse to appease me.

"Don't you dare lie to me, little fox. Whatever lie you're trying to think up, don't even bother. I need the truth." My voice is stern, yet gentle. I want her to know I'm serious. But I also want her to know I'm here for her.

Ayemeline takes a deep breath. "I need to go see my professor."

***

I should be more surprised than I am. Perhaps it is because part of me knows she has bones in her closet. After all, like recognizes like. Ayemeline told me everything. She told me about the affair with Professor Matthews. She told me about Crystal, how she had tortured and killed her, then buried her body in the woods off campus. Worst of all, she told me about Professor Matthew's little proposition.

That information fills me with so much rage, I'm ready to tear him to pieces with my bare teeth. Which is why we are in my truck on the way to Queens Inn to have a little talk with Professor Matthews. As we silently drive the pothole-filled road to the motel, the duffle bag with tools clang in the back seat. Adrenaline pumps through me as I try to imagine how this will go.

"I'll go in first. Then you can follow." Her voice finally breaks the silence.

My hand grips the steering wheel tighter. I am afraid, but not because of him. I'm afraid of me, afraid of what I am going to do to that bastard once I see him. "I'm not going to let you go in there alone."

"He won't open the door if he sees you. He's not stupid."

"I'll handle it. But you're NOT going in alone."

We pull into the decrepit motel that looks to be the breeding ground of syphilis and staph infections and park my truck.

Ayemeline turns to look at me. "Ready?"

"I'm ready," I confirm. Reaching over to the back seat, I grab the duffel bag and step out of the car, walking around to open Ayemeline's door for her.

She steps out, looking stunning. She wears a pair of skin-tight black leather pants, a sleeveless black tank top with silver circular buttons down the front, and stiletto high-heeled ankle platform boots on her feet. She is the epitome of darkness. She embraces it with every fiber of her being.

"Little fox, you make me want to swallow you whole," I purr in her ear. Leaning down, I plant a smoldering kiss on her lips. She moans into my mouth, letting her body melt into mine. "Let's get this done quickly so I can fuck you until you're so full of my cum it pours down your legs."

"Keep talking like that, and I'll be tempted to abort this mission so I can have you inside me sooner."

Smiling, I pull her in once more and kiss her forehead. "I won't be satisfied until that motherfucker gets what he deserves."

Holding her hand with one hand and the duffle bag with the other, we make our way up the concrete stairs to room 220. I pull the metal bat out of the bag and hold it in my palm. I stand with my back against the wall so as not to be seen by Professor Matthews once he opens the door. Ayemeline steps forward and gives three soft knocks.

I hear rustling on the other side of the door as the disgusting old man fights with the lock.

He opens the door and all the fury inside me springs to life. The motherfucker stands there wearing only a T-shirt stretched tautly over his girthy belly and boxer shorts.

Despite his out-of-shape physique, Professor Matthews looks like a man who doesn't have a hard time getting the women he wants. He looks every part of the distinguished gentleman who is living too comfortably to bother going to the gym. On campus, he's referred to as a silver fox by all the horny students who wait in line to suck his dick. He is a man who cares about the clothes he wears and the way he presents himself to society. The idea of him with my little fox, manipulating her to satisfy his sick cravings, makes me shake with fury. But I can't let my anger ruin our plan. I have to present a semblance of calm to ensure our plan is executed perfectly.

When Professor Matthews sees Ayemeline, a sick smile of satisfaction crosses his features. "I knew you would come. You are a smart girl, after all."

Ayemeline smiles back. To the onlooker, one could have confused her smile for one of happiness. But I know my little fox. I know that smile is the smile of pure terror and chaos, and I'm here for it.

He opens the door wider and steps aside to let her in. Before he can close the door, my hand springs out and holds it open.

"What the fuck?" Professor Matthews tumbles backward from the force of the door. I step into the poorly lit motel room and shut the door behind me, my eyes never leaving his.

"Oh," Ayemeline says through giggles. "I forgot to tell you. I brought a friend. I figured we could all have a little fun together. Won't you enjoy that, PROFESSOR?"

I would've given my right testicle for an autographed photo of the look of horror on Professor Matthew's face.

"Wh…wh…wh…", he stutters.

"Seems like you've lost your ability to speak, professor," I scoff.

"What? Why?" Professor Matthews looks back and forth between me and Ayemeline, then at the metal bat in my hand.

"Shhhh!" Ayemeline sibilates, placing her index finger on his lips. "No need to speak."

This is my little fox. She is no longer the sweet, fragile woman who sat disturbed on her sofa just an hour ago. This woman is the queen of her own fucking universe, and I love her for it.

"Get on your knees, Professor Matthews." Ayemeline's voice is like a melody as she says those words. My dick flinches.

"I will not," he retorts, finding courage. "You stupid bitch!"

I swing the bat straight toward the back of his knees, forcing him to buckle and fall to the ground. He writhes and screams on the ground, grabbing at the back of his knee. I lean down and gently tap the bat to his temple. "Watch your mouth, professor, or I'm going to have to cut your tongue out and use it to fuck your ass."

I can hear Ayemeline's sexy giggle behind me. This girl can bring my darkness to its surface with a simple laugh.

For years, I denied my darkest desires. I thought something was wrong with me. The only woman I had dared to express them to called me disturbed and ended up dead at my hands. Those memories haunt me. I'm coming to realize, however, that it isn't Julia's death that haunts me the most. It is the fact that I'd often use the memory of me inside her, choking the life out of her—the adrenaline—the uninhabited satisfaction—to jerk off. I feel shame that something so wrong makes me cum so hard. That is a reality I didn't want to face, that I was sick, depraved. Or at least I thought I was until I met Ayemeline, a woman who embraces my darkness with her own—a woman who makes me unashamed to be me without judgment, a woman who understands my deep innate desire to hurt.

I open the duffel bag and pull out a rope, Ayemeline's pink pocket knife, and my cat o' nine tails. I line each item up on the floor before Professor Matthew's face.

He scrambles to get up from his crouching position on the floor. I let him stand, knowing he won't get very far. He springs to his feet and limps toward the door.

Ayemeline reaches down and picks up her pocket knife. She slowly walks over to him while he frantically fumbles with the lock. Bending as if she has all the time in the world, she uses the knife to swipe at his ankle, leaving red streaks of blood behind.

Professor Matthews shrieks and falls to the floor once more. "Fuuuuuuuck!" he shouts.

Had this been a more reputable hotel, I would've been worried. But I'm sure the residents are used to hearing unsavory screams at all hours of the day and have been conditioned to mind their business.

"Professor Matthews," Ayemeline singsongs in a fake pleading voice, "are you trying to leave us? That's not very nice." She pouts.

"Listen," he wheezes, "I'm not gonna tell anyone what you did. We're even. Please. I have a family."

"What *I* did?" Ayemeline cocks her head in mock confusion. "What did I do?"

"I'm sorry, Ms. Cross. I…I shouldn't have…please…don't do this. You're going to get yourself in trouble. What do you think the police will do when they find out?"

"They never found out before." Ayemeline's smile illuminates the dim room. She is an extraordinary woman. I smile as I stand back, observing her. I love watching her.

Professor Matthew's eyes widen in disbelief. He is finally seeing what has always been there. On the surface, Ayemeline is a tiny, five-foot-tall girl who isolates herself and never quite fits in. She is innocent and vulnerable. That's probably what makes her an easy target for Professor Dingy Balls. But peel back the onion, and you are met with a complex being, someone who lived in darkness until it became a part of who she is, someone one should never fuck with.

"I think you should have a seat, Professor Matthews." She stands, giving him room to rise from the ground.

"Please…"

"Get. The fuck. Up," I bark, tired of his pleadings.

Professor Matthews looks at me as if he's looking for sympathy. He will not find any here.

"Would you like some help?" Ayemeline asks sweetly.

"No. Don't touch me," he stammers, trying his best to stand on his damaged ankles.

"You poor thing. You're hurt." She turns to me. "Babe, maybe you should help him to the chair."

Ignoring his pleas, I walk over to him and pull him up. I plop him down on the wooden desk chair.

The professor sobs like a child who has scraped his knee. Thick tears and snot cascade down his face and form a pool of liquid around his mouth.

Ayemeline strokes his cheeks with the back of her hand. "It's okay. Don't cry. We're here."

I can't help but laugh at her ludicrous behavior. She presents as a loving mother trying to soothe her crying child.

I use the rope to secure his arms to the back of the chair. I then secure his legs to each leg of the desk behind the chair. This gives him some mobility in his legs, but not enough to help him.

Surprisingly, he doesn't fight much while he is being strapped down. Perhaps he is beginning to accept his fate.

Once he is strapped to the chair, Ayemeline straddles his lap. Using the pink knife, she slices down the front of his shirt, exposing his hairy chest. He watches her with numbed horror while a flood of tears gushes down his ghostly white cheeks.

"You, Professor Matthews, are such a bad boy."

Ayemeline carves his skin. A smooth, straight line of blood trails from his collarbone to one pink nipple. A gut-wrenching scream tears through his chest.

"Shhh. Shhh. Shhh. Don't scream," she whispers, placing her finger on his lips. I watch her as she meticulously carves out letters onto his chest.

Pain and grief pour out of him in a flood of uncontrollable tears. "Please. Please stop."

"Don't worry. I've got you, Professor," she reassures.

Professor Matthews squeezes his eyes closed as he braces himself for the pain. She carves until all that can be seen is red. The blood doesn't gush in a constant flow like I would imagine it would after all that carving. It simply sits there, clasping the ripped flesh of his torso.

When she is done, she stands to admire her work. The words "BAD BOY" are prominently displayed on his chest in blood.

"You did a great job, little fox," I praise with a smile.

"Thank you. I'm so happy it pleases you."

Her sweet, submissive voice is making my dick hard. We stare at each other for a while, both of us trying to find the strength not to fuck the other in a pool of this man's blood. The full-throated growl of a truck followed by a dog barking brings us back to the present.

"We need to finish up here soon."

"But I'm having so much fun. I don't want it to end."

I grip her chin. "It has to end, little fox. Or he's going to have to watch me fuck you right here before he dies."

Ayemeline pouts and turns to face Professor Matthews. "Unfortunately, it's time for us to say goodbye."

"Please don't kill me. Just let me go," he pleads for his life. "Please have mercy."

"I'm afraid that's not how this is going to work. But don't worry, it'll be over very soon."

With that, Ayemeline plunges her knife straight into the side of his neck. "Goodbye, Professor. See you in hell."

CHAPTER TWENTY-ONE
AYEMELINE

That kill was invigorating—more than any other previous kill. Having Ari there for support was unlike anything else I'd ever experienced. He never interfered; he stood back and observed, giving me the space to execute punishment as I saw fit.

Before leaving, Ari carefully set the room up making it appear as if Professor Matthews was into some raunchy shit. After all, most men who frequented motels like the Queen's Inn were not upstanding gentlemen. We didn't want people feeling bad for that asshole. When the news came out about his murder, the story would go like this: "Professor Pays Prostitute to Perform Sadistic Sex Acts Goes Deadly." With a story like that, his wife would be too ashamed to push for further investigation, preferring to let the story die and not bring too much attention to her family. It's a brilliant plan, and one that would keep the cops off our tails.

When we arrive back at my apartment, we immediately strip off our clothes and get in the shower. It is a little after 1 a.m., and the air is warm. We both stand there as the water washes away all the dirt from the day. I close my eyes as the water pressure soaks me from head to toe.

A soft hand starts at my hip and works its way up the side of my body. Ari's naked frame presses into mine and I turn to face him. I wrap my hands around his neck. Reaching up, I kiss him passionately on the lips. His hand runs up and down my spine, as the water pulses down on our bodies. He pulls away from my lips and plants sensual kisses along my neck and behind my ear. He reaches between us and pinches my nipples. He rolls my nipples between his fingers. I feel his hard dick press against my stomach. His hand slides down to my belly button, stroking back and forth with his knuckles.

"Thank you for being there for me today," I say into his neck.

"I'll always be there for you. No matter what."

"I didn't think you had it in you," I smirk. "To be there and see…everything."

"I loved seeing you…the unfiltered version of you. Not many people get to see that. I feel special."

I smile at him. "It didn't freak you out? You don't think I'm…crazy?"

"You are crazy. But I love your crazy. I love every part of it." He strokes my cheek. "It's all right, love. It's our little secret. I'll protect you."

Our eyes lock, and a silent promise passes between us. This electrifying feeling sends shivers down my spine. The air is charged with anticipation and desire. The love I have for him and the love he has for me is unconditional. This man embraces all my flaws without judgment. He accepts me—the real me.

"Do you trust me, little fox?" Ari's voice is like melting honey in my ear.

"I trust you."

"Good," he growls, his husky voice coming through, "because I want to fuck you into unconsciousness. I'd like to tie you to the fucking bed and pump you so full of my cum, you'll be leaking it for weeks. I want to bend you over and pump my dick into that tiny hole until you can't walk. I want to hear you screaming my name in agony as I spank your ass until your skin is red and inflamed."

Warmth spreads throughout my body, and suddenly, my legs feel weak. "I'm all yours, Master."

***

Ari moves me from the shower to the living room. My body spasms in anticipation.

"On your knees," he demands, his voice brimming with confidence and power.

I do as I'm told, slowly descending to my knees before him. He gazes down at me with a look of pure desire.

"Good girl. Now open your mouth."

My mouth opens.

"Wider."

I open wider for him.

"I want you to take all my cock into your mouth, little fox. I want you to take me to the back of your throat. And when I cum, I want you to swallow it with one gulp. Do you understand?"

I nod my head, keeping my mouth open for him. Electric waves shoot through my spine as my anticipation rises. Before I have time to adjust, Ari is stuffing his ludicrously oversized cock into my mouth. I gag at the menacing intrusion but then quickly adjust. His dick is thick and rigid. His pre-cum soaks my tongue and I moan.

His head lifts to expose his neck and he groans into the air. His gaze travels back down to me, our eyes locking. His eyes take in every aspect of my face. He pushes his cock further into my mouth, forcing me to take him in deeper than I ever thought I could.

"You're such a complete slut, aren't you, little fox? So hungry for my cum."

I moan around his length, relishing the drops of salty liquid in my mouth. I let my tongue encircle his length while I suck. I feel him swell inside my throat, and I know he's close. I rapidly increase my thrusts, taking in his cock like it's my last meal. Ari groans, and I feel the jerk of his balls and cock. I increase my intensity, making sure to apply pressure to the sensitive head of his dick with each long pull of my mouth.

"You are a dirty girl, little fox." His hand fists around my hair as he pushes my face into his crotch. Ari roars as thick, warm ribbons spray the back of my throat. "Swallow all of me, little fox. I want to be inside of you."

I do as I'm told, swallowing his cum with one big gulp. Ari pushes out of my mouth, and I stumble backward, landing on my behind.

He drops into a crouching position in front of me. "Do you still trust me?" he asks again, using his thumb to wipe his cum from my lips.

"Yes," I croak, my voice barely audible.

His stare is intense as he bores into me; his pure hazel eyes never leave mine. Ringlets of warm blond curls stick to his forehead from either the shower or the intensity of his orgasm.

His hand travels from my lips to my bare breast, landing on my hard nipple. "Good." He rolls a nipple between his fingers. Ari helps me up and leads me to the bedroom. "I have a gift for you," he whispers in my ear.

My eyebrow cocks.

"But you're going to have to be a little more patient."

My heart drops. I can't wait any longer. "Please don't make me wait," I beg.

"You're so impatient, little fox," he chuckles. "Don't worry. It'll be worth the wait. Now, get on the bed."

I climb onto the bed and wait for instructions. I love being dominated by him.

"On your back."

I lay down on my back, letting my legs spread open slightly. The cool air felt amazing on my damp pussy.

Ari stares at me and licks his lips. "So beautiful," he croons.

He looks around the room, searching before his eyes land on my silk bathrobe hanging beside my closet door. He walks to it and pulls the bathrobe sash from it. My heart pounds in my chest as he walks back to the bed. He climbs onto the bed. Kneeling beside my head, he pulls both my arms above my head. He loops the sash around my wrists and ties my hands to my slatted wooden designed headboard.

My pussy pulses and aches as I watch him work, his semi-hard dick bobbing just above my exposed breasts.

Once my hands are secured, he moves to the foot of the bed. He spreads my legs wider and stands back to admire my wetness. His eyes burn with lust.

"You're ready for me already."

"Yes, master." His devilish grin tells me he enjoys my word choice.

His finger faintly strokes my pussy, making his way from my clit to my opening and back again.

My body writhes, dying for more. But he doesn't give me more. Instead, he licks his finger and searches the room for something else.

When he returns to the foot of the bed, he's holding two pairs of shoelaces. He stands over me, tying the laces together to make them longer.

"Do you remember the rules, little fox?" he asks as he makes tight knots in the laces.

I pause, remembering when he punished me for making a scene at the restaurant. "Yes," I pant.

"What's rule number one?" His eyes stay focused on the laces.

My breath is heavy. I try to focus, but it's difficult while he's standing there. His broad, tattooed chest flexes with each movement. I'm lost in the rich, warm tone of his reddish-brown skin.

He stops suddenly, lifts his head, and makes strong eye contact with me. "What. Is. Rule. Number. One?"

I lick my lips, my mouth suddenly dry. "Um." I swallow hard. "I will not…" I take a deep breath, trying so hard to find the strength to speak through my arousal. "Cum…without permission."

"That's my girl." He finishes the knots in the shoelaces and kneels at the foot of the bed. "What's rule number two?" Ari spreads my leg to one end of the bed and secures the shoelace around my ankle.

I try to speak through my moans, but the words fail me.

His eyes snap over to me. "Say it," he demands. His fingers brush the inside of my thigh.

"Oh my god, Master," I moaned, my head tilting back and my back arching.

A sudden surge of pain emanates through my pussy, and I yelp. "Say the fucking rule, or I will spank this pussy raw."

I try to slow my breathing and say, "I will only respond…" My chest heaves violently. This is too much for me. I want to explode.

Ari's eyes compel me to keep going.

"I will only. Respond. I will only respond to you…with…"Yes…Master."

Ari finishes tying one leg to the wooden leg of my platform bed and moves to the other leg. "What's rule number three?"

Heat radiates through my whole body. This man was going to be the death of me. "I will enjoy every minute of it."

"That's my good little fox." Ari finishes securing my other leg to the bed and stands above me. My legs are spread across the bed, giving him a perfect view of my soaking wet pussy. My arousal reflects in the pool of his eyes as his sensual gaze raked over my body.

"Master, will you please fuck me?" I beg.

Ari moves to the chair, grabs his pants and shirt, and pulls them on.

"What are you doing?" I question.

Ari smirks but doesn't answer. After getting dressed, he walks out of the bedroom. All I hear is the front door open and close. And I'm left tied to the bed, completely naked.

CHAPTER TWENTY-TWO
ARIEL

The plan was to go to the storage and grab my bag, then head back over to Ayemeline. Halfway there, I realize I don't have the storage key. I make a U-turn and head to my dorm. My dick is hard and the thought of her lying there waiting for me makes it even harder.

My phone vibrates in my pocket, and I reach to pull it out and Remy's name flashes on the screen.

"Hey," I answer.

"Could you come to Brea's place?" Remy sounds frustrated and I can hear Brea screaming in the background.

"Why? What's going on?"

"Brea says she needs you to come over now."

"I don't understand." Whatever is going on, I can tell it's not good based on the way Brea is carrying on.

"We're…we're dealing with some things. Please man, just hurry up."

"Okay, fine. I'm on my way." I hang up the phone, frustrated. I need to head back to Ayemeline soon, but I can't leave Remy hanging. Something is going on. I hope it isn't anything that will take too long.

***

I pull into the parking spot and hop out of my car, hoping to deal with whatever is going on between Remy and Brea and make it back to my little fox. At least that phone call had managed to soften my dick. *It's in the middle of the fucking night, for goodness' sake.*

I reach Brea's apartment and the door swings open before I can knock. Remy is at the door, and he gives me a look. I know that look. It's the "cover for me" look. It's the look that says, "I need you to lie for me to cover my ass." *Shit, Remy. What did you do, and why the fuck am I involved?*

I walk into the apartment, unsure of my role in this whole thing. Remy and I haven't spoken since the fair, so his calling me now is unexpected. And to be honest, fucking unwelcome. Brea stands in the middle of her living room with tears running down her face. Her eyes are red and puffy as if she'd been crying for hours.

"What's going on?" I ask cautiously, feeling like I've just walked into the lion's den.

"I wanted to look at your face when I ask you these questions, Ari." Brea's gaze bores into me.

I look at Remy for answers, but he isn't looking at me. His arms are crossed, and he's looking at the floor. The sprawling disarray of books, papers, and clothes on the ground tells me all I need to know about what transpired before I arrived.

"I want to know if you're lying," Brea says.

"Okay?" I questioned.

"I told her you didn't need to come. It's late."

"Shut the fuck up, Remy." Brea snaps.

I startle because I've never heard Brea raise her voice. She's always so quiet and docile.

"Watch your fucking tone, Brea!" Remy snaps back.

"Okay, everyone calm down." I don't know what's going on but whatever it is, I don't need it going on all night. "Just ask me what you need to ask me." I say this to Brea, although I'm looking at Remy. He still doesn't look at me.

"Don't look at him. Look at me." Brea spits.

"This is a fucking waste of time. If you don't trust me, we could just end this. Asking him isn't going to make a difference because at the end of the fucking day, you don't trust me, Brea."

"Remy, I told you to shut up. I've heard enough of your stories." Brea turns to me. "Ari, have you been sending Remy pictures of Ayemeline?"

What? What the fuck is she talking about? I look at Remy, who now stares at the wall.

"Your silence tells me all I need to know." Brea turns to Remy and shouts. "Get the fuck out of my house, Remy. I never want to see you again!"

"Wait. What?" I'm confused. *Why would I send pictures of Ayemeline to Remy? Did he say I did?*

"It's fine, Ari. You don't need to say anything else. I got the answer I needed."

"You know what? Fuck this!" Remy turns and walks out of Brea's apartment, slamming the door on his way out.

I look at Brea, a fresh coat of tears on her cheeks.

"I don't know what's going on between you two, but Remy is…" she sniffles. "He's been different since you started dating Ayemeline. You're a good person, Ari. I know you are." Her voice cracks. "But Remy…I just don't know anymore."

"I…" I didn't know what to say. I felt like I was missing a big piece of the puzzle.

"I know you didn't know about the pictures."

"Whatever is going on between you two, I'm sure you can talk it out."

Brea laughs. "Really, Ari? You think we should talk it out? Do you know what I caught him doing?"

I remain silent, not wanting to ask too many questions. Whatever was going on, Remy wanted me to cover for him, to pretend I knew what was going on. My phone vibrates in my pocket. I reach for it and check my text messages:

Remy: I can explain everything.

I slip the phone back into my pocket.

"Is that him?" She asks.

"No," I lie.

Brea cocks her head. She doesn't believe me.

"I'm sorry you're going through this, Brea. But I don't want to see you two break up over it."

She scoffs. "So you're okay with your best friend jerking off to a picture of your girlfriend while his girlfriend is in the next room?"

Her words send an electrifying jolt through my body. I gawk at Brea, unable to hide my shock.

"I was right. You had no idea," Brea mumbles the words.

I stand there unblinking. *Ayemeline? Remy hates Ayemeline, although I still don't understand why. This has to be some mistake.* "No, Remy wouldn't do that."

Brea takes a big exhale. "I'm not here to convince you. I'm just letting you know what I saw. When I walked into the bathroom, he jumped, and his phone landed on the floor. I got a good look at the picture. It was Ayemeline. Do with that as you will. But I don't want to see you hurt. So I'm letting you know. He'll lie about it. He's been gaslighting me all night. He can't even admit what he did and apologize." Her body jerks as she sobs into her hands. "I'm sorry, Ari. I need to be alone. Can you please leave?"

I stand there, eyes fixed on her. I'm unable to move for a few seconds.

"Please…leave."

I turn and leave her apartment. My head spins. I throw myself against the wall outside her door. My phone vibrates. Pulling it out, I read the message:

Remy: Are you going to let me explain?

Remy: What she thinks happened and what actually happened aren't the same.

Remy: Just let me explain.

Me: Where are you?

The response comes through immediately.

Remy: By your truck

Tucking the phone back in my pocket, I reach my truck. Remy stands there leaning against it, both hands in his pocket.

"She told you?" He asks as I approach.

I look at him, unsure if this is really Remy, the best friend I've had since we were fourteen, the one who saved me from my mother and helped me see what a normal family was. A million thoughts run through my head. None of this makes sense. He hates Ayemeline. He acts like he hates Ayemeline. He can't stand to be around her. So, what the fuck?

When I say nothing, he continues. "She did catch me…in the bathroom. But I wasn't looking at Ayemeline. I swear to you."

"So, what happened?" *Please say something that makes sense. Anything that will help us move forward from this.*

"Brea…she hasn't been…you know. She's been upset since the whole Crystal thing. I was looking at something else, and when she walked in, my Instagram accidentally opened, and it just happened to be Ayemeline's post. She sees it and freaks out, thinking I was jerking off to fucking Ayemeline. But it wasn't. I promise you, man. I wouldn't do that." He rubs his head. "I tried to explain it to her, but she wouldn't listen. She just went crazy."

"So, why'd you call me to come over?" I ask. The rumbling in the distance reminds me a storm is near, literally and figuratively.

He exhales. "I tried to tell her the truth, but she insisted I was looking at Ayemeline's pictures. Eventually, I gave up and told her you sent me those pictures."

"Why would I fucking send you pictures of my girl?"

"I panicked. I didn't know what to say. I told her I didn't know you were sending them to me. I'd just opened your messages, and the pictures were there. Then she accused me of lying, saying I changed my story. I told her I lied the first time because I didn't want to get you involved. So, she insisted I call you so she could ask you herself."

His explanation is all over the place and adds to my confusion.

"Remy, please be honest with me. Were you jerking off to pictures of Ayemeline?"

"No."

I look at him, but his eyes remain glued to the floor.

He wouldn't lie to me. Let's look at the facts. Fact number one: Remy isn't a fan of Ayemeline, so why would he even do that? Fact number two: it's more believable that he'd be watching porn in the bathroom than looking at Ayemeline, someone he can't stand. Remy has always been an avid porn watcher. He was the one who introduced me to it. He was also the one who was caught watching by his parents on several occasions. It was so often that his parents thought he was a freak and sent him to their church's youth camp so he could turn away from his "devious sexual habits," as his mother would often put it. The porn thing definitely tracks for him.

"Look, I get it." I rub the back of my neck. My brain hurts. "And I get how this is all one big misunderstanding. You and Brea need to talk."

"Yeah. I'm just going to give her time to calm down."

"I think that's a good idea. And next time you need me to corroborate your story, please give me a heads up. That was not cool."

"I know, man. I'm sorry. Thanks…for coming."

I nod my head as I climb into the driver's seat. "I'll talk to you later, man." I need to get back to my little fox. I need to relieve all the tension from tonight.

CHAPTER TWENTY-THREE
AYEMELINE

The most excruciating thing to happen to me is to get teased to death and then left alone. I'm still tied to the bed wondering if Ari will be back. The ache in my pussy is intense as I try and fail to satiate the hunger that has me reeling out of control. He tied me to my fucking bed and left. *What the fuck?* I try to determine how long I've been there. Minutes? Hours? *Where is he? Did he just leave me here? Would he do that?*

Focusing on something else in an attempt at maintaining some semblance of control, I gaze out my window. The white noise whoosh of the traffic from the interstate close by was rhythmic. It's raining—nothing too heavy—but rain, nonetheless. I watch as drops of rain slowly roll down the glass like they're in a slow race to reach the bottom. The lines of water blur the sky beyond, but I can still make out the inky blue abyss of the night sky, nature's beautiful canvas. It is breathtaking, like the sky itself is manifesting love, peace, and comfort.

My chest tightens when I think of Ari and how he told me he loved me. He promised me forever and always. And I believed him. So why am I so afraid he won't come back?

I hear the front door open and close. The footsteps approach the bedroom where I lay and relief instantly hits me. Ari stands at the door with a duffel bag in hand, his six-foot-three muscled frame making the entry look small in comparison.

I smile when I see him there and all my fears and anxieties float away.

"I'm sorry, little fox. That took longer than I wanted it to."

"It's okay." My voice cracks. "I wasn't going anywhere."

He smiles at me, a dimple forming on one cheek. Placing the bag at the foot of the bed, he makes his way to me and loosens my arms from their restraints. It takes me a moment to move my arm and when I do, I have to descend them slowly back to my side.

"Does it hurt?" he asks, kissing my forehead.

"It's fine."

"Does it hurt?" he asks again, this time his voice sterner.

I hesitate before giving him a barely audible, "Yes".

His hazel eyes lock on mine while he sits on the bed facing me. "I want you to always be honest with me. If something I do hurts you, tell me."

I bite my bottom lip. I know he didn't mean to leave me for so long. I want him to know I still trust him, but all I can do is nod.

Ari strokes my cheek, his eyes never leaving mine. "I'll never hurt your soul, little fox."

As an apology for leaving me tied to the bed for so long, Ari draws me a warm bath. He adds a few drops of eucalyptus and tea tree oils to the water. Reaching over to grab my bag of dried lavender flowers, he rubs some of the lavender petals between his hands before sprinkling them into my bathwater. My head falls back as I let the warm water and oils envelop me.

Ari sits on the head of the tub massaging my feet. I moan as his fingers work their magic.

"You keep making those noises, and I won't let you finish that bath," he teases.

I open my eyes and smile at him. "Is that a threat or a promise?"

"A promise." He leans down and places a kiss on the back of my toes.

"You have a foot fetish now?"

"No, but when it comes to you, I'll gladly suck every one of your toes." And to prove his seriousness, he sucks on my big toe.

I giggle, loving the feel of it but also finding it quite ticklish.

"You seemed to have enjoyed that a little bit too much."

I chuckle. Letting my foot rest on his lap, I ask, "So what was the gift you had for me?"

A mischievous grin decorated Ari's face. "In due time, little fox. In due time."

"You're not going to tell me?"

"You'll find out soon enough. Just be patient."

I cross my arms in front of my chest and pout like a child who didn't get their way.

"Don't be like that, little fox. Trust me, it'll be worth the wait. But first, we need to get you nice and loose."

***

After my bath, he leads me back to the bedroom. My face drops when I see what he has done. Various objects lie on my dresser.

"Uh…what's this?" I questioned.

"These, little fox, are for you."

There is a horse-riding crop that resembles a candy cane with its red stripes. Beside it is a pair of black manacles followed by a pair of silver handcuffs, a glass dildo with a purple glass heart at one end, blue tether tape, a pair of black satin blindfolds, a pinwheel, two spreader bars, a stinger electro play wand, a purple butt plug, and a black leather flogger. It's a girl's wet dream.

I stand there, speechless. This was worth being strapped to the bed for hours.

"Do you like them, little fox?"

"I love them," I say excitedly. Although I'm quite familiar with these toys, I've never gotten a chance to use them. I've never been with someone with whom I felt safe enough to explore the possibilities. But with Ari, I'd close my eyes and let him do whatever he wanted, no questions asked.

He comes up behind me and nuzzles my neck. I lean back into him, welcoming the feel of his warm breath on my nape.

"I've waited long enough to have you the way I want to. I need you now."

"I need you too," I moaned, my pussy starting to moisten up again.

"Good. Because I am going to do so many things to that body, you're going to be begging me to stop." He takes my ear between his teeth and bites down gently.

"Yes, please do," I beg.

****

The sheer amount of restraint it takes for me not to cum all over the glass dildo as he pumps it in and out of my pussy while his dick demolishes my ass is pure madness. Ari has my hands bound together and stretched out in front of me while I'm leaning over the arm of my sofa, my ass in the air. It is the perfect blend of pain and euphoric pleasure. I scream and moan as he pounds my ass harder and harder, each thrust more aggressive than the last.

"You do this to me, little fox," he drawls in my ear. "You make me lose control of the monster I've fought so hard to contain."

With one hand, he reaches around and grabs my neck, pulling me back into his body.

"You drive me fucking wild," he groans, his warm breath melting my skin.

My body tenses from his size. He feels so much bigger than he's felt in the past. Ari grunts like a wild animal behind me. The sensation of his cock up my ass, the glass dildo in my pussy, and his big, tattooed hand around my neck is too much.

"Please…master…I need…" My words are cut off as he tightens his grip around my neck. I try to scream, but the sound can barely escape past his grip. "Mas…ter…" I croak. I can't hold back any longer. My body is about to fail me.

"You want to cum for me, little fox."

I try to nod but end up looking like I'm having a seizure.

"Cum for me, baby. Soak me with your juices."

On command, I let go of the restraint I've been holding on to and cum, my juices spraying the dildo, and his hands, creating a puddle at our feet.

"My squirting little fox," he moans in my ear, and I feel his whole body tense behind me. He lets out a guttural cry so loud, I'm sure the neighbors and everyone on the street could hear.

He lets go of my neck, and I collapse on the arm of the couch in front of me, our bodies still connected. Ari pulls his dick and the dildo out of me slowly, and I immediately miss the contact. He loosens the rope that binds my hands together. Picking me up, he carries me to the bedroom and lays me on the bed.

"Spread your legs for me," he orders.

I spread my legs, feeling the mixture of our cum puddling between them. He climbs onto the bed, kneeling at my pussy. Ari gently strokes my opening before shoving his fingers inside me, reinserting his cum that leaked out of me. I yelp at the unexpected intrusion.

"Now you have all of me inside you."

***

He rests his head on my stomach, and I reach down and stroke his moist hair. We're both spent and sweaty from our early morning intense fuck session. What we just experienced together was unlike anything I've ever experienced with him or anyone else. It's as if he's finally free. He wasn't being gentle so he wouldn't hurt me. He fucked me like he had no regard for my life, and I loved it. I love the way he yearns for me. The idea that I create this lack of control in him—the idea that I make him the savage beast he is—makes me feel like I'm the one in control.

"Have you been this way with anyone else besides me and…" I pause, not wanting to say her name. I didn't want to give life to the idea that Ari was with anyone else besides me. I didn't hate her. How can you hate a dead woman? But a part of me feels envy that she got to experience him the way that should only be reserved for me.

Ari clears his throat. "No. Julia…she was the first. And then there was you."

"Why?" I ask because I simply need to know. I mean, I understand why she was the last. But why was she the first? I entangle my fingers in his hair and gently massage his scalp.

"Guilt. Shame. All the above." Ari moans in pleasure.

"Did you think it was wrong? Your…desires?"

"Yes. For as long as I can remember, I'd get turned on by pain." He strokes my arm back and forth with the back of his hand. "My mother caught me one day…watching porn. You know…BDSM porn. She walked in on me jacking off to a lady on the screen who was being flogged with a cane while bound. She went crazy. She called my dad and told him what I'd done. She even called the church minister to pray for my soul. She told me that I was prepping to be a serial rapist and that behavior was an abomination. I remember her telling my aunts about it at our family gatherings and how they'd look at me like I was the biggest disappointment. Then I remembered how everyone's look of disappointment would turn into fear when I was around. I was the boy who enjoyed watching women get tortured. That's when the shame started. I was twelve when it happened."

My heart hurts for him, for everything he went through, having to live with the feeling that he was a bad person. It wasn't fair. "I'm so sorry," I choke out.

He gives an audible exhale and squeezes my arm. "All my life, I tried to swallow it down, to pretend I was okay with mundane sex. I had to pretend I didn't have the desire to hurt. I tried to test some boundaries with other girls, but they always resisted. So I did what I had to. I locked away the realest part of who I was and pretended. That is until Julia. I think a part of me saw her as naïve and vulnerable. I didn't think she'd blab to her friends like the other girls I dated. She'd keep my secret, and I also knew that I could get her to say yes."

My hand outlines his earlobe while he talks.

"And eventually, she did say yes."

"You didn't feel like you could ask me? Did you not think I would say yes?"

"I didn't know what you would say. But I knew that my feelings for you were unlike those I've had for anyone else in the past. I knew

I didn't want to hurt you. And I don't want to lose you. You are everything to me."

"You can never hurt me, Ari."

He chuckles. "I could be so much more, little fox. Do you want that?"

"Yes. I want everything you have to offer. I can handle it."

"You say that now, but you don't know." He pauses. "And I don't want to force you to do anything you don't want to."

"That's not possible. Everything you want is what I want. I love you, Ari. I love every part of you—the good, the bad, all of it. There is nothing you can give me that I wouldn't happily accept."

He sighs a sigh of uncertainty. "I don't want you to feel powerless—like I'm dictating the narrative in our relationship."

"When you control me, when you let all your aggression out on me, it makes me feel…powerful. Because I know I did that for you. I gave you an outlet that allows you to break free and be your authentic self. And every time I watch you let go of those restraints of control you try so hard to hold on to, I feel control that I can invoke such a visceral reaction in you. My power comes from your release, Ari."

Ari lifts his head and climbs my body, planting a chaste kiss on my lips. "I really hope I didn't dream you up. Please be real."

I smile. "I'm real, baby."

***

I wake up to wetness all around me. The bed feels damp and cold. I open my eyes and strain against the sunlight coming through the window. I pick up my phone and check the time. 3:08 pm. *Damn.* We both slept through our classes. Ari's light breathing tells me he's still asleep. I pick up the sheets and look down. Red. My white sheets are stained red. *Shit. Shit. Shit.* My period chose the worst time to arrive. I can't even change the sheets without waking Ari. Fuck. Is he going to freak out when he sees I bled all over the sheets and his thigh? *Shit. Fuck. Shit. Fuck.* Blood coats the inside of my thighs, and I want nothing more than to take a shower. I'm a bloody, cum soaked mess. *Shit.*

I lift the covers very slowly off my body and try to roll out of bed without waking Ari. I can put another sheet covering the bloody spots, wipe it off his legs without waking him, and clean myself up. I can do this.

Before I can get my body fully off the bed, Ari's strong arms pull me back into him. *Fuuuuucck!*

He pushes his erection against my back and moans. "Trying to run away, little fox?" He growls in my ear.

"I just need to use the bathroom." Or maybe I should stay here. If I get up, he'll definitely see the blood.

He pushes his finger into my pussy, and, despite my embarrassment, I moan. Removing his finger, he lifts it and examines the blood that now drenches his middle and ring fingers.

"What is this?" He doesn't say it as if he's disgusted like I expected him to. He sounds…amused.

"Umm…" I don't know what to say.

This has never happened with any other guy. The sight of my period blood would repulse anyone else.

I watch Ari as he rubs his thumb and blood-soaked fingers together. "Beautiful."

"What?" I ask, dumbfounded.

"I've always wanted to see you bleed, and now I get to."

"Ari…" I shift my body to face him just in time to see him rubbing my blood onto his chest. "What…what are you doing?"

He smiles like a kid who has just opened their present on Christmas morning to find he's gotten the new bike he's always wanted. He smiled like the child who is allowed to let loose in the candy store.

"Ari…"

With one quick movement, he throws me on my back and climbs on top of me. He grabs the base of his dick and shoves himself inside my extremely wet pussy. He lets out a loud, guttural moan. "Fuuuuccccckkk. You feel so…" He pumps into me. "Fucking." He pumps harder and faster. "Wet." Ari leans down and bites my neck. He bites so hard that I'm sure he draws blood. He continues vigorously pumping his hard dick inside me. He greedily sucks my neck. His mouth is hungry and carnal, like a vampire's last meal.

I'm in a state of euphoria as Ari fucks me hard, my tits aggressively bouncing up and down. The bed shakes and groans beneath us. Ari doesn't stop. He pushes in deeper, harder until I think he's going to split me in half. With each slam into my pussy, I feel like I'm dying from pure carnal bliss. I want more. I want more of him. More of his desire. I want all of it.

He grabs my wrist and holds them together above my head. He speeds up his thrust even more. I didn't think he could go any faster but, apparently, I was wrong. He grips my wrists even tighter. The combination of his teeth and mouth on my neck sucking the life out of me, his vigorous thrusts inside my pussy, and his tight grip on my wrist is just too much. I scream, feeling the muscles inside my pussy tighten around him.

"Ari…" I moan. "May I…please cum…master?"

"Cum for me, little fox. Drench my cock with your sweet juices."

And I cum, coating his cock with my warm juices and blood, just as he'd ordered. Soon after, Ari lets out a deep guttural scream. I feel his cock pulsating as he empties himself inside of me. His body jerks and the hand gripping my arms trembles before he collapses on top of me. I know my sheets are ruined but I don't care.

"You're such a dirty whore," Ari says and I feel his cock jerk.

"Maybe you should make me clean again."

"When were you ever clean?" he teases.

CHAPTER TWENTY-FOUR
REMY

While the school is in an uproar about the scandal with the professor who was found dead in a motel room, all I can focus on is you—you, conniving bitch. You turned my fucking world upside down. I fucked up. I know I did. I fucked up with Brea and I may have fucked up with Ari, too. I have no idea if he believed me. It's been two weeks since the incident at Brea's. And it's been two weeks since we've spoken besides him periodically checking in on me to see if I've spoken to Brea. Of course, I haven't. I shouldn't have done that. I should've had more control. But, shit, it was so hard, so fucking hard to stop thinking about you. What is it about you that makes me so fucking crazy? You bring out the worst in me.

I watch you watching him. Idolizing him. Fucking him. You wouldn't have him if it weren't for me, you ungrateful bitch. Now you flaunt your relationship…your *love*—like *I'm* nothing. Like I was always nothing. Did you think I'd forget about us? I hate you so much for doing this to me. Do you enjoy torturing me? Of course, you do. I see it in your eyes. The way you look at me…it's like you enjoy my anguish. FUCK YOU! You don't deserve my pain. You don't deserve my jealousy or any part of me. You chose him. For that, I will never forgive you.

CHAPTER TWENTY-FIVE
AYEMELINE

This is a tragic incident, and our thoughts and prayers are with the family," Dean Bell stands before our class. The news about Professor Matthews has spread throughout campus. "We ask that you all refrain from gossip out of respect for the grieving family." He looks at the class through the top of his black-rimmed glasses. "Professor McCoy will be taking over the class for the remainder of the semester." Dean Bell steps aside, giving the floor to the new professor, who appears to be an old man in his early seventies, despite his full head of midnight black hair.

"Hello, ladies and gentlemen. I am Professor Donohue McCoy. Despite the circumstances, I look forward to working with you all. I promise to make this a smooth transition. Now, I understand you all are working on..." he looks down at a stack of papers before him. "The Great Gatsby."

My phone vibrates loudly on my desk causing the girl in front of me to look back at me, her lips curled up. I shoot her a deadly glare.

Picking up the phone, I see a new text from my father:

Dragon Slayer: Call me. I have something important to discuss.

I really don't want to talk to you, Father. But then I remember that I quit my job and rely on him to pay for my apartment. *Play nice.*

Me: I'll call you after class.

Dragon Slayer: Great.

Class ends and I take my time packing up my things. I see Micah making his way over to me.

"Hey," he says in a clipped tone. We need to start working on this project." He pulls his glasses off and rubs his eye before putting them back on his face.

I let out a long sigh. "Can't you just do it?"

"No."

I look at him because what the fuck? Why was he being such a butt? "No?"

"No. I'm not doing all the work for you. You actually have to work."

"Micah, why are you being such an asshole?" He'd never had an issue *helping* me with an assignment before. Although, those other times, he was getting pussy in exchange for his hard work.

"If you call me asking you to do your part being an asshole, then I'll be an asshole."

I roll my eyes. "So, this is how dudes act when they're no longer getting pussy."

Micah glowers. "You're so…" he exhales. "I'll be in the library at 6:00 to start. You can meet me there if you want." With that, he walks away.

Jerk.

I finish packing up my books before walking out of the classroom. Once I get outside, I call my father.

"Ayemeline, hi." His voice is hoarse through the line.

"Hey. What's up?"

"How was class?"

Do we really need to do this? "It was great, Father. Learned lots of things."

He lets out a heavy breath. "Anyway, I just wanted to let you know your grandpa died. We're all going to New York in a couple of days and…" he hesitates as if he doesn't want to say what he is about to say. "It would be nice if you came. The family would love to see you."

I doubt it.

"Grandma requested you come," he continues. "I'll get your tickets, and I'll email you the itinerary. But you have to tell me if you're coming. I don't want to spend the money only for you not to show up."

I don't want to go. I haven't seen my family…my father's family…in years. It's not as if I hate them. I've just always felt out of place there, like the illegitimate child of my father's affair. Oh, wait. That's exactly who I was. *Just play nice.*

"I'll go," I say quickly before any other words emerge.

"Good. I'll purchase the tickets tonight for Friday morning."

"Okay."

"Please show up at the airport."

"I will." Even if it's the last thing I want to do.

After hanging up with my dad, I call Ari. The phone rings five times before he answers.

"Hey, little fox."

My heart flutters at the sound of his deep, husky voice.

"Hey. I miss you."

"I miss you too. I want to see you."

"I'm about to go to my next class. But I wanted to tell you I'll be going to New York on Friday. My grandfather died and I have to go to his funeral."

"Should I be saying my condolences or…"

"I have no feelings about it," I say, suddenly cutting him off. "I didn't know him that well. But he was my father's father, so…" I let the words trail off.

"I get it. But it sucks that you have to go. How long will you be there?"

"Not sure. Hopefully, not long."

"I'll come to you after class."

"Unfortunately, I have to meet Micah at the library at 6:00 to do some stupid project."

Ari remains silent.

"Hello?" I stare at my phone to make sure it hasn't disconnected. "Ari?"

"I'm here." He says monotonously.

"You're quiet." I'm wary. Is he upset?

"We'll talk later. I have to go."

"Are you…upset?"

"You know I am."

"Because of New York or because of the project with Micah?"

The silence stretches before he says, "We'll talk later."

"Okay?" I say, dragging it out like a question.

Ari hangs up before I can say anything else.

Why were the men in my life so moody all of a sudden? I never told Ari about Micah. I knew he wouldn't want to know, based on conversations regarding my past. As far as I knew, Ari didn't know if he had anything to be jealous about when it came to Micah. Oh yeah. The kiss. Ari saw me kissing Micah that day outside the restaurant. Is that why he's upset? Why couldn't he say it over the phone? Spending the day wondering why he was upset with me was going to be torture.

CHAPTER TWENTY-SIX
ARIEL

I watch as she sits across from Micah in the library, their eyes on a book, except my little fox looks bored. Micah says something, and she rolls her eyes. I can't see his face or hear what he is saying, but I notice how his shoulders rise and fall as he takes several exasperated breaths. She kissed him at the restaurant, and I know no one kisses my little fox and simply moves on. *She's mine!*

I take my phone out of my pocket and send a quick text:

Me: 700-799. Come now.

I watch her look at her phone and her face scrunches up. She's typing. Three dots appear on my screen.

True Love: Are you at the library?

I watch her look around, trying to spot me.

Me: Don't disobey me, little fox.

She says something to Micah and gets up. I see him turn to watch her as she walks away. The look in his eyes tells me everything I need to know. *Mine!*

Ayemeline reaches the aisle. I'm leaning against the bookcase, hands in my pocket.

She walks up to me with her arms crossed. "You do know I have to finish this stupid project, right? I told you…"

I rapidly eat up the distance between us, and she falters, her back hitting the bookshelf behind her. I wrap my fingers around her throat and pull her toward me. "Do I need to fix that attitude?" I growl into her ear.

She opens her mouth to speak, but words fail to escape.

"Now get on your knees," I command.

Her coal-collared eyes lock on mine, and I have to restrain myself from spreading her legs and burying my face into that sweet, plump pussy.

She slowly descends to her knees, and I look at her into those deep, dark eyes. I see trust in those eyes. And fuck, does that make me hard. My little fox trusts me.

I unzip my jeans and pull them down along with my boxer briefs to just below my ass. I grip my dick and stroke it so close to her mouth they almost touch. I see the fire in her eyes, and she watches. She licks her lips. Fuck, that's sexy. I continue to stroke with one hand as I fist her hair with the other, forcing her to look at me.

"You want my dick inside you, don't you little fox?"

"Yes, Master. I want it."

I crouch down in front of her, our faces inches apart. "Tell me how much you want it."

"I want it so much, Master. My pussy is so wet for you. Please."

I smile because her begging does something for my cock. I use my fist, which is wrapped around her hair, and force her onto her feet. She lets out a soft moan. I guide her to the cart of books left in the aisle. Bending her over them, I admire the curve of her ass in her jeans.

"You are so fucking beautiful," I say, palming her ass.

I let my pants drop to my ankles. Reaching around, I unfasten her pants and pull them down.

"No panties? You are a dirty girl, aren't you?"

"Yes," she pants. "I'm dirty for you."

I spank her ass hard, and she jerks, letting out a yelp. Ayemeline covers her mouth, remembering that she's in the library. I crouch down and use my hands to spread her ass and her pussy. Her pussy glistens under the fluorescent library lights. Beads of her moisture trickle down her legs. My little fox enjoys being dominated. I stick my tongue out and lick a line from her clit to the puckered hole of her ass. She moans and squirms.

"Oh, shit," she pants.

I continue licking, starting at her clit and making my way to her ass. Once I reach her ass, I disconnect and repeat the movement. Her legs tremble, and I know she's going to cum right here.

Before I stand, I reach into my pocket and grab the small pocket knife. Ayemeline is still leaning over the book cart with her naked ass in the air. I lean into her, my cock poking her back. My lips are close to her ear, and I whisper, "I'm going to take your ass, little fox."

Her breathing is heavy and rapid. "Please, master. I need you inside me."

I chuckle darkly as I reach in front of her and collect her wetness onto my fingers. I rub it on the entrance of her ass and my dick. "You have enough pussy lube to lubricate a thousand cocks. You are so fucking wet."

I grab a few books from the shelf and place them on the ground near her feet. "Stand on these," I tell her.

Once she's standing on the books, she leans back over the cart. Her ass is higher now, the perfect height for my dick to take that ass. I line my cock to the entrance of her ass and push in slowly. I pause, giving her time to adjust to my size. I push in a little bit at a time until my dick is fully buried in her ass.

Ayemeline's moans tell me she's enjoying this as much as I am. The walls of her ass squeeze my dick, and, *fuck*, it feels incredible. I pump in her ass slowly at first before increasing my pace. Her hands cover her mouth as she tries to stifle her moans. She arches her back, pushing her ass into me.

"Do you want more, little fox? I say, low into her ear.

"Yes, please, give me more," she pants.

I grip my knife and glide the flat of the blade against her stomach. She stills as the cold, hard blade makes contact. I'm no longer pumping in and out of her, my dick just rests inside the tight cavern of her ass. I slide it across her skin until it reaches her pussy. Her breath hitches.

"Scared, little fox?"

"No," she breathes. "I trust you."

She trusts me.

I touch my lips to her neck, and she inhales suddenly.

"Tell me what you want me to do to you," I whisper.

"I…I want you to make me hurt."

"Mmmm…such a bad girl," I growl.

I push her top up higher and move the blade to her collarbone. I use the knife's edge to make several small cuts on her skin on her back, connecting the freckles there. She shudders as a droplet of blood blooms from the cut.

She lets out an open-mouthed moan as I make several small cuts on her back. I pump inside her ass again, moving in and out. Watching the collection of red on her back makes my dick even harder. My breathing is uneven and so is hers.

Moving to the front of her body, I slide lower and roughly slip the bone hilt between her legs and up inside her pussy.

Ayemeline's moans become louder. Her wetness leaks onto my knife hand as I pump the inanimate object in and out of her sloppy, wet cunt. I pump faster, my knife hand and my cock finding a rhythm. The wet, slapping sounds fill my ear and I know I can't hold out for much longer.

"Master?" she whimpers, pleading with me. "I. Need. To. Cum." She breathes loudly, taking deep, short breaths. "Please."

She begs and the last remaining remnants of my self-control snap. "Cum for me, little fox," I say, my voice coming out raspy.

Before I know it, she's coming so hard that her body seizes for a moment, and she stops breathing. Her legs tremble beneath her, and I wrap an arm around her waist to steady her. I keep fucking her with the hilt of the knife as slick streams of cum gush out of her pussy. I'm right behind her, my own orgasm seizing my body, forcing me to stop breathing. I groan from the intensity as I spray warm white liquid all into her ass. I watch as it leaks out of her ass and lands on the floor and the pile of books she's standing on.

I gently pull the knife out of her pussy and my dick out of her ass simultaneously. Ayemeline gasps.

I stand back, admiring her cum-soaked ass before I pull my shirt off. I use my shirt to clean her up and pull her pants back up. There are several wet spots on her pants where her and my cum fell, but they'll be easy to cover up with the oversized T-shirt that she's wearing.

Once she's cleaned up and dressed, I pull my pants up and return the knife to my pocket.

"You don't have a shirt." She stares at my bare chest.

"I have some clothes in the car. I'm good."

She smiles. "Thank you…for that. You always know how to take care of me."

I smile back at her. "Because I love you, little fox."

She cocks her head. "Why?"

"Why do I love you?"

"Yes. Why?"

I see the sadness in her eyes.

" 'One is loved because one is loved. No reason is needed for loving.'" I recite Paulo Coelho's words.

She gives me a small smile. She comes closer. Standing on her toes, she grabs the back of my neck and pulls me into her. She bites my neck hard, and I wince. I was not expecting that.

She pulls away and smiles broadly. "Now, *I've* marked *you*."

If she thinks I'm about to leave her with that Micah dude, she's sadly mistaken. I watch her walk back to the table where Micah sits and waits before I go to my car to grab a spare shirt. My original plan was to go to the gym, so I'd packed a bag to shower afterward. But halfway there, I'd decided to come check on my little fox instead.

They both look up at me with surprise when I take a seat at their table. Micah's surprised expression quickly shifts to annoyance. *Get used to it, baby boy. I'm not going anywhere.*

"I thought you'd left," Ayemeline says.

"Nah. I'm still here," I say, my eyes never leaving Micah's.

He adjusts himself in his seat. He's uncomfortable. Good.

"You're going to sit there and watch us?" she asks.

"Supervising," I retort.

My eyes bore into the side of Micah's face. I want him to know that I will always be watching.

Micah clears his throat, clearly uncomfortable with my presence.

"Um…" he says in a low voice. "We can finish tomorrow if you guys need to be somewhere."

"That would be great," I say quickly, not giving Ayemeline a chance to respond.

"Cool." Micah stands and places his books in his bag. "I'll…we can figure it out another time." He flings his bag over his shoulder and walks away.

Once he's gone, I turn to look at Ayemeline, who stares at me in disbelief.

"Did you think I was going to fuck him on this table?" she questions.

"Of course not. I trust you. I don't trust him," I say, narrowing my eyes toward Micah.

"Micah is harmless."

"Except he wants you. I see it in his eyes."

"Okay, Ari."

"I'm serious. He keeps looking at you with those puppy eyes. Next time I catch him looking at what's mine, I'll pop his eyeballs from their sockets."

"Cut it out, Ari. Leave him alone."

"We'll see."

She pulls my arm and gives me a serious face. "I'm serious. Don't touch him."

"As long as he doesn't give me a reason to. Now let's get out of here. I've worked up an appetite."

CHAPTER TWENTY-SEVEN
AYEMELINE

We're at a small wing shop a block off campus. The line is long, but I want some lemon pepper wings.

Ari's phone rings and he looks at the screen and frowns.

"What is it?"

He looks at me and smiles. "Nothing important. I'll be right back." He kisses my forehead and steps outside to take the call.

Who is he speaking to that he had to go outside to take it? I'd follow him out there if this line weren't so long.

I reach the front of the line and place our order to go. After receiving our order, I step outside to find Ari. I'm surprised he's still on the phone. I'm outside, but I don't see Ari. *Where did he go?* I look up and down the street but see nothing. *What the fuck? Did he just leave me?*

I stand there with the bag of food in my hand, unsure of what to do. I grab my phone and dial his number. After two rings, it goes to voicemail. I try again. This time, it goes to voicemail after one ring. I walk in the direction I thought I saw him go while sending him a text.

Me: Where are you?

No dots. No read receipts. Nothing.

"Hey, sweetheart. You waiting on someone?" A man blocks my path. He stands a little over six feet with wide shoulders and a head of long, black hair slicked back into a ponytail. He reeks of alcohol.

Ignoring him, I look down at my phone to see if Ari responded.

Through my peripheral vision, I see the man stumble closer.

"Can't speak, sweetheart?"

I continue to ignore him and keep walking. The man follows me.

"Hey. I just want to talk to you," he yells out behind me. I walk faster, trying to avoid this unwanted attention. I redial Ari's number, and it goes to voicemail.

Stop pretending like you don't want it. The rough boom of his voice bellows in my ear.

Suddenly, the man is in front of me.

No. I take a few steps back clutching my phone in my hand. *Ari, where are you?*

"What's your name, sweetheart?" He takes a few steps toward me.

Sweat forms rivulets across my body.

"You here alone?"

"N…no." My voice trembles.

A sinister smile crosses his face. "No?" He cocks his head to one side. "You look like you're here alone.

I glance around, hoping to see Ari coming around the corner. But he's not there. No one is around except this guy and his friends.

The small restaurant is now a few blocks away from where I stand. I turn to go back in the direction I came, away from him.

He gets in front of me again. The ache in the bottom of my gut tells me something is not right.

"I just want to know your name, sweetheart," he says in an insincere tone.

"I'm meeting my boyfriend."

"No…you're not."

My stomach contracts into a tight ball.

You're not going anywhere, sweetheart. Not until we're done with you.

A tight hand grips my wrists.

Cold, wet hands held my arms above my head. My mouth opened to form the word "no," but no sound came out. Waves of acid well up from my belly. Sharp, cold hands touch my skin.

"You have pretty fuckable lips," the man purrs close to my ear.

Please. Stop.

My limbs turn to jelly, and my knees buckle beneath me. I'm falling. Then I'm on the ground. A guttural scream erupts from my throat. At least I thought I screamed. But all that comes out is a strangled cry.

Open your legs for us.

Fear courses through my veins, weakening my resolve. *It'll be over soon. It'll be over soon.*

His weight crushed me. Several cold, dead hands touch me everywhere.

It'll be over soon.

A loud crunch rings in my ear. Then some grunts. I open my eyes. "Ari," is all I can mutter.

From my position on the ground, I see Ari. He slams the man's head into his face. The man stumbles backward, face bloodied. Ari grabs the man by the hair and knees him in the face. The man falls to the ground, face first. Pulling him up by the back of his shirt, Ari pulls him off the ground and sits him up to face me.

"You see her?" he says, his voice filled with rage. "She's mine. Who gave you the right to touch her?"

"I'm sorry, man. Please. I…I won't touch her. I promise. Please let me go," the man rattles on, panicked.

"I'm afraid that's not going to happen. You crossed the line. You touched what's mine."

Ari slams the man's head into the concrete.

I gasp at the unexpected crunching sound.

"Ari." I glance at the small crowd gathering around us, some with phones clutched to their ear, the rising and falling of silent conversations and whispers echo in my ear as they look on in horror. "Don't."

Ari looks around, noticing the crowd. "Leave. Now." His tone is authoritative. I freeze, unable to move.

"Ayemeline, leave. Now. Go home."

The sound of police sirens, which was faint, is now getting closer.

Ari stands and walks towards me. He lifts me from the ground. With his hands holding my face, he kisses me on the lips. "Are you okay?"

"I'm…I'm fine," I lie.

"I need you to listen to me. Go home."

"What about you?"

"Don't worry about me."

"But…if I stay, I can explain that you were just…"

"No. You have to go home. Please. I've got this."

"I don't want anything to happen to you, Ari." I now realize how wet my cheeks are.

"Nothing will happen to me. Do you trust me?"

I nod reluctantly.

"Then leave. Now!" He lets go of my face and pushes me away from him. "Run."

I turn and run as the police cars arrive. I look over my shoulder to see Ari being pushed onto the hood of the police car.

I keep running, although I don't understand why. I could've explained to them that Ari is innocent. He didn't do anything wrong. I could explain that that man, that disgusting man, deserved everything he got. Ari doesn't deserve to be arrested. He saved me.

But Ari told me to run. Even when I don't understand, I have to trust him. I'd vowed to always trust him.

CHAPTER TWENTY-EIGHT
ARIEL

The police officer looks at me in disdain as he opens the cell door, letting me out. "Ariel Yearwood, you're free to go."

"Thank you," I say to him.

He snarls at me. "Don't thank me. If it were up to me, I'd lock you away for good, you useless piece of shit. That's what's wrong with this society. Those with money get away with murder, literally." He shoots me a look of pure resentment.

I look at the police officer, dropping the pretense of kindness. I let him see the coldness in my eyes.

He looks back at me uneasily before his eyes shift to the ground. I follow him down a long hallway. He flicks a nervous glance over his shoulder at me. My eyes remain cold.

This man has no idea who I am. He has no right to judge me.

I hear my father's voice before I see him. *Shit.* I should've known he was the reason I was being let go so soon.

My father stands over Detective Tate, berating him for allowing his men to arrest me.

"Listen, Mr. Yearwood. My men had no idea. They assessed the situation and reacted accordingly.

"I don't give a fuck. You arrested my son. We had a deal."

"A deal your son hasn't delivered on." Officer Tate says with a little more confidence.

"Yeah? How the fuck do you expect him to do that when he's locked up, genius?" My father counters.

"Pop," I interrupt the two men.

My father turns to me suddenly, finally realizing I'm there. "Let's go," he says.

"Mr. Yearwood," Detective Tate interrupts, "I need to speak with Ari."

My father turns to me whispering, "What the fuck were you thinking? In public?"

"I had no choice, Pop. That man was a fucking creep."

"I don't give a fuck," he spits in a loud whisper.

"Perhaps we can go speak in my office." Detective Tate leads the way, and we follow him.

We reach his office. "I'd like to speak with just Ari."

"I believe you know how this works, detective. My son will not speak to you without me."

"Mr. Yearwood, I'm trying to help your son."

"Don't give me that bullshit. We both know unless he gives you what you want, you'll throw him in jail. Now, if you want to talk, *we* can talk. Or else, I can take my son home.

Detective Tate rubs his temples together. "Fine. Come in."

My father and I step into his office and take a seat. Detective Tate takes the seat behind his desk.

The Detective looks at me. "As I told you over the phone tonight, we believe the person we're looking for is a woman, someone you might be familiar with. Ayemeline Cross."

A ball forms in the pit of my stomach all over again, just like it did when he told me this earlier over the phone.

"Explain to me how this girl could have killed that many people. She had to have help." My father sits beside me with his legs crossed. One arm leans against the arm of his chair as he gives Detective Tate an intense look.

"We're not sure if she had any help. But we have an eyewitness who puts her at the scene an hour before the bodies were found."

I could no longer see anything but the threat. I struggle to control my quivering. I can't give anything away. Although my pulse roars in my throat, I remain a picture of calm on the outside.

"What can you tell me about her?" Detective Tate looks at me.

"Nothing," I say monotonously.

"Nothing?" He raises an eyebrow.

I feel my father's hot gaze on my face.

"I haven't noticed anything," I say, my expression unwavering.

Detective Tate takes a long inhale and lets it out slowly. "May I remind you, Ari, that we made a deal. Help us find the person who murdered those young men in exchange for a life of freedom and not behind bars where you belong."

"I suggest you watch your tone, detective," my father threatens.

Detective Tate holds up his hand. "These boys were castrated, brutally murdered, and left on their parents' doorsteps. I also want to remind you that a girl was killed recently at the university. I believe she was a friend of yours."

"She wasn't," I retort.

"Are you going back on our deal, Mr. Yearwood?"

"No. I'm telling you I haven't noticed anything." Realizing I must appease him, I add, "I'll keep an eye out for anything suspicious."

"I hope you're taking this seriously. You could be in jail for murder, but I'm doing everything I can to keep you out of respect for your father."

You mean you're doing this because my father would have your head. "I understand and I appreciate it. I promise you, I'm doing my part."

"Well, get us something."

"He said he's doing his part," my father barked. "Are we done here?" Without waiting for a response, my father gets up and walks out of the office with me following behind.

***

My father's driver opens the car door for us, and we climb in. Neither one of us speaks; the silence is thick in the air.

I break the silence first. "You didn't have to come all this way," I say quietly.

"No matter what, I will keep an eye on you. You're my son and I want to ensure you stay out of trouble. I know you don't want me to be part of your life..."

"I never said that," I interrupt, speaking through my teeth with forced restraint. I look out the window, watching cars move over the highway, their lights on full beam. The driver fiddles with the radio before settling on Grieg's "Morning Mood." I'm thankful for the noise even though it's not much.

"Not explicitly. But I understand."

"You really don't."

"Listen. You and your brother are the most important people in my life."

"Pops. Stop."

"I need you to understand that I'll do anything to protect you despite everything. You and your brother."

"And where was that urgency to protect when we were kids?" My tone is now harsh.

He glances at me nervously. "I'm sorry I left. But I couldn't handle your mother."

"And you thought we could?"

"Why are you punishing me? You still have a relationship with your mother. Why does she get to have that relationship with you, but I don't?"

"Because *you* left. You knew who she was, and you left us there. She was the way she was because she was sick. What's your excuse?"

Sitting there, misery is written all over my father's face. "I was a weak man," he says sadly. His voice is low and cracking. "I felt like I was constantly walking on eggshells around her, and I never knew when the other shoe would drop. I was in a constant state of anxiety. It's not an excuse, but I want you to understand that for me, it was hard to leave, but it was even harder to stay. Yes, I shouldn't have left you boys. But, at the time, I wasn't thinking straight. It took years of therapy and isolation to get to a place where I felt calm. And by that time, Hassan had left the house, and you were on your way out."

More than I'd care to admit, I understand those feelings. My father was my rock when we were younger. He was the parent I felt the safest with, but I also noticed how he would cringe whenever my mother was around like he was anticipating her strike. I saw how he'd fall silent when she spoke as if his words would trigger something inside her that would cause her to lash out. Yes, I understood. What I couldn't do was forgive him for leaving us behind to deal with her alone.

I remain silent because although I want to tell him I understand, I can't. He took the best parts of my childhood with him when he left. Although we speak periodically, our relationship will never be what it should be.

***

My father's driver pulls up to my dorm, and I jump out before he has the chance to walk around and open the door. As soon as I'm inside my room, I grab my phone and dial Ayemeline's number. She answers on the first ring.

"Ari?"

"Hey, fox."

"Babe, where are you?"

"I'm in my dorm."

She lets out a relieved breath. "You're not in jail?"

"No. They let me go. I explained what happened. Where are you?"

"Home. In my apartment. Why'd you tell me to leave?"

"I didn't want them questioning you," I lie.

Ayemeline is quiet.

"You there?"

"You told me to trust you. Please don't give me a reason not to."

"Fox…"

"Ari. Please. You don't beat a guy up almost to death and be free the same night. And you telling me to leave. I know you have a past, Ari. So why does it seem like you're hiding it from me now after you've told me everything? Why did you disappear from the restaurant after taking that phone call? Where did you go? And more importantly, why did you get bailed out by Elijah Yearwood?"

Shit. "Did you follow me?"

"Yes, I did. I wanted to make sure you were good. I thought you would need me. Turns out you didn't."

"I told you to go home."

"Why? Did you not want me to know who your father is? A fucking slimeball who defends assholes rapists?" I scoff. "It took me a while to remember who he was when I saw his picture at your mother's house. Then tonight, it all came back to me when I saw you two together."

A sudden jolt of electricity shoots through my veins, leaving me momentarily stunned. "My father was the lawyer who defended them?"

Silence.

"I'm coming over."

"No. I don't want you here." Her voice is shaky.

"I'm coming."

Before she can object, I hang up the phone and grab the keys to my truck.

***

I pull into a parking spot and jump out of my truck. I walk up the stairs to Ayemeline's apartment two steps at a time. I bang on the door loudly. I know how much she hates attention, so I bang even louder, knowing she'll eventually open the door before her neighbors come out to see what all the commotion is about.

Just as I predicted, Ayemeline swings the door open; angry lines decorate her forehead. "I told you…"

I push the door open wider and walk in. "I need to speak with you face to face."

"Now you want to speak to me. Were you ever going to tell me?" She crosses her arms in front of her. "Trust, right? That's what you want. You want my trust but then lie to me."

"I didn't lie to you. I didn't know my father…" I pause. "Look, the reason why I told you to leave had nothing to do with my father. It had to do with you."

Her eyebrows rise.

"You're right. I haven't been completely forthcoming with you. But honestly, I didn't know if it involved you."

"What the hell are you talking about?"

"Can you sit down?"

"No," she says bluntly.

"Fox." I reach for her.

She backs away, jerking out of my grasp. "Don't. I don't want to be touched right now. I've had enough unwanted touches for one night."

My heart sinks to the pit of my stomach at her words.

"I'm sorry I wasn't there sooner." I try to control the trembling of my voice. "I'm so sorry."

Ayemeline looks down at the ground. "I don't care anymore. I just want to be alone."

That's when I notice the small incisions on her neck. They're fresh and a small drop of blood seeps through where her old scar is. "Fox, you're bleeding." I reach up to touch her neck, but she flinches away from me.

"I said don't touch me."

"Did you…do that? Did you hurt yourself?" I try to remember if the cut was there before I told her to run. I would've noticed it. This didn't happen from the incident.

"It's not your problem." She hugs herself and looks down at the ground.

"It is my problem. You are my problem. Don't you know I'll tear the world apart for you, little fox?"

A remote coldness enters her eyes. It chills me to the core.

"Please leave, Ari."

"No. I'm not leaving you."

"LEAVE!" She grabs her phone and throws it at me, missing me by an inch.

My eyes open wide, holding a dark warning. "I'm NOT leaving." I take a step closer to her.

Her black eyes shift to a resigned sadness. She stares at me momentarily before walking into her bedroom, slamming and locking the door behind her.

I sit on the couch and cradle my face in my hands. *Fuck!* My father drove her to do what she did. He left her with no other choice. He helped those assholes.

My father is the best criminal defense attorney in Georgia. After he left my mom, he moved to California before settling here in Georgia. I knew he defended criminals and that never truly bothered me. But this is Ayemeline, my life, my whole purpose.

After Julia's death, my father recommended the best attorney in Iowa to defend me. Maybe I'm just as bad as them. I remember the disappointment on Julia's parents' faces when they found out that I wasn't going to prison for the murder of their daughter. I never got what I deserved for what I had done. I took a plea deal to save my own life. Now, it was coming back to bite me in the ass.

Five victims were gruesomely murdered: four teenage boys in Georgia and one in Iowa. It turned out that the boy who was murdered in Iowa was in the same class as the boys from Georgia. He was visiting family at the time. It wasn't until a year later that my father told me the boys were his clients. But I never made the connection to Ayemeline until now. Now, the detective is counting on me to gather enough evidence to put her away. That is not an option.

***

After three hours of sprawling out on Ayemeline's couch, I decide to go to her bedroom. I need to check on her after the night she's had. I know she told me she wanted me to leave, but how could I knowing she was hurting so much?

I slowly open the door. Ayemeline is scrunched in a heap on the bed. I inch closer to her. Her eyes fly open. In the moonlit room, I can see her eyes are bloodshot and puffy and her face is red from crying. I walk around to the other side. Her back is facing me now. I climb the bed gently to not rattle her form too much. She doesn't move. I lie down and inch closer to her. Wrapping my arm around her waist, I pull myself into her.

"I love you so much," I whisper into her ear. "And I will do anything to protect you. I recognize myself in you, fox. You are a part of me. Losing you is losing myself. You're mine, and I'm never letting you go." I pause. "Please remember that when I tell you what I'm about to tell you." I take a deep breath and tell her everything. She listens silently until she falls asleep in my arms.

CHAPTER TWENTY-NINE
AYEMELINE

Ayemeline, Age 10: Numb

I should cry. I should be angry. I should yell and rave and demand that she wake up, demand she takes me home. That's what everyone expected me to do. But I couldn't. My tears were locked inside, and they refused to come out.

My eyes fixed on the long wooden box, hoping to feel something besides this numbness. I closed my eyes and sighed. Why couldn't I feel anything? There was no sadness. No anger. It was just emptiness. I looked around at the faces surrounding me—the broken, the mourning, the distraught. But for me…there was nothing. It was as if my mind was wrapped in wool.

The scene before me flickered and faded like when my mom would show me that old film reel that kept skipping frames. I didn't feel close to anyone here. Rain pebbled my skin and my mother's sister pulled me into her under her umbrella, squeezing tightly. My body remained stiff.

"It's okay to cry," she said but her voice sounded distorted and distant.

I squeezed my eyes shut, coaxing the tears to fall. Nothing.

After leaving the cemetery, we headed to my mother's sister's home. Too many people. My mother's aunt and grandmother traveled from Haiti to attend her funeral. They stood with a group of two other family members speaking Creole. They'd periodically look over at me with a look of sympathy, and although I didn't understand what they were saying, I knew they were discussing me.

My mom loved to tell me about her life in Haiti before coming to the States when she was sixteen. She shared some of her family's traditions with me—traditions that were now buried deep with her. My mom didn't speak Creole with me often except to sing me a lullaby from her own childhood. I closed my eyes and could still hear her soft, melodious voice singing:

<blockquote>

"Dodo ti pitit manman

Dodo ti pitit manman

Si li pa dodo, krab la va manje

Si li pa dodo, krab la va manje"

</blockquote>

When I opened my eyes, they were all staring at me. I turned away quickly and climbed my aunt's steep stairs to the upstairs bedrooms. I needed to hide.

I opened the door of my aunt's bedroom and walked inside. The first thing I noticed was the pink pocket knife sat on my aunt's nightstand. It was so pretty, with engraved pink roses decorating the hilt. My fingers touched the cold metal of the blade's edge. I felt a light sting on my fingertip. A dot of red sat on the tip of my finger. I admired it. It was a nice distraction from the events downstairs. My breathing got heavy. I ran my fingers over the edge again and produced more red liquid. It didn't pour out; it just sat there on my skin.

I felt something and that made me want more. I lifted the blade and pushed it against the skin below my ear. I pushed in a little more. My sharp intake of breath almost stopped my heart for a second when the blade bit into the smooth skin. My skin parted to the sharp blade, and a line of red ran from my ear to my collarbone.

Then it came, like a wet towel thrown in my face. Sadness seeped through my veins like ice. A silent scream lodged in my throat, and I could feel the sting in my eyes like shards of broken glass. And just like that, my tears fell like raindrops. My body shook like a violent storm, and I let the knife fall to the ground. I followed it down, burying my face in the carpet. I clenched my fists as I pounded them on the ground, letting my cries and screams bounce off the walls of the bedroom.

My aunt opened the door and gathered me into her arms until my sobs subsided, and all that was left was a lingering headache and rawness in my throat. A man stood behind her, watching. I could barely make out his ginger-red hair and pale skin through my blurry vision. But I saw how his green eyes looked at me with pity and fear, and I knew this was my father.

*****

I don't think I've seen so many family members in one place. Although my mother was very popular and respected in the community, not even her funeral had this many attendees. After the funeral service, we all go to a banquet hall for the wake. My dad stands with his brothers, Uncle Finn and Uncle Ronan, talking. Mother sits with my grandmother and appears to be comforting her.

It blows my mind that my grandmother would even grieve my grandfather's death. Their relationship was rocky. Rumor has it that my grandfather never officially married my grandmother. They lived together for thirty years, had three children together, and lived a life together, but never made it official. He then met Georgianna. Georgianna is…was…my grandfather's mistress turned wife, making my grandmother the new mistress. It gets so confusing. He left my grandmother and married Georgianna. They married and adopted a daughter together since Georgianna may have been nearing fifty at the time. Shortly after that, they moved to France, where they've lived ever since.

My grandfather would make yearly trips back to the States, and whenever I visited my grandmother in New York or whenever my father needed a break from fatherhood and sent me to my grandmother's, my grandfather would be there in her house. I even caught him in her bed once. His marriage to Georgianna and moving to another country never stopped my grandfather from spending time with my grandmother. She loved that man and could never let him go, even in death, apparently.

I don't know much about Georgianna except she is about twenty years younger than my grandfather and she loves to talk. The few times I've met her, I often found myself trying to hide so I wouldn't get caught in her excessive ramblings. That woman is so chatty. I think she loves hearing herself speak.

My grandmother sits beside my stepmother, dabbing her eyes with a tissue while Mother Dearest rubs her back. I've always wondered why my mother didn't go into acting. She's really good at it.

"Ayemeline, how are you, child? It's been so long since I've seen you. You are turning into quite a beautiful young lady. Oh my God, I can't believe I finally get to see you. It seems we never see each other. How's school? You're in college now, right? How is that? Are you liking it so far?" Georgianna approaches me with a glass of amber liquid in her hand. I shoot her a look for interrupting my alone time in the shadows. Doesn't she see I'm trying to hide from unwanted conversation?

Even with my stilettos, she towers over me at five feet eleven. She is dressed in a knee-length black fitted dress with a shallow neckline—too low for someone her age, sheer black stockings, and red, six-inch stilettos. On top of her long blonde hair sits a black church Kentucky Derby hat fit for a British bridal tea party. She is beautiful and elegant—the opposite of my grandmother, a four-foot-eleven, stubby redhead who resembles a high school English teacher who should've retired years ago but is staying on for the children.

I give her a faint smile. We haven't had much conversation with one another. I've only seen the lady a couple of times. And here she is, approaching me like I mean something to her.

She leans in closer to me and speaks in a whispered tone. "Now that your grandfather is…gone…I would like you to…" She pauses. "There's someone who would like to meet you," she says hurriedly, as if she is trying to get the words out as quickly as possible before someone steals them.

My eyebrows raise in curiosity. "Now that he's gone?" I ask, wondering what his being gone has to do with me meeting this person.

Georgianna looks over her shoulder to ensure no one can hear before leaning in closer. I step back because this proximity is making me very uncomfortable. "Look, your grandfather didn't want anyone to know. He was keeping this secret for your father. But now that he's gone, I think you deserve to know. I'm really doing this for her. She wants to meet you. She's wanted to meet you for a very long time. But with us having to keep this secret and living so far away from one another…you know. It wasn't feasible. And your father insisted that you two not get too close. I guess he feared you'd know the truth and rat him out."

"What are you talking about?" I'm getting impatient with her babbling. *Just spill it already.*

"You have a sister. Well, a half-sister."

My eyebrows furrow in disbelief. "What?"

"She's eighteen, two years younger than you are. He actually knew about her before he knew about you."

"I don't understand," I say cautiously.

She looks around again to make sure we're still out of earshot of anyone. Georgianna is quite the gossip queen. But this is one piece of information I'm curious to know about. "When her birth mother got pregnant with her, unlike your mom, she told him right away. She also told him that she didn't want to keep the baby and she wanted him to take her. Since your father was married, he didn't want his wife to find out about his infidelity, so he agreed to find a home for her. Your grandfather and I agreed to adopt and raise her as our own. But we weren't to tell anyone who her father was. We've kept the secret from everyone but her. We felt like we shouldn't lie to her. She needed to know the truth about who her parents were. We told her about five years ago. And she's been wanting to meet you ever since."

"But…" I pause trying to find the words to the question I wanted to ask.

"Why'd he take you in but not your sister?" she asked, reading my thoughts exactly. "Well, your mother made sure his wife knew about you. So, once she knew, there was no point in hiding the fact that you existed. Your sister, on the other hand, no one knows about her. I don't think he wants his wife to know it wasn't just that one affair, poor woman."

I looked at Georgianna curiously. Did she not know her husband cheated on her as well? The Kennedy men all have a reputation for sticking their dicks in random pussy.

"Anyway, my baby girl, Auria, wants to meet her big sister. I promised her I'd introduce you two. She's here, you know. Your father is not very happy about that. But what did he expect? For her not to attend her father's funeral? The man that raised her? He'll get over it."

I look around, trying to spot the girl who is my half-sister. There are so many people here it's hard to pinpoint who she could be. The place is filled with people I've never seen in my life. It was obvious that several people flew in from France, Ireland, and different parts of the U.S. to attend my grandfather's funeral based on the languages and accents permeating through the large banquet hall.

"Would you like to meet her? You know your father will be pissed if he sees you two speaking."

I smirk at that. My specialty is pissing my father off. It's something I've always been good at. "I'd love to meet her."

"Great. She's going to be so excited."

"Who's going to be excited?" My father stands beside me. I didn't see him approach us.

Georgianna tightens her lips.

"We're having a private conversation, Father," I say, turning to face him.

"I want to know what you two were talking about. I want in."

Before I can say anything, Georgianna jumps in. "We were discussing school, Bradan. Your daughter was telling me about her friend from school," she lies.

My father looks at me. "You have a friend?"

I narrow my eyes at my father.

He holds his hands up, reading my expression perfectly. "I don't mean to offend. I've never met any of your friends. I always thought you preferred to be alone."

He's right. I do prefer to be alone. But he doesn't need to point it out like I'm some epic loser who can't make real human connections, like I'm unwanted by my peers and my family. It's all true, but he doesn't need to spell it out like that.

"You've never met anyone because it was never your business," I shoot back. You go low, I go lower. *I thought you were supposed to be playing nicely. I know, but he deserved it.*

He lowers his eyebrows before looking away from me. "How's France?" he asks, turning to face Georgianna.

I use this opportunity to walk away. I do not want to get caught in a three-way conversation with anyone, much less my father. I walk to the food table and grab a plate. I fill it with foods I know I won't eat but need something to do right now.

I grab a bacon-wrapped date and take a cautious bite. It's sweet, smoky, salty, and spicy all at once. There are so many flavors, I don't know which one to focus on. I spit it out into my napkin.

"I made that, you know. It's actually quite delicious."

I look over at the girl with a heavy French accent. As soon as I see her, I immediately know who she is. She is me. A more refined, sophisticated me, but still me. Her hair is the same copper ginger as mine but hers is straight and neat compared to my unruly curls that I try so hard to tame. Her skin is fair like the silk of white rose petals. Georgianna told me about my half-sister, and she told me she was here. Yet, seeing her was still as unexpected as snow in the summer.

I watch as she picks up a crab-stuffed mushroom and places it on my plate. "Try these. You'll like them."

I continue to stare at her. She grabs a gougères and adds it to her already filled plate.

"I am Auria, by the way. You are Ayemeline, yes?"

I say nothing.

"I am so happy to finally meet you. I'm sure my mother told you about me." Her accent makes her seem so much more polished than I am. And I realize besides our appearance, we are very different.

She pouts when I fail to respond to her. "I, euh…I'll let you finish your meal. It was very nice meeting you, Ayemeline." She pauses, still standing there waiting for my reply. When I say nothing, she gives me a shy smile and walks away with her plate of food.

Is it possible to feel bad for not conversing with someone you know nothing about? Because that's how I'm feeling at that moment. Something about her makes me want to hug her. And that's not common for me. Perhaps it's that we both shared the same father who didn't want either of us. Perhaps it is because she wears my face. Or perhaps it is the idea that she is someone I could've been in another life, and I wanted the opportunity to explore that life through her.

I've never been a girl's girl. I've always been the outcast of any girl group. For girls my age, I've always been an easy target to be picked on and ridiculed. To boys my age, and to be honest, grown men, I've always been seen as easy to manipulate. Friendships aren't something that ever came easy for me. For Auria…my sister…to just start talking to me was, how would I say, unfamiliar territory. So, I froze. I shouldn't have, but I did.

"Ayemeline, we're leaving." My father startles me out of my thoughts. Wrinkles form on his forehead.

"I think I'm going to stay." Did I just say that?

He gave me a stern look. "I think it's time for us to go."

"You can go without me."

"You came with me. I'm your ride. So, let's go."

"I'll get a ride. Or I'll take the subway. It's not a big deal."

"Why do you always have to be so difficult?" he says in a loud whisper.

"Just because you want to leave does not mean I have to." I assume my father saw Auria speaking with me, which is probably why we have to leave suddenly.

He stares at me for a long moment, probably trying to think of a way to get me to leave with him. Nothing he says will work. Although I'm not sure what I want to say to Auria, I'm positive I won't get the opportunity if I leave now. I have a sister. It's something I've always longed for but never got. To say I'm curious is an understatement.

"Ayemeline," he sighs heavily.

I decide to end this with honesty. "I already know about her."

A quick flash of a frown crosses his face before it disappears. With a shaky voice, he says, "Let's step outside and talk."

I follow my father outside because, honestly, I'd love to know what he's going to say. Is he going to threaten me? Is he going to tell me everything I know is a lie?

"I have a favor to ask," he starts once we're outside. "You're an adult now, so I'm going to be honest with you. Your mother doesn't know about…her…and I want to keep it that way."

I watch him closely. Is he asking me to keep his secret? No excuses, no threats, just keep his secret?

"Look," he continues, his voice getting softer. "I made a mistake. I'm not perfect."

I scoff.

Ignoring me, he continues. "But I've worked hard to be a better person. I hope you can see *that?*"

I narrow my eyes at him.

"Ayemeline, please," he pleads.

"Did you ever love my mom?" I ask honestly. My mom had so much love to give, and I'd love to know if she received that love back.

A vertical wrinkle appears between his eyebrows.

"I figured, *Father.*" I walk back inside, leaving him standing there to stare after me.

***

The rest of the afternoon is spent dodging Kennedys' left and right. After two hours of meaningless small talk, I manage to sneak away to the bathroom. I wish Ari were here.

Before I left for New York, Ari explained everything to me. Although part of me is still a little upset, there's no one I want more right now.

I pull out my phone and stare at the red blinking light. I put in my pin to unlock it. I know right away the message is from Ari. We have not spoken since that night in my apartment. He had agreed to give me some time to think.

The devasting part isn't that the police knew what I had done, and they were trying to gather more evidence to lock me away. It is the fact that Ari is supposed to be helping them do it. He told me he'd never give away my secret, and I believe him. But that doesn't extinguish the fear. What if he has no other choice but to help them? What if he must choose between saving himself and saving me? Will he pick me? And even if he does choose to save me, can I really live with that? Could I live a life without him? Could he live a life without me?

My heart stumbles over its own rhythm when I think of life without Ari. Because no matter what he decides to do, it ends with us being apart. Time slows as the gravity of the situation weighs me down. I clench the phone in my hand tightly. I can't lose him. Death would be a much better option.

I press my trembling, sweaty hand against my phone screen, pulling up my messages and trying to distract myself in an attempt to still my frantic thoughts. They whirl inside my head like a never-ending twister I can't escape.

I click on Ari's message:

Ari: I'm here whenever you're ready. I love you.

This man can warm my soul with just a few words. He is my sun, illuminating even the darkest corners of my world. I wish I were with him right now.

I press the "call" button to dial his number. He answers after two rings, his calm, husky voice coming through the phone.

"Hey, fox."

"Hey," I say shyly. I feel like I'm speaking to my crush for the first time over the phone.

"I'm glad you called. I miss you," he says sweetly.

"I miss you too."

"How are *you* doing? Everything going okay up there?"

"Not really. I wish you were here."

"If you want me to, I'll be there. I can get on a plane right now."

I smile at that. "You don't have to do that. I'm just…" I let out a breath. "I found out I have a half-sister."

"Seriously?"

"Yup. Apparently, my father is a serial cheater, and I wasn't the only child he fathered outside of his marriage."

"Holy shit, love. How did you find that out?"

"My grandfather's wife told me. It's a long story. But my grandfather and his wife adopted her when she was a baby. But now she wants to get to know me, apparently."

"What are you going to do? Are you going to meet her?"

"I already have. Kind of. I don't know. I want to get to know her but…I don't know."

"It's up to you. Would you be okay with never getting to know her?"

"I…I don't know. Probably not."

"Well, that's your answer. And if you don't like her, you can tell her to fuck off, and you never see her again."

I giggle. "I'll try."

"Good. You know, if you let people get to know you, they'll actually love you, just like I love you. You just have to give them a chance."

"Okay. I'll try."

"You do that. Now, I need to tell you how much I've missed you over the last few days. And you know who else is missing you, little fox?"

"I can take a guess," I say, smiling coquettishly.

"I need to see you. Answer the video call."

I pull my phone away from my ear and swipe to answer. His face looks tired. His beard is thicker than when I'd seen him, and it's no longer groomed to perfection. His beautiful hazel eyes have a ring of red around them.

"Ari, are you okay?"

"I am now that I get to see you. Don't ever disappear on me like that again. I don't think I can handle it a second time."

"I'm sorry, babe." My heart aches to see him this way. I never want to know that I'm the source of his pain. I would never intentionally hurt him.

"Don't be. You did what you had to do. You're entitled to time to reflect after everything I told you."

"It was a lot."

"I know. But we'll figure a way out. Together. I promise. Do you trust me?"

"Yes. I trust you, Ari."

"Perfect. Now, on to other matters. How's my pussy, little fox?"

CHAPTER THIRTY
ARIEL

earing her voice again is like all the rays of a thousand sunshines rolled into one. Getting to see her face is like the gates of heaven opening. I never wanted to go through that again. The last few days, she had not communicated with me. I wanted to give her the space she requested. I wanted her to know I respect her wishes. Today, however, I couldn't handle another day of no Ayemeline. I'd sent her a text this morning. It took her five hours to finally respond, but she did.

I watch as she squeezes her eyes shut, coming so close to her orgasm.

"Did you get my permission to cum, little fox?" I grip my cock tighter, trying to hold on to my own orgasm.

"Ari…please," she pants, her eyes rolling to the back of her head. "I need to cum."

"Beg me some more, baby. Beg me to let you cum."

"Please, let me cum, Master. Please."

"Fuck, baby. You sound so sexy when you beg." I pump my cock faster. "Let me see that pussy, little fox. Let me see you squirt all over your phone."

She moves the phone down to her pussy. Her pink lips glisten under her fingers. Her clit is engorged from her arousal. The pretty red landing strip of pubic hair on her pussy is moist from her wetness.

"So beautiful," I say in admiration. "I want to taste you, little fox. I want to circle my tongue around your soft, sweet clit. I want to lap up all your juices."

She moans in pleasure. "I want you so bad. I'm going to cum."

"Cum for me, little fox."

Her fingers pump in and out of her pussy, making loud, wet sounds. I watch more moisture accumulate as she thrusts her index and ring finger in and out in a quickening rhythm.

I feel a familiar spark of electricity run through my spine and into my head. I feel tears squeeze out of my eyes as she grinds her pussy into her fingers. Her back arches as her hips thrust to meet each stroke of her finger. My cock pulses under my hand. Her fingers are so deep in her pussy. With each stroke of my cock, I climb closer to the edge.

Her body begins to convulse, and sweet liquid squirts from the depths of that beautiful, wet cunt.

"Fuuuuck, baby," My body begins to lose control. My muscles tighten. My body freezes up as I reach the peak. In a euphoric rush, my body convulses as thick white ribbons spring from the head of my cock, collecting in a pool on my stomach.

I'm left dazed and panting. My body continues to shutter as waves of my orgasm linger. Ayemeline is a desperate, wet, and overstimulated mess. I love seeing her this way. Her breathing is heavy as she tries to catch her breath.

"You are so fucking gorgeous," I tell her once I'm able to speak again.

That fucking smile of hers. "Yeah?" She says, giving me a conspiratorial, seductive look. "You'll have to show me when I get back."

"Gladly, little fox. We have some lost time to make up for."

CHAPTER THIRTY-ONE
AYEMELINE

After cleaning myself off along with the mess I made, I snuck out of the bathroom, hoping no one would see me. A body slams into me, knocking my phone to the ground.

"I'm so sorry. I...I didn't see you," the French accent stutters. She reaches down and picks up my phone, handing it to me.

"Thanks," I mutter.

"You do speak. I thought you were a mute woman."

Oh, she's funny. "I speak when I have something to say. I know you're used to people rambling on and on like your mother, but we aren't all that way."

She laughs. "She does talk a lot." She continues to laugh.

"It's really not that funny."

She tries to control her laughter. "I thought it was."

"Well, it's not." I keep a serious expression on my face, although I want to laugh at her ridiculous laugh.

She laughs like an old engine turning over. Then, just as quickly as it started, it stops, her face turning serious. "I'm sorry. Today was a rough day. It felt good to laugh."

I suddenly remember she had just lost the man who played the role of her father all her life—her dad. I didn't have the relationship with my grandfather that she had. But I do remember the way it felt to lose my mom. It sucked.

"I'd really like to talk. I have some things I want to know…about you." I tell her.

She smiled the widest smile. "I would love that."

✳✳✳

We agree to leave the wake and meet at a small gyro joint near the train station. After placing our orders, we sit across from one another.

"I have questions, too," she begins. "I want to know what our father is like."

I scrunch up my face. "You didn't miss much in that area."

"That's unfortunate." She takes a bite of her gyro and swallows quickly before taking another bite.

I could've sworn she had a full plate at the funeral. Why is she eating like a starving child in a third-world country? I mean, I love my food just as much as the next girl, but, geez. She's already halfway done before I take one bite of my food.

"They have strawberry cheesecake here. I want to try one. Do you want one?"

I look at my untouched food. "No. I'm still working on this."

She gets up and walks to the counter. A few minutes later, she's back with two slices of cheesecake and an order of cheese fries. "In case you change your mind," she tells me when I eye the two slices of cheesecake in front of me.

She uses her fork to take huge bites of cheesy fries. This girl has already eaten half a gyro and a whole side of fries, and now she is halfway through her plate of cheesy fries. I watch her in awe.

"How much do you know about me?" I ask her.

She swallows quickly and grabs another forkful of cheesy fries before answering. "I know you were raised by our father and his wife. That your mom…you know. And left you with them." She dabs her mouth with a napkin before biting into her gyro. "That's about it," she says with a mouth full of meat. "How about you? What do you know about me?"

"Nothing," I admit. "I just found out you existed a few hours ago."

"I wish we'd met each other sooner. You're so nice."

"Am I?"

"Yes, of course. You do not have to sit here with me, but you do. You are nice."

I squeeze my lips together. *I'm nice? That's interesting.*

"Your parents. Were they good to you?" I want to know if she had the same life as I or was hers filled with love and attention from adoring parents who pampered her and was always there for her.

"Yes. Papa was…" Her shoulders slump, and her face turns downward. "He was the best Papa one can ask for. Mama always said he was spoiling me. I knew he will always say yes to anything I want. But, most importantly…" she says quietly, "he was the one person in the world I can talk to about anything. Mama will give advice, but Papa will always listen. He will not judge. He will not tell me I do things a certain way. He will just listen. That is what I love about him."

I felt a little jealous of her. She had a father—a real father. Not someone who felt forced to take care of a daughter he never wanted. My grandpa wanted Auria. He truly loved her, which is more than I can say about the man I call father. "You're lucky," I tell her.

She looks at me empathetically. "Let us focus on us getting to know one another. What is your favorite food?" she asks, changing the subject.

"My favorite food? I don't think I have one," I admit.

Her jaw drops. "You don't have a favorite food? That is not possible."

"What's so impossible about it? Not all of us can enjoy bacon-wrapped dates garnished with jalapeños."

Auria giggles. "They are so delicious. But nothing beats warm baguette."

"Bread? Really?"

"Eh, the French are serious about their bread. It is one of the best things to eat in France." She takes the last few bites of her gyro and cheese fries and moves on to her cheesecake.

"Do you like living in France?"

"Yes. But I love New York. This is my first time here. It is very exciting. Do you live in New York?" She asks between bites.

"No, I'm just here for the funeral."

"Where do you live?"

"Georgia."

"I'm not familiar."

"It's not special. How did you learn to speak English?"

"We mostly speak English at home. Mama and Papa speak French sometimes, but they are more fluent in English. I have to learn. Some English phrases do not make sense to me. Like 'ballpark figure.'" She says the two words very slowly. "It has nothing to do with a ball or a park. It is a financial term? That is *ridicule.* And 'table that.' Mama says that a lot when she does not want to talk about something anymore. English is a funny language. And…"

"Okay. I get it. I think you may have gotten your talking skills from your mother," I tease.

"No! Do not say that." She giggles. "This is fun."

I give her a slight smile.

"So, what do you do for fun besides go to school? Do you go to school? Yes, you do. I remember Mama telling me this."

"Just to be clear, I do not do school for fun. It's an obligation."

"Of course. I mean that college is to be fun, non? I am going to graduate, and I want to go to college in the States, but Papa says I have to stay in France. Now that you are here, I want to come to the States for school even more. You can show me around and introduce me to new people."

I scoff. "I'm not the person to introduce you to new people. I don't like people."

Her laugh sounds like her car engine.

"I'm serious."

"It is fine," she says, rubbing the tears from her eyes. "People do, euh…suck? *En tout cas*, I am only interested in getting to know my sister." She smiles at me. "Are you going to eat your cheesecake?"

"You can have it." I push it toward her.

She pokes it with her fork and takes a big bite.

"You must really like that cheesecake," I say, confused as to how she can put away so much food in one sitting and still be so small.

"Not really. I have better desserts in France."

I cock my head at her. "Are you serious? You ate two slices of cheesecake for it to be just okay?"

"Food is for eating," she responds, as she takes another giant forkful of cheesecake.

We continue to meet every day in New York for the rest of the week. Auria is on a mission to try every pizza place. She hears about this place called Angelo's in Brooklyn. We take the number two train to Flatbush and walk one block to Angelo's.

This girl orders two slices of cheese pizza, an order of zeppoles, and a beef patty with cheese. We do this every day while we discuss everything about our lives. Okay, she may have talked more about her life than I did. I learned that she goes to a private school, that she recently broke up with her boyfriend because he didn't have aspirations, that her favorite food was anything she could put in her mouth, and that she was a virgin. That last piece of information was provided to me in the middle of a conversation about the different types of cherries there are.

I make it back to my hotel room exhausted, yet feeling accomplished. I had met my sister. And surprisingly, she is someone I'd love to get to know more of.

CHAPTER THIRTY-TWO
ARIEL

ulling up to the airport pick-up lane, my heart flutters at the sight of her. One week. It's been one week since I've seen her in person, and fuck, did I miss her. I pull up to the curb, jump out of the car, and take huge steps towards her. I reach her and grab her face, pulling her toward me. I close my eyes and whisper into her neck, "I missed you so much, little fox."

Her mouth opens to speak, but only a moan escapes.

My tongue flicks out to taste her sweet, vanilla-scented skin. My heart pulses. Her fingers slip under the waistband of my pants, pulling me into her.

"Keep playing with me, little fox. I'll fuck you right here. I don't care who's watching."

Her beautiful dark eyes flare with excitement. "Mmmm…sounds promising." Her fingers leave my waistband and climb up my body, exploring the smooth and rippled muscles on my chest.

I inhale sharply as my cock hardens. "You're playing with fire," I drawl so close to her ear that my lips vibrate against her earlobe.

I don't remember when we started kissing, her lips meeting mine. I kiss her softly at first before it turns ravenous. I coax her lips apart with mine. Her tongue slides into my mouth, and I relish the sweet flavor of her mouth—sweet and velvety like honey. I suck her tongue, devouring all her sweet flavors.

I rub my cock against her stomach. I can feel myself soaking through my boxers. I growl into her mouth. I am dangerously close to the edge.

Ayemeline pulls away slowly, suddenly aware of where we are. She looks around nervously before her eyes dip to the tent in my pants. "People are watching," she whispers.

"Is that a problem, little fox? I don't care who watches."

She chews on her lips and shifts her weight from one foot to the other.

"Keep biting those lips," I warn. "I'll have them wrapped around my dick right here."

Just then, a woman who looks to be in her sixties passes by. She stares at me in silent horror before walking away quickly.

Ayemeline's eyes bug out.

I smile at her playfully before cupping her chin in my hand and gently kissing her lips. "I'm going to have to help you come out more," I say, giving her a conspiratorial look.

Her eyes flicker with excitement and apprehension at the same time.

"Don't worry. I've got you," I promise her.

"I have somewhere I want to bring you tonight," I tell her once we're in my truck.

"Really?" She asks, her eyes twinkling.

"You are so fucking beautiful, you know that?" I can't help but remind her. The way her eyes light up. She gets excited before even knowing what it is.

She flickers a nervous glance at me.

I reach over and hold her hand in her lap.

"Where are you bringing me?" She asks softly.

"You'll find out tonight."

"Give me a hint. Please?"

"Patience, little fox. Patience."

***

After dropping her off and reluctantly leaving Ayemeline at her apartment, I head to my dorm to change. I quickly shower and get dressed. I wear a black pair of slacks and a black button-up dress shirt. I leave the top three buttons undone and roll my sleeves three-quarters of the way up. Throwing on a pair of white leather sneakers, I finish off the look by spraying some of my Dark Lord cologne on my neck before heading out the door.

I'm full of energy. Tonight is about exploration and liberation. It's something I've always wanted to do but was made to feel ashamed for it. But now…now, because of my little fox, I no longer feel shame. She loves me for me—darkness and all.

I pull up to her apartment and she's waiting outside. *Fuck, she's gorgeous.* She's wearing a sexy black low-cut dress. It's a backless halter dress with a wrap hem. The V-shaped slit in the hem of the dress reveals most of her thigh on one leg. The waist is made of sheer lace, revealing the skin under her breast to her navel. On her feet are sexy, black, strappy stiletto sandals that cross over, forming a bow at the back of her calf. Her toes and fingernails are painted white. Her big, curly, copper ginger hair frames her face. She has it parted on the side with one side pinned up and held back by a gold jewel-encrusted hairpin. She finishes the look with a pair of yellow gold stud butterfly earrings.

I climb out of the car and kiss her lips, inhaling her sweet vanilla scent, before opening the car door for her.

"I don't think we're gonna make it to our destination with you looking like that."

She looks at me up and down, her eyes dark and wild. "I think you might be right," she says mischievously. "I didn't think you could look any sexier, but here you are."

I plant another kiss on her lips. "You ready for tonight?" I ask as she climbs into the car.

"I hope so. I don't know where you're taking me."

I smile. "I think you might like it. But if you don't, please let me know. I want you to like it, but I also want to make sure you don't feel forced to do anything you're uncomfortable doing."

"I think you've sold me. I'm excited now." Her eyes gleam.

"Yeah? Well, that's good."

She bites down on a smile, taking my hand in hers.

***

We arrive at the club and pull up to the valet parking. The building looks like a factory building on the outside. The bricks are painted black, and the words "The Red Door" are illuminated outside.

Her eyes form a question.

I say nothing. Taking her hand, I lead her inside. Our IDs and memberships are checked at the entrance. This is a membership-only club. I purchased a two-month membership for her and me in the hope that we will use this club more than once. I was given a tour of the place afterward, and I knew this was an experience I wanted to share with Ayemeline. After being checked in the front, we're led through a door into the main part of the club. There is purple lighting dimly illuminating the space. To our left are tables where various members sit down for dinner. Beyond the restaurant is a dance floor adorned with two poles, one on each side of the dance floor.

"What is this place?" she asks before her eyes flicker to the television screens strategically placed throughout the food area and dance floor. Each screen shows various couples engaged in sex. On the screen in front of us, there is a woman hog-tied with a gag in her mouth while a mask-wearing man proceeds to fuck her ass. Another screen shows a woman suspended from the ceiling while she is spanked in the ass with a riding crop. "Oh," she says, realizing what this is.

I look at her, attempting to find any hint of discomfort. I want my little fox to trust me, and part of that trust is not putting her in situations that make her feel helpless.

All I see is the heat in her stare. "I think I like it here."

"I'm glad you like it so far. But there is more."

"More?" She asks with hooded eyes. I can tell my little fox's pussy is soaking wet right now. That sends a shot of electricity through my body.

I take her hand and lead her through another set of doors. There are several rooms here, each housing a different type of dark fantasy. I pass by the first room. This room resembles a strip club. There is a stage in the middle of the room surrounded by leather sofas. Except there is no pole in the middle of this room. On the stage, a woman is on her knees. Her feet are tied together and her hands are tied behind her back. Before her is a line of men. They each have their cocks in their hand stroking it as the woman is throat fucked by the man in front of her. They seem to be all waiting their turns.

Ayemeline watches with hooded eyes as a stream of drool and cum leaks out of the woman's mouth onto her bare breast. Several guest sit around the stage observing the scene before them, most with noticeable bulges in their pants. A spectator has a woman kneeling between his legs sucking his cock. Another man's hand is under a woman's skirt as he fingers her pussy. Her eyes stay on the scene before her as he pumps faster into her.

"You ready to see more?" I ask her.

"Oh, definitely," she says breathily.

I lead her to the next room. This room is a Victorian and Gothic-inspired playground. It is equipped with a king-size bed in the center of the room. To the side is a cage where a naked man is tied to the bars. He's wearing a wrist restraint and scrotum clam combo. The restraints are securing his hands while clamping his scrotum. Any movement of his arms will squeeze his scrotum. It also acts as a ball stretcher, pulling his balls downward.

"Whoa. I like that," she says, pointing to the man in the cave.

"You're getting ideas, little one?"

"So many ideas."

I have never been on the receiving end of pain. My obsession has always been inflicting pain. When it comes to sex, I prefer to have control. But if my little fox wants me to bow down to her, I will gladly do it.

The room also houses several spanking benches, a large bondage table, and a web prism.

Several scenes play out in this room. A man sits on a bench. A woman is draped over his lap while he spanks her with a wooden paddle. Several options are laid out and available for the guests to use, including rulers, hairbrushes, straps, canes, and whips.

Another woman is sprawled out on a sofa, completely naked. Her legs are spread open. Her labia is held open with a spreader clamp. The oval jaws of the clamp stretch her labia wide, exposing her clit.

Another woman is wearing a black faux leather underbust buckle corset. Her breasts, which are absurdly huge, are completely exposed. Her breast repeatedly smacks the woman in the face as she uses a red candle to pour hot wax on the first woman's breast and torso. The woman in leather pauses periodically to administer harsh licks to her partner's pussy. Her partner moans loudly with each lick.

Ayemeline stands there, transfixed.

"I can smell your wetness, little fox," I say into her ear.

Her breath hitches as I nibble on the scarred skin on her neck. Her lips part, and she lets out a soft moan.

I trail a finger up the hem of her dress until I reach her panties. I massage her engorged clit through the fabric of her lace underwear.

"Ari," she moans.

"I want everyone to watch me fuck you." Slipping my fingers into her underwear, I insert two fingers into her pussy and pull them out. I place my wet sticky fingers into my mouth and suck. "But first, we have to finish our tour."

She lets out a frustrated moan. "I don't think I can handle anymore. I feel like I'm about to explode."

"Let it all build up for me. I want you to cum on my face today." I take her hand and lead her to the next room.

This room is not as big as the others. There are two bondage tables in each corner of the room. A woman is strapped down on one of the tables, her hands and legs spread wide. Five men stand around her pumping their cocks. The woman is covered in white fluids from her face to her legs. One man cums, spreading his seed all over the woman's body. Once he's done, he moves out of the way, and another man takes his place, pulling his cock out of his pants and begins to pump it vigorously on top of the woman. The woman is glazed over with various men's cum. She licks her lips and moans as another man releases himself onto her face.

On the second bondage table, there is a man strapped down in the same way the woman is. The man has a penis restraint. The thick bands hold the base of his cock and balls simultaneously, maintaining his firm erection while separating his testicles from the shaft. Pre-cum leaks from the man's cock as a woman squats over his head. She rubs her pussy on his face as he sticks his tongue out to lap at her juices. Another woman slaps his cock while a third woman is on her knees, feasting on the second woman's pussy. The first woman reaches her orgasm and climbs off. A fourth woman, patiently waiting her turn, immediately takes her place over the man's face. As the fourth woman rides the man's face, the first woman proceeds to shove a large dildo in the fourth woman's ass. She lets out a cry, and the dildo settles in her ass.

"Are you ready, little fox?"

"Yes." Her voice is breathy and barely audible.

I take Ayemeline's hand and lead her to another room.

This room is a giant dance floor. Couples are rubbing their bodies against each other while they dance to the sultry music playing through the speakers. Red and purple lights flicker throughout the dance floor.

I lead Ayemeline to the middle floor and pull her into me. As the thrumming rhythm of the music plays, we sway back and forth. I can't remember the last time I did this with anyone. She falls into me, my strong arms wrapping tightly around her waist.

My lips brush against hers as my hand lifts the back of her dress. I hook my fingers in her panties and pull them down. Pulling away from her, I crouch to my knees in front of her. I pull the panties down to her ankles.

She looks around the room warily, a nervous expression on her face.

"Eyes on me," I tell her in a demanding voice.

She complies, fixing those dark eyes on mine.

"Good girl. Now step out of these panties."

She lifts her legs and steps out of them. I put them to my nose, taking in the smell of her arousal, before stuffing them into my pocket. Pushing her legs open, I use my tongue to flick her clit. She moans and places her hand on the top of my head.

I'm in the middle of the dance floor, on my knees, devouring my girl's pussy. I position my index finger at her opening and gently slide it in. Her body tenses as she takes a fistful of my hair. Fuck, she is wet and warm. The muscles in her pussy clamp down around my fingers. She moans and spreads her legs even wider for me. I bend my fingers downward while my tongue laps at her clit.

Her moans get louder as I take her clit in my mouth and suck. Her pussy is creamy from her arousal. Each time I slide my finger out, her wetness oozes out of her pussy, and her thick cream coats my fingers.

"OHHHHHH, Ari!" She moans loudly, no longer concerned about the people around us.

I slide my finger out and quickly replace it with my tongue, tasting her sweet nectar deep inside her. I pump my tongue in and out of her pussy as my thumb makes soft, light circles around her clit.

Her hand grips my hair tighter as she pushes my head into her pussy.

My cock throbs in my pants, but this is not about me. It's about her, my little fox. My sole purpose in bringing her here today is to allow her to let loose, to be free.

Ayemeline is liberated when she's with me, but outside of me, she hides in her shell. I need to get her out of that shell. I need to show her that she doesn't have to hide from the world. She doesn't have to shrink herself or make herself invisible. I want to show her it's okay to let go of the fear of being seen.

When that asshole attacked her outside the restaurant, I knew she could've handled him herself if she was in the right headspace. But she wasn't. She can be fearless at times. She solves her own problems, and that's what I love about her. Then there are other times when she allows her fears to cripple her. Once she stops being afraid to be seen, there will be no stopping my little fox.

Ayemeline lets out a loud, guttural sound as her body tightens up. "May I cum, Master?" she pleads.

"Cum for me, baby." I dip my tongue back into her pussy and pump faster. Her body jerks as she has a very wet orgasm.

Cum drips down her thigh, and I lick it off. Her body jerks a few more times before relaxing. Her legs wobble beneath her. I pull her dress down and stand. I pick her up in my arms and carry her to the bondage room. I have so much more to share with her.

CHAPTER THIRTY-THREE
AYEMELINE

Last night was nothing short of amazing. The Red Door is unlike any place I'd ever been to. It felt liberating to be in a place with so much free expression, where you didn't feel judged, where people watched you with admiration and not disgust. Ari and I spent the night exploring the many toys and furniture the place offered.

I snuggle close to his warm, hard body, completely spent and hurting in all the right places. His breathing is shallow. I watch the rise and fall of his chest. My fingers run along the welts and scratch marks that now decorate his chest and neck, and I smile, enjoying the fact that I put those there.

He rolls over to face me, his face so close to mine. I plant a light kiss on his pillowy lips that are slightly parted. He moans against my mouth but doesn't wake. I push my body into him and close my eyes.

The loud screech of the phone startles me out of sleep. Ari grunts before rolling over and picking it up. He exhales deeply before picking it up.

"Hey, Ma," he says, his voice groggy with sleep.

"It's 2:00 in the afternoon, and you're still sleeping?" Her raspy voice penetrates the speaker. It's as if she's right here in the room with us. Imagine that! I shudder at the idea of ever being in a room with that woman again.

Ari sits up and uses the sheets to cover his bottom half. "I had a long night," he says.

"Doing what?"

Ari looks at me and smirks.

"Not important. Did you need something, Ma?"

"I hope you didn't spend the night in jail again."

"What?" A genuine look of confusion crosses his features.

"You know what I'm talking about. I heard about you beating up the poor young man in the street. Do you want to spend your life in prison? Is that your destiny, Ari?"

Ari remains silent, his brows drawn together.

"I'm speaking to you."

"He wasn't a poor young man, Ma. He assaulted Ayemeline. I had to…"

"Of course, that girl was the cause of it. I knew when I saw her that she was bad news. She's the devil."

My vision swims and I have the sudden urge to hurt someone. How dare she? She's a much bigger devil than I am.

Ari's jaws clench. He spreads his fingers like claws before balling them into a fist. "You know nothing about her."

I see he's trying hard to hold on to a semblance of self-control.

"If you want to continue talking to me, you will respect her. She's the best thing that ever happened to me."

"Oh, please. You know I'm right. It would be best if you got away from her. I'm your mother. I know what's best for you."

Rage pulses through my veins.

"Do you? Because it seems like the only thing you ever cared about was what's best for you."

"This is exactly what I'm talking about. You never spoke to me this way. Now you've got your little girl, you've grown some balls. I'M YOUR MOTHER! Maybe I should've let you rot in jail," she shouts, and Ari moves the phone away from his ear.

"You know what, Ma? I gotta go."

"I'm not done with you yet. Don't you dare…"

Ari hangs up the phone, cutting her off mid-sentence.

Ari is visibly shaking by the time he gets off the phone with his mother.

I place my hand on his arm. "Are you okay?"

He remains silent while he stares at the wall. Then, without saying a word, he gets off the bed, walks to the bathroom, and shuts the door. I hear the lock click.

My anger spikes. How dare that woman call and fuck up our morning? Whenever Ari is in the presence of his mother, there is an invisible cloud on top of him. I know he feels weighed down by the burden of taking care of her alone and dealing with her temper tantrums.

I want to go after him, but I know he wants to be alone. My soul hurts for him. I want to take away his pain. I want to see him happy. But he can't seem to let go. He tries so hard to please her, and all he gets in return is aggravation and hurt feelings. I know the resentment he feels toward her. It grows inside of him like a tumor. If he doesn't cut it out, it will surely be the death of him.

Sorrow and anger stir inside me. I love him. I can't watch him go on like this. I know he won't do anything to make it better. It's my job to make it better for him. I can be his savior in the way he's been mine.

*****

We go to dinner later that night. Ari is somber while we eat, responding with just a couple of words at a time.

"I'm sorry, fox. I…need to go home. Only for a couple of days."

"No, you don't," I say, my face serious. "She doesn't deserve you. She doesn't deserve anything you do for her. She's a miserable old bitch who wants to make sure you're miserable. I'm sorry, but it's the truth. And you need to hear it." My anger boils to the surface.

He stares at me, a blank expression on his face. He remains quiet.

"Ari. Say something. Please."

He stares down at his plate.

"Babe."

"You just don't understand."

"No, I don't. I don't understand why you prefer to punish yourself."

"Ayemeline. Stop."

"If I don't?"

"ENOUGH," he yells. The other guests turn around and look at our table. He lowers his voice. "I don't want to talk about this." His voice gets even lower. "I'm sorry. I can't talk about it. Not now. So, please." He pauses. "Stop." His voice cracks at the last word.

A ball forms in my throat as we sit in silence, barely touching our food. After a very tense dinner, Ari drops me off at my apartment and drives back to his dorm, leaving me to figure out what to do next.

***

My apartment is darker than usual. The moon's light seems to be hiding, leaving a heavy, almost eerie darkness. I quickly reach for the light switch and flick it on. The room floods with soft lighting. I immediately drop my keys. They make a muffled clang sound as they hit the rug.

"Hello, beautiful."

My eyes widen in alarm. *What the fuck?* My lips part in silent surprise, and my heart hammers in my chest.

"Wh…what are you doing in here? How did you find out where I live?"

Remy hops off my kitchen counter and walks toward me. I back up instinctively.

"I made the mistake of not doing my homework before. I won't do that again." He picks up a book from the table, flipping it over and examining it before laying it back down.

"Why are you here, Remy? Does Ari know you're here?"

"DON'T FUCKING SAY HIS NAME!" He lunges at me. He eats the distance between us in two large steps, causing me to stumble backward. He is close, his breath warming my face. "Don't say his name," he says softer now.

"What. Do. You. Want?" I try to insert steel into my voice, but it comes out weak.

"I want you. I've always wanted you." He strokes my cheek with the back of his hand. "But you never wanted me, did you? You used me."

"I didn't use you, Remy. I didn't know Ar…" I stop, catching myself. "I didn't know him when we met."

"Exactly. You were mine first. Mine. But I wasn't good enough for you. Tell me something." He grips my chin. "Does he fuck you better than I do?"

I say nothing.

"Does he?"

"No," I say in an attempt to calm him.

He moves away and laughs. "Of course he does. That's why you chose him." He walks toward the door. He turns and faces me once more. "All I wanted was for you to choose me." And then he's gone.

I release the breath I'm holding and drop onto the sofa.

CHAPTER THIRTY-FOUR
ARIEL

The way I reacted toward Ayemeline has been eating away at me. She doesn't deserve that. She only wanted to help. I know that. It's hard to justify something to someone when you can't really justify it to yourself. I don't know why I put up with my mother's antics. I could've cut her off, like everyone else had. But I couldn't do that. Maybe it's because I believe no one deserves to be completely abandoned, or maybe it's because part of me feels like I owe her something. She fought for me when the whole thing with Julia went down. Yes, my dad put us in touch with his lawyer friend, but he wasn't there during most of the ordeal. He was dealing with his own cases and trying to stay far away from my mother. She was there. Maybe that's why I feel this impeding sense of loyalty for her.

I sit on a bench outside Gregor Hall. Ayemeline's class should be ending soon, and I want to see her. I need to apologize.

I reach for my phone and send her a text:

Me: Are you done with your class yet?

True Love: I don't know. Are you done with your temper tantrum yet?

Touché, little fox.

Me: Behave, little fox.

True Love: or what?

Me: Are you asking to get choked?

True Love: Maybe.

True Love: You're going to get me yelled at. Stop texting. I'm in class.

I smile and place the phone back in my pocket. Ten minutes later, Ayemeline walks out of the building, books held to her chest. Her hair is in a messy ponytail on top of her head. She is wearing a pair of leggings and an oversized hoodie despite the weather being warm. Her books fall, and she bends down to pick them up. Her round ass points toward me.

I stand and walk toward her, but something catches my eye. Beside a tree, dressed in a black hoodie with the hood covering his head is Remy. He's…watching her? Why is he watching her? My mind replays the night at Brea's place—the accusation towards Remy, the explanation he gave me afterward. Since that night, I tried to put it out of my head. But now…now, I'm not sure.

I change direction and walk toward Remy. I come up behind him so that he doesn't see me approaching.

"What the hell are you doing?"

He jerks around suddenly at the sound of my voice.

"Hey, man. What's going on?" he asks calmly. He pulls his hoodie off his head. His dark hair cascades down his face and lands on his shoulders.

"Were you…watching Ayemeline?"

He tilts his head quizzically. "What? No. Why would I…?"

"I saw you watching her." This may have been purely a coincidence. But something tells me it's not. I haven't heard much from Remy since that night at Brea's apartment. He was the one always checking in, making sure I was good. But lately, there's been nothing.

"Bro, I wasn't watching her. What's wrong with you?" Remy avoids my eyes, choosing instead to focus on a bird perched on a branch above us.

"You want my girl, man? Was Brea telling the truth?"

"Are you fucking kidding me right now?" he barks, still failing to make eye contact with me. He pulls at his ear. "I think you're paranoid."

"You know what? I gave you the benefit of the doubt the first time. I let it slide each and every time you treated her like shit. You hated her since day one. I don't understand why. Now, you're fucking watching her like a fucking creep." I pause, realization hitting me. "If you touch her, I will kill you."

"You think I hate her?" He chuckles. "Nah, man. I don't hate her. I fucking love her. But she chose you."

I stop breathing. "What?" I asked, confused.

"She was mine first, but she chose you. Congratulations. You won."

***

Remy, Four years ago: Dibs

"Yo, we should go. I'm not supposed to be here. I have court in the morning."

"Come on, Ari. Just enjoy the night."

"I'm not trying to enjoy the fucking night. I'm trying to leave." Ari's tone was serious.

I looked at my friend. He's changed so much in the past year dealing with the backlash of Julia's death. He's lost so much weight, and his forehead has developed permanent lines. I just needed him to relax. Honestly, I didn't know if I would get this opportunity for us to hang out like this after his trial tomorrow. This might be the last time. That's not something I wanted to voice, but it was in the back of my mind.

"Fine. Let me say goodbye to the boys. Go grab one last drink."

"Just please, hurry up." He turned and walked toward the bar.

After letting the guys know we were heading out, I walked over to the bar. Ari wasn't there. I looked around to see if I could spot him. He was nowhere. I walked outside. The rain pounded against the pavement. I pulled my hood over my head to shield myself from the rain as I looked up and down the streets. I couldn't find Ari anywhere.

Thunder roared followed by a flash of lightning.

"Shit." I turned toward the voice. She stood behind me, trying to get her umbrella to cooperate. The wind swept her umbrella out of her hand and toward the street. I ran and caught it right before it hit the car whizzing by. I walked over and handed it back, doing my best to fix the broken umbrella.

"Thank you," she said. Her voice was sweet and quiet.

"You're welcome. This weather is crazy, huh?"

"Yeah," she said, failing to make eye contact.

I looked in the direction she was looking at. "Are you waiting for someone?"

"Just trying to catch the bus."

"Yeah, that bus could be slow. I can give you a ride."

She looked at me and cocked her head. "Are you some sort of serial killer?"

I laughed. "No. I just don't want to leave you out here in the rain. It's late."

She stared up at me. Her eyes were big and dark. They were so beautiful. She pushed her wet hair out of her face. "What kind of non-serial killer offers a girl a ride when they've just met her? Sounds suspicious to me."

"I promise, I'm not a serial killer. I'm just trying to do a good deed. I'm Remy." I put my hand out.

She reached out and shook it. "Ayemeline."

"Nice to meet you, Ayemeline."

She gave me a soft smile.

"I can get my car and give you a ride to wherever you need to go."

She gazed down the street again. "Fine. I guess being killed isn't the worst thing to happen to me tonight."

I chuckled. "I won't kill you. I promise."

We drove, making small talk until she finally said, "To be honest, I don't want to go home."

I snuck a glance at her. "Why not?"

"I just don't." She sat with her hands in her lap, fidgeting her fingers.

"We can go to my place until you figure out where you want to go. I can always drop you off later."

"Fine. We can do that."

"You must've had a pretty shitty night to choose murder over going home."

"Only I can make that joke. Not you."

"Oh. I'm sorry. I guess I didn't understand the rules," I chuckled.

"I have to warn you, I live on campus. So, I'm gonna have to sneak you in."

"Cool." That's all she said.

***

In my dorm, I gave her a pair of my sweats and an oversized T-shirt for her to change into. Her clothes were drenched from the rain, so we laid them out across my desk. Now that we were in the light, I could better see her features. She had the most beautiful freckled face and curly red hair.

"Thank you for this," she said as she pulled on my T-shirt.

"It's no problem."

She looked me up and down before her eyes landed on my crotch. In one quick movement, she was straddling my lap. Our lips locked. Her tongue tangled with mine as we shared a passionate kiss. She reached into my pants and gripped my dick.

I let out a breath. Her hand was warm. It felt so good. She stroked me while she kissed me. Unable to control myself, I broke our kiss, picked her up, and flung her onto the bed. I pulled my sweats off her body, exposing her naked pussy. I kissed my way up her thigh before burying my tongue inside her sweet, wet pussy.

She moaned as she pushed my face further into her. Standing up, I made quick work of removing my pants and boxers. I spread her legs further, watching her as she watched me. Her eyes widened at the sight of my cock. I leaned in and kissed her again while I lined the head of my cock to her pussy.

"Oh, yeah. That feels so fucking good, beautiful," I grunted as I pushed in and out of her wet pussy. Her body tensed with each of my strokes, but I was too far gone to analyze the situation. I just wanted her at this moment.

She was so much tighter than any woman I've ever been with.

"Fuuuuck. Your pussy is so tight."

She squeezed her eyes shut and whimpered softly. "You're…too…big. It…hurts."

I continued to pump her pussy, moving faster now. Her hands gripped my back, and her nails cut into me.

"Don't come inside me," she begged.

"I can get you Plan B," I pant between strokes.

"No."

Her pussy tightened around me and I lost all control. Before I knew it, I was cumming inside her.

"I told you not to do that," she said softly.

"I'm sorry." I collapsed on top of her. "I couldn't control myself. Your pussy is so good." I kissed her neck.

"I need to use the bathroom," she said, turning her face away from me.

I pulled out of her and rolled onto my back on the bed. She pulled on the pair of sweats that we'd discarded along with the T-shirt. After telling her where to find the shared bathroom, I rested, still trying to catch my breath. I knew nothing about this girl, but I knew I wanted to keep her. She was so beautiful with the most innocent features.

She came back to the room, and I sighed a sigh of relief. She hadn't run away.

"You could rest," I told her. "I'll be right back."

I made my way to the bathroom to clean up, leaving her to rest on my bed. Once inside, I pulled down my pants and stared at my semi-erect dick. Was that blood?

***

By the time I reached my dorm, Ayemeline was sprawled out on my bed, fast asleep. I climbed onto the bed and fell asleep beside her. The next morning, we woke to the regular morning ruckus I was used to waking up to living on a floor full of guys.

Her eyes cracked open, and she stretched. "Thank you for letting me stay here last night."

"You're welcome, although you could've told me you were a virgin."

She bit her bottom lip. "Was it a problem?"

"No. I just would've been more…cautious had I known."

She said nothing.

"Can I see you again?" I asked.

She looked at me. "Maybe. We'll see."

I smiled. "Oh. It's like that?"

She climbed over me and off the bed.

"Where are you going?" I looked at her, confused. I wasn't ready for her to leave.

"I gotta go."

I got out of bed and grabbed her wet clothes from last night. I examined them to make sure they were fully dry before handing them to her. I grabbed her jeans and a card fell out of her pocket. I bent down to pick it up and my jaw almost hit the floor. On the card were the words, Hunter Davis High School. It was her school ID.

"You're in high school?" I looked at her silently, begging her to say no.

Instead, she nodded her head.

My stomach contracted into a ball. "How old are you?" I was afraid to ask, but I was hoping she would say eighteen. Maybe she was a senior. That wouldn't have been that bad.

Instead of answering, she grabbed her clothes, holding them in a ball against her chest. "I think I better go."

***

"You fucked Ayemeline?" A wave of acid wells up from my belly. Remy was Ayemeline's first. A chill runs up my spine as I put the pieces together. Remy met Ayemeline when she was sixteen. The assault occurred when she was sixteen. Then she got pregnant. Could the baby have been Remy's? I want to throw up. "You fucked Ayemeline," I say again, unable to believe my own words.

Remy remains silent now.

"She was sixteen. She wasn't yours. She didn't pick me over you. She was FUCKING SIXTEEN!"

"She picked you," he says quietly. "Three years later, she picked you."

"What the fuck are you talking about?"

Remy exhales deeply. "Jansen's party at that bar. She was there. We spoke. Then she saw you, and she started asking all types of questions about you. It was obvious she was interested in you. She treated me like shit. Like I was no one and she just moved on to you."

"You're sick," I hiss.

Remy bursts into laughter. "I'm sick?" he says, pointing to himself. "When it comes to sick individuals, I believe you wear the crown on that one."

My nostrils flare as I stand there with my fist clenched by my side, shoulders rolled back, praying to God he gives me the control I need not to punch him.

Remy looks down at my fist and backs up instinctively. Smart.

The onslaught of information has my body feeling like I might pass the fuck out. Shock has momentarily stolen the sound of my voice. And then, finding my voice again, I say the words I never thought I'd say. "Stay the fuck away from us."

CHAPTER THIRTY-FIVE
AYEMELINE

My phone vibrating in my hand startles me awake. I look around me. Most of the passengers on the flight are either asleep or reading a book. I gaze down at my phone. It's Auria. I swipe to answer.

"Hey," I whisper.

"Bonjour, sister. Guess where I am?" Her voice is giddy and loud. I have to pull the phone away from my ear.

"Where are you?"

She squeals on the other end of the line.

Auria and I have been texting back and forth ever since my grandfather's funeral. One thing I can say about my sister is that she loves to talk and she doesn't keep anything to herself. I'm pretty sure I can predict when her period is set to arrive based on every detail she's given me.

"I am in Georgia. Mama and I."

"Really?"

"Yes!" She hollers excitedly. "We can go out to eat."

Of course, we can.

"I have so many new outfits I want to show you. Oh! And guess what?"

It's so much easier texting with her as opposed to talking on the phone. I have a hard time matching her energy.

"What?"

"Mama says I may go to school with you."

"What?"

"Oui. We can go to school together. Once I finish Lycée, I can come. We can live together."

"Really?" I don't want to tell her that's never going to happen. Auria has grown on me, and I enjoy the way our relationship has been developing. However, living together isn't something that would work for us. Besides, my father isn't aware that we've been speaking to one another. I'm afraid once he finds out she's living with me, he might decide to stop paying my rent—not a risk I'm willing to take.

"Are you not excited?" I can hear the big grin in her voice.

"So exciting," I say, trying to push some excitement into my voice.

We end the call after she tells me about her latest flow and how she had to change her tampon three times in one hour. I wonder if she gives everyone she meets as much information as she gives me or if I'm just lucky.

I settle into my seat for the remainder of the two-hour plane ride. I told Ari I needed to go home for the weekend, but in reality, I needed to take care of more pertinent matters.

His mother has been a huge weight on his back. I needed to have a serious talk with her. Ari is the man that I love. I can no longer sit by and watch him deal with her on his own. My job is to protect Ari, even if it's from his mother. I hate that woman. As much as I wanted to kill her, I couldn't do it—for Ari's sake. I don't think he'd ever forgive me. So, we just talked. I dished out threats that I had no intention of ever keeping, but she didn't need to know that. All she needed to know is that I have Ari's back, and I always will. I warned her that she would not continue to treat him like shit, or I would come back to deliver on my threats. I finally saw the look of terror in her eyes, and it filled me with so much joy.

CHAPTER THIRTY-SIX
ARIEL

My rage nearly consumed me as I made my way back to my dorm after my conversation with Remy. I needed time to think. It was just too much. The thing that got me the most was the fact Ayemeline didn't tell me that she met Remy before me, that they'd fucked. We'd poured our hearts and souls into one another, and she didn't think to tell me this.

She texted me, asking if I wanted to come over once she was done with class. I didn't respond. The following day, she texted me saying she was going home. That, too, went unanswered. I needed time to think. Between my mom, who had been ringing my phone nonstop since our last conversation, and this, it's just too much.

It's been three days of me isolating myself in my room. My mind swarms. I rub my temples, trying so hard to rationalize what happened. My best friend and my girl had a secret that they were keeping from me. Why did she feel like she had to keep this from me? We've been through hell and back with each other. Was she afraid of what I might say? Was she afraid of destroying my and Remy's friendship? Did she think I wouldn't look at her the same?

The rage that had thrummed through my veins has subsided to a flicker of irritation. I need to know. I reach for my phone and pull up Ayemeline's contact.

Me: Why didn't you tell me about you and Remy?

Dots appear on the screen and then disappear again. Then appear and disappear.

Me: Just answer the fucking question.

Dots and they're gone. I throw my phone across the room. It slams into the wall before falling to the carpet. Rage grips me as I hold my head and scream. After screaming for what felt like hours, I grab my bag and slip on my shoes. The only thing that can help me now is pain.

CHAPTER THIRTY-SEVEN
AYEMELINE

I step out of the airport and am greeted by the pale bluish white of the full moon overhead. Despite it being night, it is surprisingly hot. Even with a light breeze, the Georgia air remains thick and hot.

I carry only a small duffle bag. I cross the street, making my way toward the covered parking. The parking garage is empty and quiet. I feel a dizzying sense of anxiety, realizing that I'm here alone. Panic rises in my throat, and I hurry my steps. My steps sound doubled, like someone is walking at the same time as I am. I turn to look around me. Nothing. I continue my fast pace to my car.

The chilling feeling I'm being followed crawls up my neck. I build up the courage to turn around. Maybe I'm just being paranoid. I check my surroundings suspiciously while I continue moving forward.

I reach my car and fidget with the door handle. I get it open and fling my bag onto the passenger seat before climbing inside. But before I can do that, I'm shoved backward into a hard body. A towel-covered hand covers my mouth, and all I see is black.

I awaken to darkness and a soreness in my limbs. My eyes are covered. I try to move but find that I can't. I take a quick stock; my hands are tied above my head to a contraption overhead, leaving my body dangling. My feet are secured below me, leaving my thighs spread. I feel a tight band around my breast and stomach. Rope? The way the air hits my skin tells me I'm naked. I open my mouth to scream, but my screams are muffled. Something is around my mouth. It feels like a ball. Fear crawls over my body, prickling my skin. My stomach churns, and my throat squeezes shut.

I jerk my body forward and backward, trying to free myself. It's no use. The rope around my wrists isn't rough against my skin, but as I tug on them, they seem to be getting tighter. I stop moving, realizing I'm making my situation worse.

I try to sense where I am. A hint of cologne that's vaguely sweet and musky. The scent of the cologne mixes with the putrid stench of mold and decaying wood. I listen. The sound of a siren is far off in the distance. *Where am I?*

A cold hand is suddenly on my bare thigh, and I gasp, trying to move away from the touch. A deep chuckle rings close to my ear. I want to plead for the hand to stop but I can't get any sound out through the ball-like object in my mouth.

A warm breath is at my neck. I feel my captor inhale my scent. The hand runs up my stomach to my breast. It pinches one of my nipples and then the other. The body walks around me. Suddenly, my nipple is absorbed into a warm, dark space. Teeth bite down hard on my nipple, and I writhe through the restraints.

Big hands find their way down my body to my opening. I try to squeeze my legs closed, but the restraints make it impossible. Fingers find my slit, and I whimper, my body betraying me. My captor slowly works a finger inside of me even as I shake my head violently. Fingers hook into my pussy, and my head and eyes roll back. It is a slow, firm taking of my body. Despite everything my brain is telling me, I can't stop my body from reacting. I feel my pussy getting wetter as the fingers slide in and out in a painfully slow rhythm.

The fingers are thick. I writhe and moan as he pumps, slowing his pace even further. Why is my body doing this to me? I can't enjoy this. It doesn't have my permission to react this way. A little pressure is added to my clit, and I'm silently screaming as my body convulses. Great. Now this asshole thinks I'm enjoying this.

The fingers are withdrawn. I feel them against my lips, and I turn away. The fingers push through the ball in my mouth. I can taste myself on my tongue. A deep chuckle escapes from my captor.

I shut my eyes against my blindfold and tears well up in them. A single tear rolls down my cheek, and a cold tongue licks the tear off my face.

"Don't cry, little fox. Just accept your punishment."

My body slumps at the sound of his voice as the tension dissipates.

He slowly removes the ball from my mouth. I lick my dry lips.

"Ari." My voice is hoarse.

A hard slap lands on my back, and I yelp.

"Did you forget the rules already, little fox?"

I shake my head from side to side. "No, Master. I'm sorry."

"That's better." He passes the soft fronds of what I can assume to be a flogger along my breast before walking around my body. "You lied to me." *Snap!* "You were keeping secrets." *Snap!* "And now…" *Snap!* "You need to be punished." *Snap!*

With each stinging lash on my back, I scream.

I hear his footsteps retreat. I try to catch my breath while I anticipate the next sensation. My whole body trembles, and I can feel the moisture pooling between my legs.

Suddenly, a belt is looping around my neck. He tightens the belt and pulls back, causing my head to fall backward. He stands behind me, his erection poking my back. I draw in a sudden breath as desire consumes me. He pulls the belt with one hand as his other hand splays across my pussy, cupping me aggressively. Two firm fingers spread my pussy lips, exposing my engorged and needy clit.

"Look how wet you are," he croons into my ear from behind. I sigh heavily as my arousal becomes more evident in the wetness that seeps through his fingers. He strokes firmly along my hot core. He makes dangerous circles just inside, and I moan with each stroke. He sinks several fingers deep inside my dripping pussy as he tightens the belt around my neck. I struggle to catch my breath. His breaths are shaky behind me as he moans his own pleasure. The coupling sensation of the leather straps around my neck and his intense strokes are too much.

"Don't you dare cum."

"Please," I beg for my release.

"Not yet, my horny little pet. You don't deserve to cum yet."

He pulls his fingers out of my pussy, leaving me empty. A hard whack hits my ass again and again. My sobs and moans are muffled as the belt cuts off part of my air supply.

He breathes deeply. His voice is heavy and laced with desire. I can feel the rawhide-laced handle move up between my thighs. "Mmmm…I love punishing you."

Pulling the handle away, I feel him back away, the belt loosening around my neck. My heart pounds in my chest, and my hands tremble in their restraints. Not being able to see what's coming is the worst type of torture and also the most delicious. I try to control my fast, shallow breathing as I hear him approach me. My skin tingles and burns.

He moves closer, and a stingy smack hits my pussy. I scream at the unexpected burn.

"This…" Another smack lands on my pussy, "is a dragon tail whip. It's my new toy." Another smack, this one harder than the last.

I pant and wheeze. My whole body is on fire.

"Do you like my new toy, little fox?" He asks a hard object is inserted into my ass.

Through deep, ravenous breaths, I say, "Yes…master."

He pumps my ass inexorably close to the edge before pulling out and reinserting the object.

His husky voice whispers, Tell me you want to feel the sting of my whip on your pussy. Tell me you like the pain. Tell me how wet it gets you." He pumps harder into my ass. "Tell me, or I'll stop."

"I…I want your pain, master. Please…" I breathe. "Hurt me. Make me wet."

His cock grows stiffer on my back before he pulls away. He stops pumping my ass, but the object remains lodged inside me. He swings the flogger. I can hear it swishing through the air before the leather strips splay across my filled ass. I gasp. My body stiffens at the stinging needles of pain. He strokes my clit. I accept the pain as my body nears another orgasm while it relaxes and accepts the pain. The flogger smacks me again, warming my ass. The fusing of pain and pleasure eats through my fogged mind. I cry out as pain and pleasure start a war inside me.

My mind tries to understand how I can feel so aroused as my pain increases. One shouldn't go with the other. There should be a clear distinction. But, for me, there isn't. My mind struggles trying to sort the fear and pain from excitement and arousal.

I feel my pussy leak down my thigh. I whimper and sob, begging him to let me cum. "Please, Master. May I cum?"

"No." His voice is gruff and angry.

My tears soak into my blindfold. "I'm…I'm sorry. I…I didn't want to lie to you. I didn't want to see you hurt. I was…" I sniffle. "I was selfish. I thought you wouldn't want me. I thought…" I choke back a sob and my voice cracks. "I thought if you knew how he felt, you'd back away. And I didn't want to lose you." My eyes sting with tears. "I never want to lose you."

Ari is silent. I don't feel him near me.

"Please." A wave of sadness wraps itself around me.

Then, the blindfold is removed. It takes a few seconds for my eyes to adjust. When they do, I see Ari standing in front of me, dressed in all black. He tracks the tears on my face before leaning in and kissing me. Hot, salty tears run down my face to my mouth.

His voice is thick with his own tears. "I will never not want you." He kisses me again; this time, it is a deeper kiss. He wraps one arm around me while the other arm reaches overhead, loosening my restraints. My hand falls limply to my side. Looking down, I can see my legs are restrained with a spreader bar. "Those will stay for now," he says, referring to the spreader. "I'm not done with you yet."

I smile, happy to finally see those bright hazel eyes.

"I have a surprise for you." He strokes my tear-stained cheeks before stepping away.

I gasp, and my eyes widen immediately. Only a few feet away from us, is a man. Not just any man. The man Ari beat up and got arrested for me. He sits in a chair with his hands tied behind his back. A rope is looped around his ankles, securing them to the leg of the chair. He's wearing a face muzzle, which has an attachment for a mouthball. *Ari and his toys. I love this man.*

"This, little fox, is for you." He stares at me with a wild and dangerous glint in his eyes.

My heart melts for this man. "You did this for me?"

"Anything for you, love. You see, I didn't think it was fair for him to walk around freely with no consequences after what he tried to do to you. I figured you'd want to fix things."

I look at the man. He's hardly recognizable. His eyes are swollen and purple. His lips are severely bruised and three times their original size. Beads of blood and sweat roll down his forehead.

"It looks like you started without me," I say.

"I couldn't help it. But you can finish the job."

Adrenaline surges through my body. This man has managed to combine my favorite things: sex, pain, and torture. He did this all for me even when I knew I didn't deserve it. I don't deserve his forgiveness. I don't deserve his unconditional love. But here he is, giving it to me freely. It is more than I could ever imagine, more than I've ever experienced.

"This is going to be fun," he says as he walks up to the man. He lands a fist on the man's nose, breaking it. Blood shoots out like rivers of fire. The bright crimson fades quickly as it mixes with his tears. The man thrashes his body around on the chair, but he isn't going anywhere.

He walks over to me and hands me a knife he picked up from a nearby table. "Remove any part of his body you want, little fox. But don't kill him yet."

He places the knife in the palm of my hand before crouching down to remove the spreader bar, giving me back the ability to close my legs.

I walk to the man. He gives me a quick, nervous glance. He makes a terrible strangled sound as I cut through his clothes. My knife makes a clean line from top to bottom until his chest is exposed. Then, I move to his pants and boxers, repeating the same motions. His tiny, exposed dick hides in its shell. I run the blade of my knife along the side of his dick. I see the panic in his eyes—the pleading. None of that means anything to me. He didn't care about my pleadings as his friends held me down. He didn't care about my cries.

Cold, sweaty hands gripped my wrists tightly. My screams became hoarse.

"Hold her tighter."

"You know you like it."

"Such a tight pussy."

My mind shifted to the sixteen-year-old boy sitting before me. His hands were bound to the chair, and his gaze went through me like a blast of ice.

"You stupid bitch. Touch me, and you'll die."

I cocked my head. "I don't think you're in a position to make threats, TYLER. I'm sorry, but I'm the only one that holds that power."

He spat in my face. I wiped my face with my sleeve.

"That wasn't nice, Tyler. You know how unsanitary that is?" I look at him with a smirk. "Now, you can't just die. No, I need to make sure you

suffer first." With one quick movement, I lifted my knife and swung. It's a clean cut. His dick tumbled to the ground with a soft thud.

A piercing, gut-wrenching scream reached my ears.

Ari rests his hand on my shoulder, and the scream fades into the background. I look down at the pool of blood on the man's crotch. The thick and viscous blood coats his skin like a warm blanket. A metallic scent invades my nostrils. I take a deep inhale, savoring the aroma. I see the man's muffled cries behind the face muzzle.

Ari gently takes the knife from my hand and sets it down. He cups my face in both of his large hands and kisses me. "You're here with me."

I blink up at him through blurry vision.

"Stay here…with me."

I nod. He plants another kiss on my lips before moving down to my neck. He sucks my scar. I can feel the pinch of his teeth as he bites down. My cries become moans of pleasure.

"I love the taste of your blood," he moans into my neck.

He pulls away and lifts his shirt over his head, flinging it to the ground. I watch as he lays his body flat on the ground.

"Sit," he demands.

Obeying, I straddle him, one leg on each side of his head. I crouch down until my pussy hovers teasingly above his mouth. He uses two hands and pulls me into him, slamming my pussy onto his tongue.

His hard dick forms a noticeable bulge in his pants. I yearn to see his hard, glistening cock stand at full mast for me.

"Oh, Master," I moan as his tongue penetrates my pussy. He jabs his tongue deeper. His finger toys with my ass. That's when I realize the object he placed in my ass earlier is still there. He toys at it, pushing it in and out while his tongue alternated in my pussy. He starts to build a good rhythm, and I can feel my pussy leaking onto his face.

He reaches down and unzips his pants with one hand, freeing his hard, rigid cock. Fuck, that looks appetizing.

I make eye contact with the man before me and smile. His eyes bulge as he stares at us, a streak of blood and tears running down his face. Had he not been gagged, his screams would've alerted anyone who was near. I lean forward and grip Ari's cock. It's wet with his precum. I slowly put it in my mouth. Starting slowly, I kiss and lick up and down his cock before taking it into my mouth again. He kisses my pussy lips and licks up and down my slit. He takes my clit into his mouth, and I almost black out from the immense pleasure. I lightly grab his balls with one hand while I use the other hand to stroke his dick, my hand and mouth working together to make an up-and-down motion. He grunts, and the vibration of the sounds emanates through my pussy.

I suck faster, rubbing my pussy on his face. He sticks a finger inside my pussy, almost pushing me over the edge. My pussy clamps down on his finger as I moan loudly with his cock still in my mouth. His thighs tighten. He thrusts his hips into my mouth. His body spasms as his tongue penetrates my pussy again, becoming more intense. He loses control as thick spurts of his cum floods my mouth. I keep sucking as he jerks and thrashes beneath me.

The taste of his salty juices causes me to lose control as my orgasm flows through my body. It gets increasingly intense as my body goes into spasm after spasm. My ass contracts and squeezes the object that is lodged in my asshole.

I moan as I lick up every drop of his cum.

"Mmhhh…you taste so fucking good." He growls beneath me.

I get up, my body completely spent after my second orgasm. I flip around and stare into his eyes. His face glistens with my arousal. He slowly licks his lips, and I instantly feel my pussy getting wet again.

I lean over and kiss his lips. "I want you to punish me now."

A devilish grin crosses his face. "With pleasure, little fox."

He picks me up and flips me to my hands and knees so I'm facing the man on the chair. He holds my head down with one hand while he uses the other hand to remove his pants. My ass is pinned in the air.

"You're a bad and dirty slut." The object goes in and out of my ass. I savor the sensation. "You deserve to be punished." *Smack.* His hand collides with the already sensitive skin of my ass.

I yelp as my skin stings and pulses.

He lines up his throbbing cock directly in front of my dripping pussy. My forehead is resting on the ground, giving me a clear view between my legs. A puddle of my juices rests on the ground between my legs. Another drop stretches from my pussy before disconnecting and landing on the ground. I watch as he pushes his big head inside of me. He pulls my hips toward him as he rocks back and forth. I watch with excitement as his cock disappears deep inside of me, making slopping wet sounds. I feel so incredibly full. With each of his thrusts, the object vibrates inside my ass.

Ari grabs my hair and pulls my head back as he continues to fuck me. I moan as he pumps into me harder and harder.

He fucks me aggressively and with no mercy. My scalp stings as he continues to pull my hair. My eyes water, and my entire body weakens. His hand reaches around and finds my neck. He squeezes. I can't breathe. He pushes my head back, forcing me to look at his face. He looks down at me sadistically. My wetness spurts around his cock. I'm so close to cumming. I feel my air supply running out.

"Cum for me. Cum all over my cock, baby."

I shake as my orgasm takes over. The spasms start deep, and they stretch out into my limbs and up to my brain. I get lightheaded as I gasp for air, my hand reaching out to claw at his wrist. His hand doesn't move.

I cum hard, drenching his dick with my juices.

"Oh shit," I hear him growl behind me. His body spasms and his dick grows and pulsates inside me. He lets out a loud, guttural scream as his orgasm wracks his body.

The pleasure twists itself inside me as he squeezes my neck even tighter. Then, I'm cumming again. My orgasm is powerful. It shakes me to my core and leaves me panting as he continues to brutally thrust his cock inside me.

This man is not human. Every guy I've ever been with has never been able to keep pumping through his orgasm. But Ari is different. He releases my neck, and the scream that was trapped now escapes.

I collapse, but before hitting the ground, he catches me. Pulling out of me, he rolls me onto my back. I can't open my eyes. I can't speak. I can't think. I've never experienced anything like that before with anyone. I love that I get to experience it with him.

Ari rubs my cheeks. "Wake up, baby. We're not finished yet."

I moan under his touch. My lids feel heavy. My body is sore.

His hand runs down my breast. "I think it's time to say goodbye to our little voyeur friend over there."

I smile at that while I gather my strength to open my eyes. I can't lay here all day. I have a body to fillet.

CHAPTER THIRTY-EIGHT
REMY

*Y*our perky tits swing from side to side as he fucks you from behind. I can see the sweat forming on your eyebrows. I should've been the one to put that there. You part your lips and whisper his name. It should be my name. You're enjoying this, aren't you—his roughness?

I didn't intend to follow Ari. And I never thought I'd run into you like this. I knew he was fucked up. But you? You, I had no idea you had so many layers. But that doesn't stop me from wanting you. It should be me behind you pounding into your honeyed pussy. But you don't like the nice guy, you crazy bitch.

Peeking into the small window of the old, abandoned warehouse, my hands reach down into my pants as I fist my cock. Fucking hell. I should be appalled at the bloody body of the man in the chair. But all I can focus on is you, my sweet, sweet, fucked up little doll. Precum pools at my tip as I pump my dick. I can't hear the sounds you make, but I know they are sweet and velvety and full of lust. I want to fill your mouth full of my cum. My muscles tighten as I near my release. Oh fuck!

He pulls you into him and plants a sloppy kiss on your lips. Suddenly, my release is gone. Fury springs to life as I watch him consume what was mine first. Do you think he's better for you than I am? Do you think he can love you more? Life isn't always fair, but I've never been one to give up. You will be mine.

CHAPTER THIRTY-NINE
ARIEL

Carrying Ayemeline from the tub to the bed, I put her on the towel I had placed on her bed. She rolls from her back to a face-down position. Her eyes are half closed, and I know she's worn out from the night we had.

After leaving the warehouse, we drove several miles to bury his body in the woods. I knew the warehouse was the perfect location to execute my plan. It had been abandoned for some time and was set to be demolished in a couple of weeks. That's what made it so perfect. Finding the right place wasn't easy but my research had paid off.

It has always been difficult for me to cope with my emotions. Anger always left me with the need to hurt. But that was something I suppressed for so long. I was afraid to lash out, scream, or express my anger the way normal people would for fear that I might lose control of myself. Had I let my full anger out, Remy would've been dead. That is something I would never forgive myself for.

My decision to hunt down that low life was made to save Remy's. A life for a life. It felt so good to throw punch after punch into his face for touching my little fox, for thinking he could have what's mine. I beat him for what he'd done and for what Remy had done as well. It was a two-for-one special.

Welts line the skin on Ayemeline's back. I gently touch the red, raised skin, and she flinches slightly. I lean forward and place soft kisses along her back. She moans softly at the feel of my lips on her skin.

"How do you feel?" I ask her.

"Sore," she moans.

"I'm sorry, baby."

"Don't be. I love every second I get to be with you." She lets out a soft yawn.

I smile at her words and wonder how I got so lucky. "Just relax. I've got you."

Reaching into the bowl of warm water, I grab the small washcloth and squeeze the water out. I apply the warm cloth to the area several times before applying an antibiotic ointment. By the time I'm finished, Ayemeline is asleep. Her curls cascade onto her face, completely covering it. I push her hair back and lie down beside her. I stare into her angelic face. She looks so peaceful sleeping. She has a scratch on her face connecting one freckle to the next, and I wonder how she got that. I made sure not to touch her face. I never want to scar my fox's face.

***

I must've fallen asleep because the next thing I know, I'm startled by a faint knocking on the front door. I look over at Ayemeline, who is still asleep. I roll out of bed as slowly as possible so as not to wake her. Throwing on a T-shirt, I go to the door and look through the peephole. I can only see the top of a girl's head. I disable the lock and open the door a crack. I would've asked who it was before opening it but I don't want to wake Ayemeline.

As soon as the door is open, the girl's all too cheerful voice comes through. "Hello. I am looking for Ayemeline."

I stare at the girl who is a replica of my little fox except she's different. This girl looks a whole lot more bougie, whereas Ayemeline is more down-to-earth in her looks. She has a thick French accent, and I wonder if this is the sister Ayemeline told me about.

"Who are you?" I ask.

"Pardon," she says in French, holding her hand to her chest. "I am Auria. I am, euh, the sister of Ayemeline."

I cock my head. I'm pretty sure Ayemeline wasn't expecting a sister today. Or perhaps she was, but she didn't have time to tell me about it.

"Is she expecting you?"

"Non. She does not expect me. This is, euh, surprise. What is your name?"

"I'm Ari."

Her face lights up when she hears my name. "Bon, oui! Ari. You are her boyfriend, yes?"

"Yes, I am."

"It's perfect to meet you, Ari. I kiss you?"

I squint my eyes in confusion. Is she asking me to kiss me? "No." As soon as the words leave my mouth, I realize what she meant. The French will greet people by kissing them on both cheeks. Maybe she's asking to greet me? Either way, I don't think it's a good idea.

I open the door wider for her. "Please come in." She practically dances through the door.

"Merci, Ari." She said, making both words rhyme.

"Ayemeline is asleep right now. I don't want to wake her."

"It's okay. You don't have to wake her. So, Ari, you live here?"

"Um. No. I'm just…visiting."

"You are very tall. There is a boy in my class that is tall like you. We always tell him his mother breed him with a giraffe." She giggles. "Alors, the instructors always ask him to get high objects. He always complain. I say maybe you should be shorter then no one will ask you to help all the time."

I suddenly have the urge to wake Ayemeline but think better of it. After what I put her through, I should let her rest.

"What do you study, Ari?" She stares at me intently, eagerly awaiting a response, like my answer will solve all her problems.

"I study music."

"Ah, music. Okay. You play instrument?" she says excitedly.

"Yes. Violin."

"Violin? That's exciting. I play harp. I wanted to play violin, but my papa wanted me to play harp. En tout cas, harp is very beautiful. I enjoy it. You can show me to play violin, oui?"

"It's a possibility," I say cautiously. "How long are you staying? Where are you staying?"

"I want to stay here. I will ask Ayemeline, of course. Mama came with me. She is in a l'hotel."

"Would you like something to drink?"

"Non. I am okay. Do you have food? Bread, perhaps?"

"Yeah, sure. I can find you some bread." I walk to the kitchen to search Ayemeline's pantry for some bread. What a weird request.

"And do you have cranberry juice?" Auria asks from the couch.

"I doubt there's cranberry juice," I respond, even though she said she didn't want anything to drink.

She gets up and walks into the kitchen with me.

I grab a loaf of French bread. "Is this okay?"

"It is okay. Do you have cheese?"

"I think so. You can check the fridge if you'd like."

"Merci," she says as she opens the refrigerator door. She pulls out the bag of Gouda. "In l'hotel, my mama ask for two beds. The worker tell us they don't have any more rooms with two beds. We have to take one bedroom. Mama says no, she pay for two beds. For one hour Mama fight with the man. I am so tired. She says to get us a room with two beds sinon she will leave. We never get two beds. Just one.

That is why I prefer to stay here with Ayemeline. My mama snore so loud. I cannot sleep."

"Yeah, that can make it difficult to sleep."

Auria is very different from her sister. She seems to be the type of person that can only be tolerated in small doses. She is a sweet girl. But Lord, does she talk! And, if I'm being honest, I only caught a little bit of what she says due to her heavy accent and the random French words in her sentences.

For two hours, Auria talked to me about her trip, the hotel, her father's funeral, school, and, although I didn't need to know this, that she's a virgin. Yeah. I really did not need to know.

Despite all that, I enjoyed my conversation with her. I can see why she is the only person, beside me, Ayemeline is trying to form a relationship with.

***

We are in the kitchen as Auria talks and scarfs down her third helping of bread and cheese when Ayemeline walks out of the bedroom stark naked.

"Oh, mon Dieu." Auria's eyes bulge when she sees her.

Ayemeline must've not noticed her at first because she startles by her voice before hurrying back into the bedroom.

"I'm sorry. I'll be right back," I tell Auria.

I enter the bedroom, and Ayemeline stumbles into a pair of pajama bottoms.

"Your sister is here," I say in a matter-of-fact tone as if she hadn't already seen for herself.

"No, shit," she responds incredulously as she attempts to locate the neck hole in her T-shirt.

"She's been here for two hours, but I didn't want to wake you. Did you know she was coming?"

"No. I mean, she said she would come, but I didn't know she was already here. We spoke yesterday."

"Well…surprise."

Ayemeline exhales. "Did she come alone?"

"It looks like it. She wants to stay here."

Ayemeline looks at me as if she's asking for permission.

"It's your apartment."

"What about you?"

"I have my dorm."

"I mean, it'll be hard to spend time…together. Doing stuff." She smirks.

I chuckle. "If we have to, I can sneak you into my dorm."

"We're too loud to fuck in a dorm."

"We'll figure it out." I walk over to her and plant a chaste kiss on her forehead. "Take care of your sister. By the way, I learned a lot about your sister—more than I ever needed to know."

She laughs. "I'm so sorry. All she does is eat and talk."

"Oh, I know." I kiss her again. "Go. I'm going to jump in the shower."

CHAPTER FORTY
AYEMELINE

*H*aving Auria here in my apartment was a strange feeling. But it also felt nice. I've never had a girlfriend whom I could bond with. I finally see what I've been missing. Although Auria is always like a kid in a candy store on Christmas morning, I truly enjoy being around her.

While Ari showers, I decide to cook. Cooking has never been my thing, I'll admit. But I have the only two people who mean something to me here, and I want to do something special. Besides, Ari really took care of me last night with the warm bath, the massaging of my feet in the tub, and tending to my wounds. He deserves something in return. I decide to make rice and chicken partly because the recipe seemed simple enough and partly because those were the two ingredients I had on hand.

While I cook, Auria tells me that she arrived here the day she called me on the plane, but she wanted to surprise me. It definitely was a surprise.

I grab three bowls and scoop some rice into each bowl. I top the rice off with a piece of chicken breast. It doesn't look exactly like the picture in the recipe, but I'm not surprised. Most of these food pictures are fake, and they never look like what real food is supposed to look like.

Ari emerges from the bedroom just as I'm placing the bowls on the table.

"What is that smell?" he asks, his nose scrunched up.

"I cooked."

He arches an eyebrow. "Really?"

"Yup. I wanted to do something special for you guys."

"I didn't help," Auria volunteers.

"I wanted to do it myself," I tell Ari. "It's my first time cooking a whole meal, so be gentle."

"I'm sure you did great." Ari kisses me before walking to the table.

Auria stands from the couch and joins him at the table.

I take the third chair. "Tell me what you think," I say to them.

Ari and Auria stare into their plates. Ari uses his fork to examine the chicken.

"How did you make this?" he asks, putting the chicken to his nose and sniffing it.

"I followed the recipe for chicken and rice."

"This is chicken and rice?" Auria asks. "Oh, mon Dieu. I thought it was soup."

Ari stifles a laugh. He looks at me and notices the serious expression on my face. His smile vanishes.

"Fox. I, um…I don't understand why the rice is so…moist."

"I don't know, ARI. Because that's what the recipe told me to do." I roll my eyes.

"To make it moist?"

"To add water. Would you prefer crispy rice? Rice is supposed to be moist."

"Rice is supposed to be moist. You're right. Thank you for this, babe."

Auria is the first to take a bite. She pokes the chicken with her fork and puts a big piece in her mouth.

I watch her. "How is it?"

She holds up one finger before standing up and heading to the trash can. She spits the chicken out into the trash and comes back to the table. "I could not talk with my mouth full," she explains.

Ari stifles another laugh.

I glare at him. "Is something funny?"

"No. I'm just eating my dinner."

"You haven't taken a bite."

"We all have to make sacrifices, oui? So, eat, Ari." Auria nods toward his plate.

Ari glares at Auria. "Why don't you take another bite of chicken?"

"Non. I eat too much bread. I feel so full."

I watch Ari as he moves his food around with his fork. He sees me staring and picks up a piece of chicken. He slowly puts it in his mouth. He holds it there. Then he chews slowly. He chews for what seems to be forever before swallowing.

"Did you use any of the seasoning in the pantry?" he asks.

"Yes, I did. I used salt and pepper."

"Is that it?"

"Yes. That's all the recipe said to use."

"Number one rule of cooking: Use more than just salt and pepper."

"So you don't like it?"

"Non." Auria chimes in.

"It's just…different. But it's ok, fox." I say, glaring at Auria and silently telling her to shut up. "It was your first time, and I appreciate all the effort you put into making this. Next time, we can do it together."

I roll my eyes at him. *How dare he not like my cooking?*

"We can eat at a restaurant?"

"I thought you were full of bread." I furrow my brow at Auria.

"I was lying, of course."

Ari chuckles. "It's okay. You're good at so many other things." He winks at me.

"What things?" Auria props her face onto her hands as if she was ready to hear a story.

"It's none of your business," Ari teases. "Let's get everything cleaned up, and we can go out to eat."

***

Auria picks a random restaurant for us to have dinner. She claims she likes the purple neon lights they have outside, so she wants to try the food. Ari side-eyes me during the whole ride to the restaurant. I told him my sister was special. I guess I didn't warn him enough. But he indulges her. He engages in conversation with her no matter how random or inappropriate. Auria seems to have trouble differentiating between need-to-know and keep-it-to-yourself-because-no-one-needs-to-know.

We place our order once the waitress comes back with our drinks. I order an appetizer for my meal, Philly cheesesteak eggrolls. Ari orders a medium steak, sauteed mushrooms, and rice pilaf. Auria can't decide what she wants, so she orders almost the whole menu. Slow roasted salmon with raclette-gruyère mac and cheese with pickled shallots, loaded cheese fries, fried mozzarella, beer and cheddar soup, and a side salad. I wonder how her poop is. I'm sure she'll tell me eventually.

Ari stares at her with raised eyebrows when she finishes giving the waitress her order.

"I will pay for my food," she says as if that is the problem.

Ari pulls at his ear. "Who else are you planning on feeding tonight?"

"I don't understand." Auria furrows her eyebrows.

"It's all for her. She'll eat everything," I volunteer.

Ari looks at me in bewilderment. "I want to see this."

One thing about Auria, she loves her food. But you wouldn't guess by looking at her. Although her body is thicker than mine, she's nowhere near overweight, considering the amount of food she eats. She's all ass and thighs. Her curves are accentuated in all the right places. I wonder if Ari notices her body.

Ari reaches under the table and squeezes my hand. "How are you feeling?" he whispers to me.

I know he's checking in, and it makes me feel good. My body has never been subject to that amount of pain-pleasure combo. It was so different. I still feel a dull ache on my back from the lashing Ari administered. But, shit, did it feel amazing.

I smile at him. "I'm good."

The waitress passes by with a plate of food for the table beside us.

"That looks delicious," Auria comments. She waves the waitress over. "Excuse. What is that you put on their table?"

The waitress looks over at the nearby table. "Oh, that's a grilled cheese with corn and Calabrian chile."

"May I try?"

"Would you like me to put in an order for you?"

"Yes, please."

The waitress hurries away with her order.

"You do know this restaurant is not all you can eat, right?" Ari grins.

"Every restaurant is all you can eat. They will never tell you no."

"She does have a point," I say.

Ari rolls his eyes.

The rest of dinner is filled with talk about Auria moving in with me once she's done with school. She doesn't exactly ask. It's more of a suggestion.

She's only here for a couple more days, then she has to go back to France. Part of me feels sad to see her go. Having Auria and Ari with me makes me feel complete. They each play a role in my life, and I wonder how I ever survived without the feeling of true love and family.

***

We're in Ari's truck, driving back to my apartment when Ari's phone rings. Ari declines the call. It rings again. On the third ring, he picks up.

"I'll call you back later."

A deep, baritone voice comes through the speakers. "Your mother is dead."

CHAPTER FORTY-ONE
ARIEL

I reach out and clasp Ayemeline's hand. She stands beside me in a flowy black dress and matching black shoes. The black suit I wear feels suffocating as I watch them lower my mother's casket into the ground.

There's no way to describe the way I feel at this moment. Sad? Angry? Relieved? My mother was a burden, but she was my mother. We didn't have the best relationship. As a matter of fact, our relationship was horrible. Despite all that, the feeling of relief isn't as big as I thought it would be when I no longer had to be responsible for her all on my own. It feels more like…lost. Loss of hope. I always hoped we would have a better relationship. I always longed for the relationship Remy had with his mother. The type of relationship where you come home and tell her how hard your day was, and she comforts you, tells you everything will be all right, and tells you you're the best son in the world. But that was never my mother.

Now that she's gone, it hurts even more. When she was alive, I hoped we'd get there one day. I hoped that she'd wake up one day and forget to treat me like shit. Every day I kept hoping and wishing. Now, that's gone. The hope died with her. I'll never have that type of mother. We'll never have that type of relationship. And that hurts so fucking much.

Hot tears course down my face despite my fight to hold them in. Ayemeline squeezes my hands and leans in closer. Her warm body gives me a sense of relief. She had her reservations about attending the funeral, but she's here, nonetheless.

My father rubs my mother's sister's back as she covers her face with shaking hands. My mother's family always made it a point to stay away. Sure, they called to check on her, but those calls were usually a minute or two before they'd rush off the phone. My mother always had a way of making people want to run away from her.

What I'm more surprised at is the fact that my father attended. The fact that he called me to tell me about my mother's passing says that he's been keeping tabs on her from a distance. The person whom I couldn't find was Hassan.

Mrs. Winthrop, our short, stocky neighbor from next door, approaches me.

"Oh, Ariel." She spreads out her arms and embraces me in a big hug. "I'm so sorry. Your mother…she'll be missed." She rubs my back before pulling away.

"Thank you," I mumble.

Mrs. Winthrop looks over at Ayemeline and then at our clasped hands. "Hello. We haven't met. I'm Mrs. Winthrop." She reaches out a hand for Ayemeline to shake.

"Hi, I'm Ayemeline." She shakes Mrs. Winthrop's hand.

"Ayemeline? That's such a pretty name, dear."

"Thank you," Ayemeline responds shyly.

"Is this your girlfriend?" She looks over to me.

"Yes, Mrs. Winthrop."

"Oh, how nice." A look of concern crosses her features before it's quickly replaced with a faint smile. "Your mother adored you, Ariel. She spoke about you all the time. About what a good son you were, driving back home to take care of her and to clean the house. You're very blessed, dear. You have such a good soul. She always said she didn't know what she would ever do without you. It's so sad that your brother abandoned her. But you…you did the Lord's work. You can have peace knowing that you did everything for your mother. And she knew that too." Mrs. Winthrop leaned in close and whispered, "You were her favorite, you know?"

I smile politely. "Thank you, Mrs. Winthrop."

She pats my arm. "If you need anything, I'm right next door."

"Thank you."

She walks away to talk to my father and aunt.

Mrs. Winthrop has always been a sweet old woman. She is one of the few people who experienced a different side of my mother—a kinder side, and I wondered what made her so special and not me.

I see Remy's parents on the other side of the crowd. They were our neighbors for a while before moving away. Nevertheless, I'm surprised to see them here. They were never fans of my mother.

"I'm going to say hi to Remy's parents," I tell Ayemeline.

Her eyes widen. "Remy's parents? What are they doing here?"

"They were our neighbors until about four years ago. They lived right next door."

Her eyebrows furrow.

"I don't think they know you."

"Is Remy here, too?" She's concerned about running into him. Actually, she looks scared.

I pull her to the side, away from the crowd of people. I caught Remy watching her, and now, based on her expression, I wonder if she also had a run-in with him. Remy certainly hasn't acted like himself since Ayemeline came into the picture. But lately, it's been so much worse, and I wonder how deep his obsession goes. At first, I figured it was a pride thing, her choosing me over him. But now, I feel like it's so much more.

"Is there something you're not telling me?"

Ayemeline pinches her lips together.

"We talked about this keeping secrets shit."

Her lips quiver slightly. "I'm sorry. I'm trying so hard not to get in the middle of your friendship."

"That doesn't matter anymore. Just…just tell me, Ayemeline."

She flinches at her name on my lips.

"I…I came home one day, and he was in my apartment."

My stomach stiffens and my teeth hurt from clenching my jaw.

"We can talk about this later. It's not that important."

"What happened?" I ask between clenched teeth.

Her voice cracks. "Nothing. He was upset. He said I was his first and asked if you were better than he was."

"Did. He. Touch. You?"

"No," she says hurriedly. "He didn't. He left after that. I was freaking out because somehow, he got into my place. I don't know how. He's never been to my apartment before."

I take a long inhale and let it out slowly, trying to calm myself. Remy is…was my best friend. For years, he's had my back. Now, he's gone too far. What was he planning on doing? I shudder at the thought. Would he really hurt her? This isn't the Remy I've known for so long.

"I need you to tell me when things happen. You can't keep things like this from me."

She looks down at the ground. "I know. It's just…"

"I know," I say. I lift her chin up so she can look at me. "But it's me and you. Trust, remember."

She nods. "What are you going to do?"

"I don't know. But I'll do something. I just have to figure it all out."

Just then, a hand clasps me on the shoulder. I turn to see my father standing there in a black suit and red tie.

"Ari," he says to me but he's looking at Ayemeline.

"Hey, Dad." I have no enthusiasm in my voice. Today has been a tough day, and I feel broken. I can't even fake it at this point.

"Can we talk? In private?" His eyes never leave Ayemeline's.

"Sure." I look at Ayemeline. "I'll be right back. Are you good here?"

"I'm good."

I plant a kiss on her cheek before walking away.

***

"What do you think you're doing?"

"What?" I sigh heavily and cross my arms.

"What? Why did you bring her?"

"Because I needed her here."

My father draws a breath and releases it before he speaks. "Ari."

"Dad, I'm good."

"You're not good. You know what she is. You're supposed to be helping the police put her away for her crimes."

I want to ask him if he was aware that those boys raped her, that they held her down and forced her. But if I do that, I'll be admitting to him that she killed them. I'll do anything to protect my little fox. So, I don't ask.

"She didn't do it. It's just speculation. They want someone to pin the murders on, and they chose her."

My father briefly closes one eye. "Look, I know you guys have this thing going on, and you don't want to…"

"It's nothing like that. They asked me to find something to pin the murders on her, and I found nothing. She's innocent."

He furrows her brow. His voice is soft now. "Please, Ari. Don't do anything that will compromise your own life."

"I won't, Dad."

His eyes are sad. "I love you, son," he says, the fight leaving him. He leans in and gives me a bear hug. "Please take care of yourself.

****

Hassan did not attend the funeral. He never showed up to pay his respects. The whole day was filled with questions about why he wasn't there. I didn't have an answer for them, which is why I'm surprised to walk into my mother's house three days after the funeral to find him there.

"What the fuck are you doing here?" I glare at him.

He has a trash bag in his hand.

"I'm just getting some stuff out of here," he says nonchalantly as if it's completely normal for him to be here. He hasn't been home in ten years.

"What do you mean, you're getting stuff?"

He stops packing things into his trash bag and stares at me for the first time since I walked in. "Is there a problem, Ari?"

"Are you fucking serious?!" I shout. "You don't show up to the funeral, but you're here in her house getting stuff?"

"Are YOU fucking serious? Did you expect me to show up at that woman's funeral? For what?"

"She's your mother."

Hassan laughs. "Even after she's dead, you're still her little lap dog. You, more than anyone, should be celebrating right now."

I lunge at him. "Fuck you!" I spit. He's about two inches taller than I am, and I'm not sure I can take him. Since he left home at eighteen, he started to train as an MMA fighter. He's pretty good. I've never won a fight against him. But I'm willing to try.

"What are you gonna do, Ari? You gonna beat me up?" he patronizes.

I stop short of punching him right in the face.

"Go ahead," he says, watching my balled fists at my side. "It's what she always wanted, for us to fight each other, for you to hate me just as much as she did. So, go ahead. Deliver her last dying wish."

My fists relax at my side. My mother always had tried to turn us against each other. She would always tell me how Hassan had treated her so poorly and how she never deserved such treatment from him. She'd even shed a few tears. And each time, I'd feel sorry for her. I'd give her a hug and tell her I wasn't going anywhere. I kept my promise, too, until the very end, no matter how hard it was.

"No? You don't want to fight anymore? Okay, let me know when you're ready." Hassan goes back to gathering things around the house and placing them in the trash bag.

I look at the trash bag and realize he's not packing things to take. He's cleaning up.

"Why?" I say slowly. "Why are you here? Doing this?" I point at the bag in his hand.

"I figured it would suck for you to clean up this place alone."

"I thought you were taking things."

He scoffs. "There isn't a damn thing I want from this house."

I grab a black trash bag from the box and throw things in there.

"You should've at least come to the funeral." I say quietly, having calmed down a bit. "We had the same childhood. We both went through the same things."

He shakes his head like I'm the ridiculous one here but says nothing.

"Do you think she treated me better?" I ask

"Yes, Ari. She did."

"That's bullshit. Do you know the shit I had to put up with?"

"You're lucky that's all you had to deal with."

"What do you mean?"

"Don't worry about it. Just keep pretending your mother was the best mother in the world. Continue to live in your bubble."

"You haven't been here the past ten years. You have no idea."

"I have some idea. I know that your experience and mine were completely different. Had they been the same, you would've never stuck around for so long."

"I'm not you, Hassan. I don't just abandon my responsibilities."

"She wasn't your responsibility. You were hers. *She* was supposed to be taking care of *you*." He glares at me. "You know what, man? I'm happy for you."

We clean in silence for the next couple of hours, moving from room to room trying to clear out as much of the clutter as we can. I pack old family photos in boxes along with trophies and artwork we created as children. My mother kept everything.

Three hours later, it feels like we've accomplished nothing. The house has an overwhelming amount of junk. Hassan and I talk about his latest fight and his plan to move to Columbia in the next few years.

"So, do you have a plan for when you're actually going to move?" I inquire.

"Not sure. Still trying to figure it all out. Lana is..." He stops abruptly.

I pause and look at him with a grin. "Lana? Who's Lana?"

In all the years since Hassan left home, I've never known him to date. Sex? Yes. But he's never mentioned any of these women by name. They were usually one-night stands, and he hardly knew their names.

"No one." He shifts his attention to the mountain of boxes by the door. "What are we going to do with these boxes?"

"Don't try to change the subject, man."

"Why are you in my business?"

"Dude, you know about my girl."

"Yeah, but I've never met her."

"You can meet her today if you'd like. She's waiting for me at the hotel. Now, back to the topic. Who's Lana? Are you seeing someone?"

Hassan rubs his forehead. "I…just met her, actually. She's my…" he inhales and lets it out slowly. "Daughter."

I stare at him, awaiting an explanation. When he doesn't explain further, I say, "What the fuck? Are you going to explain how you have a whole fucking daughter?"

His shoulders slump as he stares at me with a blank stare.

"Hassan?" I have so many questions, but I don't know where to begin.

"I haven't told anyone about her because…" he pauses, "I'll have to explain…everything, and it's just too fucked up."

"I get that, but you haven't told me. You were the first person I called when my shit happened. And I had a niece, and you never told me? Mom would've been excited to know she had a grandchild."

"Please don't bring that woman up to me. You really need to stop idolizing her."

"Showing respect and idolizing are two different things, Hassan."

"Not for you, they aren't. And just so you know, your mother did know about her."

My brows rise in a surprised arc.

"Yup. She knew about her. And, no, she wouldn't be excited to know she had this grandchild because she tried to make sure she was never born."

I'm coming to the realization that Hassan's relationship with my mother is rooted in so much more hate than I realize. The look of hate in his eyes when he talks about her says it all.

"Who's her mother?"

Hassan winces. "Rebecca Porter."

I search my mind for a face to go with that name. The name is so familiar. Rebecca Porter. Then it comes to me. Mrs. Porter was one of my mother's friends. She would come over when we were younger. Every time she'd come over, she'd bring gifts for the both of us. She was my favorite person back then, and I always looked forward to her visits. But then, I started to realize that Hassan's gifts started to get better than mine.

One day, she came over and gave me a twenty-dollar bill. It was like Christmas morning. That is until I saw the new gaming system she'd given to Hassan. I was so upset that I threw a tantrum and broke dishes, mugs, and anything else I could get my hands on. I ended up getting my money taken away, and that was the last time she brought anything for me. But Hassan's gifts never stopped.

"Ms. Porter?" Realization hit me. "How old is your daughter?"

"She's twelve."

"Mom knew?" A wave of acid wells up in my belly.

"She knew. She just didn't care. Whenever I told her I didn't want to go there, I would get a beating for being unappreciative."

"She sold you," I speak so quietly I'm not sure he hears me. Although this is news to me, I knew my mother. When it came to money and things, she'd sell her soul to the devil. This time, the devil was Ms. Porter, her forty-year-old friend.

"Ms. Porter wasn't the only one. Her house was full of fucked up psychopaths—men, women, it didn't matter. And your mother pretended not to know what was going on over there. Always sending me over."

"So, all those gifts she'd get you…the money?"

"All went to your mother. She took all of it. You were the only one that got to keep everything. She wanted to ensure she always had your loyalty if shit came out."

"Shit, Hassan. I'm…I'm sorry." Molten anger ran through me. How could a mother…? But she was my mother. I knew my mother. I knew the person she was. She was vindictive and evil. I was the only one who stuck by her, who held on to the hope that one day, she'd be a mother. But now, all I'm filled with is guilt—guilt for coming down on Hassan for leaving, for not taking care of her once she got sick. He was the one who needed me. He was a fucking kid. The one person that was supposed to protect him failed to do so.

I'm his brother. I should've had his back, but all I did was blame him for not being like me. "Kid, I'm sorry."

"Listen, we can let it go. She's gone now. I never came back because I knew if I ever saw her again, I'd kill her. My only regret is that I didn't get to watch her suffer."

Usually, Hassan's brutal words would have invoked anger in me. Now, however, I could relate.

"Anyway, the old hag got pregnant, and your mother tried to get her to abort, but she wouldn't. She gave my daughter up for adoption. About a year ago, her foster parents helped her find me. I've been trying to get to know her."

"How is that?"

"Hard as fuck. She's a reminder of everything I tried to run away from. I keep reminding myself that she's a child like I was. She's innocent. None of that shit has anything to do with her."

"What happened to Ms. Porter?"

"She went to prison five years ago. Secrets always come to the surface no matter how deep you dig."

Hassan shows me pictures of his daughter. She looks just like him. He gushes when he talks about her.

"Is your plan to move to Columbia with her?"

"I'm hoping I can. I have to sort some things out first. I don't get to see her much because of the distance, but we talk every day. I want to do things right. The last thing I want is to pass on any of our fucked-up upbringing. I want to be a good dad, you know?"

"You already are. Just make sure I get to meet my niece before you leave."

After getting the house cleaned up, which took nine hours, I send a text to Ayemeline letting her know I'm on my way to get her so we can go to the gym. It's been an extremely rough few days, and I need to get a good workout in.

Ayemeline responds with a crying emoji. I know working out isn't her favorite thing, but I need her right now. Some days, just having her close is all I need. I don't really care if she only pretends to work out this time. I need her with me.

CHAPTER FORTY-TWO
AYEMELINE

I hate the gym. Ari insists on dragging me here. I get it. He likes to work out. But, why do I have to suffer? Although, the view is quite delicious.

"Are you going to sit there and watch me the entire time, or are you going to work out?"

"Watch you," I say honestly.

He smirks before putting the dumbbells down and walking over to where I sit on the weight bench, taking up space. His crotch is directly in my face.

"Are you going to whip it out for me?" I tease him.

"Don't test me. I don't care who's watching."

I feel the warmth on my cheeks. His shirtless, chiseled body glistens with his sweat.

"Now stop staring and get to work," he says, pulling away.

"I don't wanna," I whine.

He pulls me up off the bench and pulls me into him. "Are you being a bad girl?" His growl heats my blood, and I have the sudden urge to drop to my knees.

"No, sir." I can't help the smile that crosses my face.

"Good. Now get on the mat so I can help you stretch." His mouth says he's going to help me stretch, but his eyes say he wants to fuck me. His hands brush against my exposed stomach.

I'm wearing black yoga pants that end at my calf and a gray sleeveless crop top hoodie with an exposed black sports bra underneath. His hand rises up and hooks onto the bottom of my sports bra. He reaches up and brushes my curly hair out of my face.

"You should really tie this up. You're going to sweat a lot."

My hair has gotten really thick in this humidity. "I wasn't expecting to sweat."

"Always expect to sweat with me, little fox."

"Are you flirting with me?"

"Mmmm." His lips brush against mine. "We've got work to do."

He guides me down to the mat and lays me down on my back.

"We're going to start with some stretches."

I lie flat on my back.

"Place your left foot over your right knee."

I comply. Ari rests my right foot on his stomach and gently pushes himself toward me, drawing my thigh closer to my chest with every exhale.

"Good girl. Now switch sides," he says after holding the pose for what felt like forever.

When I switch legs, he does the same thing. This time, his fingers brush my inner thigh and trails down toward my pussy.

"Ari," I breathe. "You're gonna get us kicked out of the gym."

"I didn't do anything," he teases.

By the time he's done stretching me out, I'm wet, and it's not from sweat. I lean in and kiss him.

"I'm so wet," I say into his lips.

His grin is wide. "Maybe it's time to jump in the shower then."

"It's definitely time to jump in the shower."

Ari helps me to my feet and escorts me to the showers. The family shower is empty, which is pretty lucky since the gym only has one family shower available.

As soon as we're inside, Ari kisses me passionately. "I love you so much, you know that?"

"I love you too."

He descends to his knees and presses his mouth against the crotch of my yoga pants. I can feel my heat radiating from my core. My hand finds his hair, and I grip it, pressing his face firmly into my crotch.

He uses both hands and hooks them to the top of my pants, pulling them down to my ankles. I lift each leg so he can take them off completely.

"No underwear?" he groans into my pussy. I feel the heat of his breath against my clit. His lips touch my pussy while his tongue toys with my folds. I grip his hair more firmly and guide him precisely to where I need him. My wetness feels so thick. He reaches around and grips my ass. I can feel his nails digging into my ass as he laps at my pussy.

He takes my clit into his mouth and sucks. I push him away, gasping. "I'm gonna cum," I moan.

"Good," he growls. He uses two fingers and spreads my lips apart as he slides his tongue up and down my spread pussy.

"Ohhh," I moan as I tilt my head back. My knees begin to buckle beneath me.

At the sound of my moan, Ari doubles his efforts. I feel a finger penetrate my tight asshole, and he forages my pussy. His tongue goes deeper into my hole as his finger pumps my ass. Wet noises fill my ears, and I have to close my eyes tight not to cum. I feel a thick trail of my cum or his saliva cascade down my thigh.

"I need to cum." I cry out.

"Cum for me, baby."

The sensation of Ari's finger in my ass and his tongue buried deep in my pussy is too much. My whole body trembles from my orgasm. My legs give way, and I collapse. Ari catches me before I hit my face on the shower floor. Holding me close to him, he sits on the floor of the shower and pulls me onto his lap. My body still shakes from my orgasm. I rest my head on his chest, and he holds me there like a baby.

He rubs my arm up and down. "Are you good?"

I respond with a kiss. I can taste my arousal on his lips. "I'm always good when I'm with you."

CHAPTER FORTY-THREE
ARIEL

yemeline lays beside me on the bed. Her head is resting on my chest while she watches TV.

"We need to talk," I say.

She lifts her head and looks at me, and a look of concern crosses her features. "About?"

I exhale. "About you. Us. This whole thing."

"What do you mean?" She sits up.

I sit up too. "I love you. And I promised you I would keep you safe. But…" he rubs the back of my neck. "We need to figure a way out of your situation."

"My situation?"

"They want to put you away for the murder of those assholes. And they think you have something to do with that girl on campus's murder as well."

She looks down at her legs. "Why do they think that?"

"Well, they say there's a connection with all the victims. They all went to your school. You were all in the same class."

"So, make them believe that I'm a victim too. Make them think it's someone else, and I'm the next victim."

"It's not that easy. They've moved past 'if' you're guilty and are trying to collect evidence to prove that you did it."

She remains silent.

I understood why she had to take care of those boys. But Crystal? Was it an act of jealousy?

"Why'd you kill Crystal?" I have to know.

"I should have done it years ago. She was the one who invited me to that party. Those boys were her friends. She stood there and laughed while she watched them. She deserved it, the evil bitch." Ayemeline's dark eyes turn black.

My eyes widen. I notice her starting to leave and drift back to the past. I take her hand in mine to make sure she stays with me. "We are going to get out of this. We'll figure it out. Together."

Her eyes turn soft. "Would you really sacrifice everything for me?"

"Definitely. If anything happens to you, it happens to me. We're going to find our way out of this. We're in this together."

Ayemeline smiles shyly. "When you said we needed to talk, I thought you were done with me. I got so scared."

I furrow my brows. "That will never happen. Ever. You know too many of my secrets for me to ever let you go." I tease. "You're bound to me for eternity, little fox. And when this is all over, I'm going to put my babies inside you."

Her expression is pained as a single tear races down her cheek. "I could never have your babies. I'm not…"

"You're everything," I say, cupping her chin in my hand. "You are my everything, little fox. And you will carry my babies. We will be a family."

"I'm not worthy of you." A flood of uncontrollable tears pour from her eyes. "I can never bring a life into this world. I'm…I'm so broken. I don't have anything to offer to you or a child. I'm nobody. I can never…"

"You can't say that. You can't say you're nobody when you are everything to me. You say you have nothing to offer, but you've given so much of yourself to me. I was broken too, but you were my missing piece." I squeeze her hand.

"I just don't ever want to hold you back. You have so much potential. You are going to do big things. I don't even know what I like to do for fun. I'm so fucked up that I don't even know who I am or what I like."

"I know who you are. And if you have trouble finding her, I'll help you search. You are amazing, little fox."

She wipes her tears with the back of her hand. Her face is now red, and her eyes are swollen. Her lower lip trembles. "You're the only one that says that."

"I'm the only one who matters, aren't I?" I tease.

Her lips quirk up in a small smile.

My chest tightens, and I can feel my tears form, but I won't let them fall. My heart hurts for my little fox. I want her to know how special she is. She may have gone through some shit, but she's still working through them. That doesn't mean that she isn't everything to me.

"I'm going to end up pulling you down with me," her voice cracks.

"That's okay."

"No, it's not. I should've never let you get involved with the professor and that guy. Now you have blood on your hands. If they find out…it isn't fair to you."

"And I'll do it again…for you."

"You shouldn't say that."

"I am saying it. I'll burn this whole fucking world down for you."

"I just want to be somebody. Not just somebody that fucks things up for you."

"You are somebody to me. Some people need a little time to find themselves—to realize their own potential. That doesn't mean that it isn't there. It just takes some searching. You…" With my thumb, I trace the tears on her cheeks, "are my greatest gift. I know what true love is because of you. You love me unconditionally. You don't judge me. You don't make me feel ashamed of who I am. I'm so much more when I'm with you. So, if you think I have my shit together, it's because of you. I'm going to spend the rest of my life making you realize that everything that you are is everything I'll ever need. Forever and always."

I kiss her tear-stained lips.

"And don't you ever talk about my little fox like that again."

CHAPTER FORTY-FOUR
AYEMELINE

Ari's finals are keeping him occupied, which is why he isn't at the library right now supervising Micah and me while we wrap up this annoying project. Micah sits across from me with his nose buried in a book, his long legs splayed out casually, as he jots down notes in his notebook.

"This is soooooo boring," I groan.

He looks up at me through the top of his glasses.

"Don't look at me like that. You know it's boring."

"I don't care if you think it's boring. It's not boring to me." He blusters in a throaty voice.

I pout and cross my arms across my chest. "Nerd," I whisper.

He looks up at me again, this time rolling his eyes.

"Not you, of course," I lie.

He breathes deeply. "Can we just finish?"

"Can *you* just finish?"

"What part of 'group project' do you not understand, Ayemeline?"

"What part of 'this is boring' do *you* not understand, MICAH?"

"You're acting like a child."

This time, I'm the one who rolls my eyes. "You sound like my dad."

"Geez", he says under his breath. "Why do you insist on making things more difficult than they already are? You think I want to sit here with you?"

My eyebrows lower. "So, you hate me now." It's more of a statement than a question. Ever since that kiss, Micah has been distant. He often acts as if he doesn't want to be near me. I used him to make Ari jealous. I get that. But get over it already.

"No, Ayemeline. I don't hate you." His tone is warm and soft, almost mellifluous. "Quite the opposite, actually. But it really doesn't matter now."

"Micah."

"It's fine. I'm…working through it. But it's hard. I've always had a crush on you. I was just too slow…or scared. I don't know. I know I never told you how I felt. I made it seem like you were just a hook-up for me. But you've always been more. That's what I get for being too afraid to speak up. I know, I'm an idiot."

I stare into his glassy emerald green eyes, unable to think of something to say in response to his confession.

"I don't know why I said all that." He rubs his arm. "Yeah, just ignore me. I know you're in a relationship, and I respect that. I'm not looking for anything from you. It's just hard to be around you without wanting to kick myself. Don't take it personally. It's nothing you did and everything I didn't do."

"I'm sorry." I truly am. I never realized that Micah had true feelings for me outside of sex. The sad part is even if he told me how he felt, it would have never made a difference to me. I never saw Micah as anything more than someone to fill a void at the moment. But I would never tell him that.

He gives me a shy smile. "It's cool. Really. You deserve all good things, and I hope you have that in your relationship."

"I do," I mumble.

"Then that's all that matters."

***

The silver-white moon hangs low in the sky. The crisp air and clear sky make it the perfect weather to walk back to my apartment. It's the perfect excuse to reject Micah's offer to drive me home after our session.

It's a quiet night, with only a couple of students making their way to their dorms. I cross the quiet street officially leaving campus. Besides the barking of a dog somewhere in the distance, the silence is piercing. It's usually not this quiet so early on. But with everything that has happened on campus with Crystal and Professor Matthews, students are opting to stay indoors.

Muffled music pulses from a nearby building. It grows quieter as I walk further away. And it's silent again except for the crunching of leaves at my feet. It's too quiet. I'm suddenly hypersensitive to the sounds around me. My muscles tighten. Maybe I should've taken that ride from Micah.

I increase my speed, eager to make it back to my apartment. The crunching of the leaves grows increasingly louder. Sweat prickles over my skin, and I get a dizzying sense of anxiety. *What's wrong with me? There's no one here.* I turn around to look behind me. The street is empty. I take a deep breath. *Just relax. You're fine. No one's here.*

I pull out my phone and dial Ari's number. He caught me off guard once. I won't let him get me a second time. At least if he's behind me again like he was at the airport, I might hear his phone ringing. I bring the phone to my ear, and it rings. I pull the phone away from my ear and listen carefully for a phone ringing in the distance. Nothing. Then Ari's husky voice comes through the speaker.

"Hey, little fox."

"Hey," I say, a little out of breath. "Where are you?"

"Just getting out of class. Are you running?"

"No. Just walking to my apartment."

"Want me to come over?"

"Yes, please."

"Just get ready for me."

"How do you want me, Master?" I say in my best seductive voice while completely out of breath.

"First, I want you to get some water, old lady. Maybe some Bengay for those joints after all that walking."

I smirk. "Ha. Ha. Ha," I say dryly.

"Then, I want you to take off all your clothes and get on the bed face down. I want your ass up in the air. I want it to be the first thing I see when I walk into that room. I want your pussy wet and dripping for me." He croons in my ear, and my panties melt.

"Yes, Master. I'll be waiting for you." I'm practically panting now, but I'm not sure if it's from the walking or his delicious words.

"That's my good girl. I'll see you soon."

We hang up right when I reach my apartment. I make my way inside and close the door behind me, relieved to be inside. Quickly jumping in the shower, I wash every inch of my body. My pussy pulses in anticipation.

****

I hear when he enters the apartment. His steps are slow and steady. I'm on the bed, naked, exactly the way he asked me to be. I make sure I am his obedient girl.

The cool air caresses my opening while my ass and pussy are exposed to him. He's in the bedroom now. My face is buried in the sheets. I hear the rustling of clothes, and a surge of electricity jolts through my body. The bed shifts, and he climbs behind me. His finger traces my opening. My legs tremble. His warm breath caresses the skin on the back of my neck.

"You're about to get exactly what you deserve," a distorted version of Ari's voice says. His voice is muffled as if he's speaking through a mask.

He grips my hair and forces my head to lift from the sheet. A cloth covers my eyes and is secured tightly behind my head. My breathing is labored. I am ready to cum, and he hasn't even touched me yet.

Suddenly, he slams inside me. Deep, rough thrusts in and out of my ass as his fingers grip my hair. My scalp stings from the pressure. I scream out in pain. His thrusts grow increasingly rougher and more erratic. I feel like I'm about to be split in two.

His cold hand grips my neck and squeezes. My screams die down. He squeezes harder and harder, cutting off my air supply. Steadying myself with one hand, I reach up with the other and grip his arm. His grip gets tighter. Despite the pain, I begin to thrash under his weight, but that only causes him to increase his punishment on my throat and ass. His long fingers feel like tendrils around my throat.

"Ari," I choke out.

He groans in my ear. "You like my pain, don't you, little FOX?" He spits out his nickname for me as if it left a bad taste in his mouth.

My head spins as I try to gasp for air to no avail. I can't breathe. I can't think. And the stabbing pain in my ass is becoming too much to bear.

Ari has never been this way. Even in his roughness, there's always a gentleness about him. He never fails to check in to make sure I'm okay. This, however, is not my Ari. My heart slows in tempo. I try again to pry his fingers away, but I'm becoming increasingly weaker. His palm presses more firmly around my throat. Desperation to take a breath overtake me. My vision darkens. My hand falls to my side as the energy leaves my body.

Ari. Please. A tear trickles down my face. Panic surges through me. I'm going to die. Emotions stir inside me, and a torrent of warm tears pour from my eyes. *Help. Me.* My body starts to give up. My movements become slow and spasmatic.

My eyelids flutter as I reflect on my life, on everything that has happened up to this point. If this were before Ari, I would have willingly accepted it. But now—now I don't want to die. I think about Auria and the life I could have had with her. I think about Ari and carrying his babies. It's a life I was excited for but now will never have.

My brain is starving for oxygen. I no longer feel the pain. All I can see is Ari's bright hazel eyes looking at me. *I love you, little fox. Forever and always.* Closing my eyes, I give myself away to the darkness. I can't fight anymore.

EPILOGUE
EIGHT YEARS LATER

Rustling behind the bush piques my curiosity. A fluffy white bunny hops from behind the bush and dashes through the flower beds. I chase after it, and it disappears behind a row of trees, but not before stealing a trophy from my garden.

Beautiful dogwood trees flank the garden. I close my eyes and allow myself to take in the fresh, crisp morning air. My home isn't much—a chair, a table, a couple of lamps, and a bed—but my favorite part of this place is my garden—the garden I've created. Earth's nature song wakes me each morning and reminds me that I'm still alive.

The garden is filled with vibrant colors. Lipstick-pink peonies line the edge of the white picket fence. A blackbird perches on a nearby branch. And the scent of this place—it's the scent of rebirth. But my absolute favorite part of this garden is the purple foxgloves that line the edge of my porch.

I make my way to the far side of the house where the food is planted and pick an apple from the tree. I sit on the bench under the Dorsett golden apple tree and use my dress to clean my apple. As I bite into it, I marvel at the butterflies flying majestically above the milkweed.

I'm alone in this place I've called my home for the past eight years. It's also been my hiding place ever since I woke up in a box and had to claw my way out.

Ari had tried to kill me that night. He'd tried and failed. I'd been hiding from him ever since. He promised me he'd find a way out of our situation. He promised we'd do it together. But he took the cowardly way out by trying to get rid of me. I thought he loved me. He promised me forever and always. He lied. For eight years, I've been trying to muster up the courage to do what I know needs to be done. But I loved Ari. I *love* Ari. That's what makes it so hard.

I stand and straighten my sundress. Today is the day I stop hiding. No matter how hard it's going to be, Ari needs to know how it feels to die. He needs to feel how it feels to have his heart torn from your chest and burned by the person who promised to love you forever and always. I vow that Ari will burn in hell with me.

Ravenous: Book 2 of the Unhinged Trilogy Coming Soon!